9 DECEIVING FACES
The ChristOn M Larson Story
I0596946
THE INVASION OF B.R.A.Z.O.S ALIEN FORCE IN CHICAGO. WHO IS THE MYSTERIOUS ENFORCER, LARCENNI
SEAN ALEMAYEHU TEWODROS GIORGIS
9 RUBY PRINCE INTERGALACTIC AMBASSADOR

9Deceiving Faces The Christon M Larson Story
The Invasion Of B.R.A.Z.O.S. Alien Force In Chicago
Who Is The Mysterious Enforcer, Larcenni

HARD COVER CASEBOUND BOOK ISBN: 978-1-7350361-5-1
SOFTBOUND PERFECT ISBN: 978-1-7350361-9-9

ORIGINAL PUBLICATION DATE: **1997** A.D.

LIBRARY OF CONGRESS CONTROL NUMBER: 2022902424

COPYRIGHT: © 2022 SEAN ALEMAYEHU TEWODROS LINZY
ORIGINAL COPYRIGHT: © 2005 (SEAN ANDREW LINZY)

EDITORIAL IMPRINT | GEORGE WASHINGTON KING GIORGIS IMPRINT

TRADEMARK |
SEAN ALEMAYEHU TEWODROS GIORGIS
9RUBY PRINCE PRESIDENT INTERGALACTIC AMBASSADOR™

PUBLISHER |
Intergalactic Ambassador Prince President Giorgis

WASHINGTON DISTRICT OF COLUMBIA | CHICAGO - CHAMPAIGN ILLINOIS | PARIS FRANCE EUROPE | BAHIR DAR ETHIOPIA

9Deceiving Faces

The ChristOn M Larson Story

The Invasion Of B.R.A.Z.O.S

Alien Force In Chicago

Who Is The Mysterious Enforcer, Larcenni

Sean Alemayehu Tewodros Giorgis

9Ruby Prince Intergalactic Ambassador

9Eyes 9Deceiving Faces
9Mecca Chicago The Wrath Of
Qaddisin & The Angelic Wars
Sean Alemayehu Tewodros
9Ruby Prince of Abyssinia
5 Years O

Presented To | ____

____

Given By: ____

____

Date | _____________ **20 __** **In The Nation / State Thereof** | _____________

As A Gift Of Respect And Honor Of | ____

____

____

In The Love Of The Most High Heavenly Father Creator Of The Boundless Universe
Genesis Chapter 14 Verse 18

Thank You and Kind Regards... And May You Be Blessed..

Sean Alemayehu Tewodros Giorgis
9Ruby Prince President | Intergalactic Ambassador

Her Majesty, Secretary of Business Affairs
Royal Office of Tiruwork Tewodros
Negest of Abyssinia

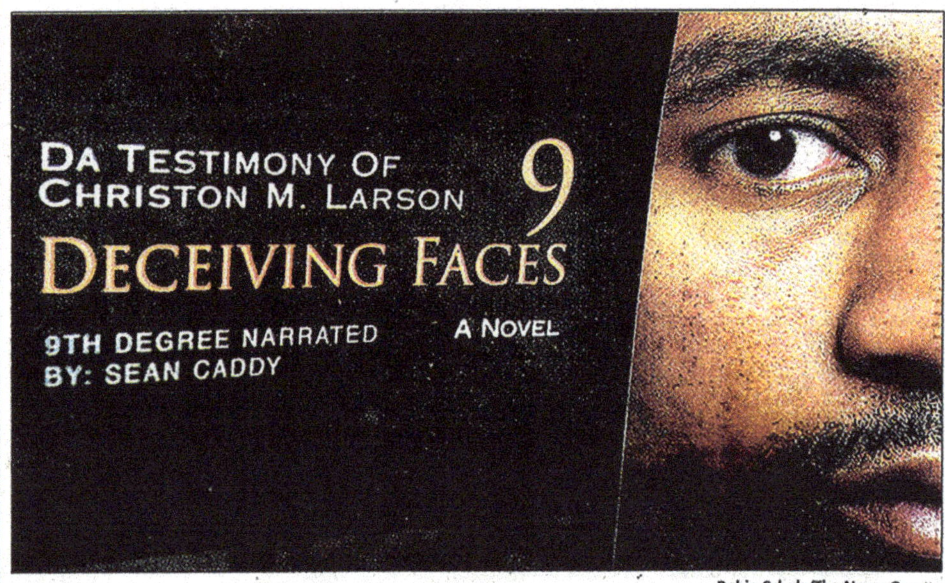

Robin Scholz/The News-Gazette

Champaign native Sean Caddy is the author of the novel '9 Deceiving Faces.'

STAFF SGT. SEAN CADDY

In midst of war, soldier finding time to create

Champaign native has written novel, made hip-hop album

By PAUL WOOD
pwood@news-gazette.com

CHAMPAIGN — Staff Sgt. Sean Caddy doesn't waste his free time while serving in Iraq.

The Champaign native has written a novel, "9 Deceiving Faces," and created a hip-hop album with military overtones. He's trying to market them both, which isn't easy for a guy who has six months to go in Iraq.

Caddy, 29, who served in Kuwait after joining the Army in 1999, is now in the reserves.

His real name is Sean Linzy. The author listed on his novel is S. Andrew Linzy, and the main character is FBI Special Agent Sean Michaels.

And the DVD is titled "Cadillac Jumpin' 2007."

As the book's ebookmall.com page tells it, the mystery describes:

"June 6th 2009 in the world of deceiving faces, friends become enemies. Enemies become friends and revenge can strike in the most gruesome way. Deep in the shadows, truth is not often seen with the eyes. It is only through betrayal and manipulation reveals that ultimate double crossing."

Caddy also has a sort of best-of called "A Day in The Life ..." which features military-tinged songs like "Enter Da Soldier," "Camouflage Infantry" and "International Girls," available at cdbaby.com.

Caddy got into hip-hop in 1995 when he was sort of a roadie for his cousins, who had a rap group named the B210 Clique.

Over the years, wherever he's been stationed, Caddy has returned to Champaign as his home base.

"I learned to be intergalactic," he says.

Between Army Reserve engagements, Caddy was a staff member for MTV's "Music in High Definition" and has assisted in sound production, lighting and stagings for such artists as Cheyenne Kimball, Gary Alan, Dashboard Confessional and the Goo Goo Dolls.

Last week, he was here to see family and promote his creations, documenting the events on digital video.

His "9 Deceiving Faces," subtitled "Da Testimony of Christon M. Larson," is published by iUniverse and available at local bookstores as well as amazon.com.

Some of the DVD cuts can also be seen at youtube.com, he added.

MULTI-NATIONAL SECURITY TRANSITION COMMAND-IRAQ

CERTIFICATE OF APPRECIATION

Presented to

Sergeant Sean A. Linzy

Your outstanding support, professional knowledge, self-motivation, and determined tireless efforts made an excellent contribution to the efficient functioning of the Iraqi Army units that you supported. The maintenance and supply support you provided in support of the Cascavel, an armored personnel carrier used by the Iraqi Army, was marked by integrity and initiative. The most impressive part about your willingness to lend your talents to getting a mission essential piece of equipment operational was that you volunteered to take on the mission. Your uncompromising standards of conduct and professionalism have left a lasting and positive impression on your Iraqi Army counterparts. Because of your actions soldiers in the Iraqi Army will be better able to take the fight to the insurgents. In sincere appreciation to you and your unit, thank you for a job well done.

Thank you for your contributions.
Given this 16th Day of March 2007

MARTIN E. DEMPSEY
Lieutenant General, U.S. Army
Commanding General

Testimony Chapters of Life

9Deceiving Faces

The ChristOn M Larson Story

The Invasion Of B.R.A.Z.O.S

Alien Force In Chicago

Who Is The Mysterious Enforcer, Larcenni

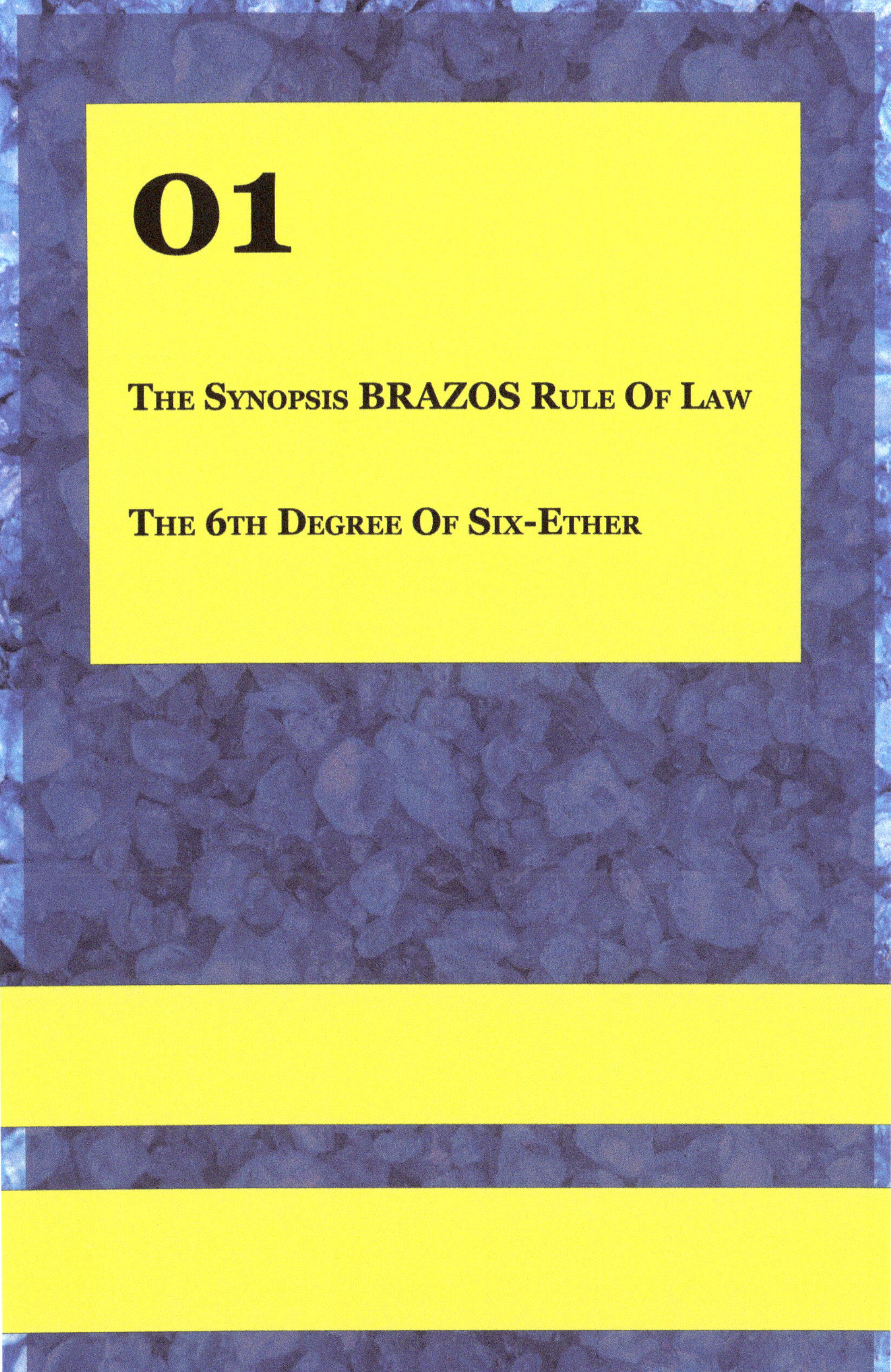

01

THE SYNOPSIS BRAZOS RULE OF LAW

THE 6TH DEGREE OF SIX-ETHER

In September 2027 D.A.,

ChristOn M Larson Returned Unexpectedly To His Hometown Of **Occupied Chicago**. To Experience The World Of Spiritual Eyes Of Deceiving Faces, Where There Was No Such Reality As Good And Evil, Due To The Illusion That The Evil Man Was Good At Being Evil And The Good Man Was Evil At Being Good.

There Was A Time When The Five Elite Families Selected Their Agents As Supplanted Leaders, As They Boldly Desired To Control The Masses Within Their Time And Location Called Trapped Knowledge. This Event Illustrated How The Spiritual Beings Charged With Revenge Began To Strike In The Most Gruesome Way.

Who Is This Spiritual Soul Known As ChristOn ChristOn M Larson? A Man Illuminated In A Twinkle Of An Eye, **Da 9Sacred Eye** To Be Exact.

Larson Became An American War Hero Who Served During The Iraqi Wars Just Years Before The Robotic Soldiers. The Fake Alien Invasion. Were Unleashed Out Of Control That Caused Mass Hysteria On A Global Stage Of World War Three. A Short Time After, Larson Engaged Nine Million Warring Angels Known As Former Gang Members Against The Sorcerers Of Deception Causing The War Of Tribulation Starting In **Occupied Chicago**.

They March Throughout The City United And Of One Mind, Da Spiritual Mind To Be Exact! They Became The Inheritors Of The Planet Earth, Qi. Some Of The BRAZOS Rebels Sided With Castoni And Larson Was Given The Title The Sarge With The Staff That Only Desired To Live In Peace, After Serving And Retiring From Armed Forces Honorably.

In The Year 2024 D.A.,

Shortly After The Appearance Of The 13th Planet Nibiru, The Crystal City Released Itself From The Massive Planet Located On The Outside Of The Photon Belt, Traveling Two Years To Go Through It. The Crystal Ship And Child Of Its Mother Nibiru Hovered Eerily Within The Earth's Atmosphere For Over Three Years. The Ship's Presence Caused The Entire World To Be

In Fear, And Its Energy Made The Emotions Of Revenge, Hate, Sorrow And Regret Within All Sinners Come To A Complete Stop Due To The Confusions Within Them.

In June 2024 D.A.,

48 Months After The Retirement Spiritual Laws Of Abraham Musa, The City Of **Occupied Chicago** Embraced Mayor Elite Donal James Finley, A New Foreign Leader During The Time Of Political Unrest. He Introduced A New Foreign "Entity" Called BRAZOS. That Brought In A New Economic Order. After Orchestrating The Major Economic Collapse. BRAZOS Gained Fascist Control Having A Direct Influence Over All Public Official Police, International Airports, The Teenage Army Of Civilians, Banks, Hospitals, Attorneys, The Union System And Other Major Organizations. Banking, Medical And Food Supplies Became Micro-Chipped Productions Under The BRAZOS System. The Cost Of Living Heightened By The Orchestrated Recession, The BRAZOS Job Pay Rates Remained Lower Even To The Highly Educated, And Citizen Poverty Levels Were Peaking.

Under The Rulership Of BRAZOS' Foreign Changes, They Allied With Five High-Powered Elite Families Of **Occupied Chicago**. The Wicked Families Began To Revitalize Abandoned Buildings And Repossessed Houses Invaluable Neighborhoods Throughout The City. They Cleaned The Streets Of Notorious Gang Members, Drugs, And All Other Illegal Operations Because They Needed Full Control, And No One Was Able To Use Paper Money Any Longer. Instead Of Giving **Occupied Chicago** Citizens A New Hope For The Future,

However, Mayor Elite Donald Finley And BRAZOS Picked Up Where The Newly Incarcerated, Powerful, And Disgraced Criminals Left Off.

"Soon After, The Elections Were Once Again Canceled To Keep The Mayor Elite In Power."

All Manipulations Peaked In June 2022 D.A., Four Years Before The Very Last Election, And 9Mecca Chicago's Mayor Elite Abraham Musa, Known As A Great Man, Was Mysteriously And Aggressively Being Forced Into Early Retirement Due To A Secret Force That Had Been

Running The City In The Shadows. Now That The 9Mecca Chicago Was Without A Mayor, The Passing Away And Mayhem Reached A New High.

Through It, All, An Ancient And Unfamiliar Anunnaqi Surfaced For Revenge On The City's Tyranny And Penetrated Lightning Strikes As A Wrath Throughout The Streets Of 9Mecca Chicago. The Mysterious Anunnaqi Of Judgment Had A Name…Da Qaddisin…Divine Authority And The 13TH Of The 24 Elders. Da Qaddisin Was Summoned From The Da 9TH Chamber Of Nibiru And Had Begun Releasing Vengeance Upon The Planet Qi… The Ancient Title For Planet Earth. The Summoning Occurred Three Years Before The Visual Appearance Of Nibiru In The Sky.

B.R.L. (BRAZOS Rule Of Law) Illiana's Arch Chief Sham Michaels Was Summoned To Investigate The Wicked Oppressors Within The City After The Appearance Of The Crystal City. The Rumor Was That ChristOn ChristOn M Larson Had Been Seen Nine Months After The Mysterious Emergence Of Da Qaddisin.

Along With The Many Changes Occurring In The City, The Foreign BRAZOS Was Making Plans Of Assembling Military Assassins. However, Larson Campaigned Against The BRAZOS Enlistments For This Covert Operation. Marquis Castoni, The Head Of One Of The Five Elite Families, Also Rebelled Against It. Castoni Began To Realize That His Alliance With This Foreign Entity Might Have Happened Too Quickly.The BRAZOS, They Have No Past," He Thought, "They Came From Nowhere! Who Is This Foreign Entity? Castoni Secretly Tried To Unite With Various Mob Bosses In The City Without Letting Them Know His True Intentions, Only To Discover They Were Already Under The Manipulation The BRAZOS' Deceptions.

Castoni Heard Of Larson's Campaign And Approached Him Because Of His UnGreground Connections Called Da Ill-State Enforcers. Made Up Of Lorenzo 'Chaos' Larson, Andre 'Da Drego' Jones, Castoni JR, Jr., Cleni JR Cleni And Joe Da Posey.

Who Were All Known For War Campaigns. The Connection Was Formed Privately And Planned Out By Larson, With Castoni As Its Overseer. Infiltration By Mayor Donald James Finley And The BRAZOS Entity Was Rampant.

Mass Quantities Of Uncut Cocaine Were Found Destroyed In Warehouses During The Recent Police Raids. BRAZOS Workers Penetrated Former Government Agencies, And No One Was To Be Trusted From Within, Causing More Groups To Denounce The Entity. 9Mecca Chicago During This Reign Became A City-State Having Its Own Jurisdiction.

Arch Chief Sham Michaels, B.R.L-Illiana, And His Elite Team, Began Preparing To Fight A War Unlike Any Civil War. While Mob Bosses And Some Renegade B.R.L-Illiana Police Chiefs Began Uniting Against BRAZOS. These Events Sparked The Return Of Mayor-Elite Mayor Elite Donald Finley. Whom Was Previously Known As Mayor Abraham Musa.

****

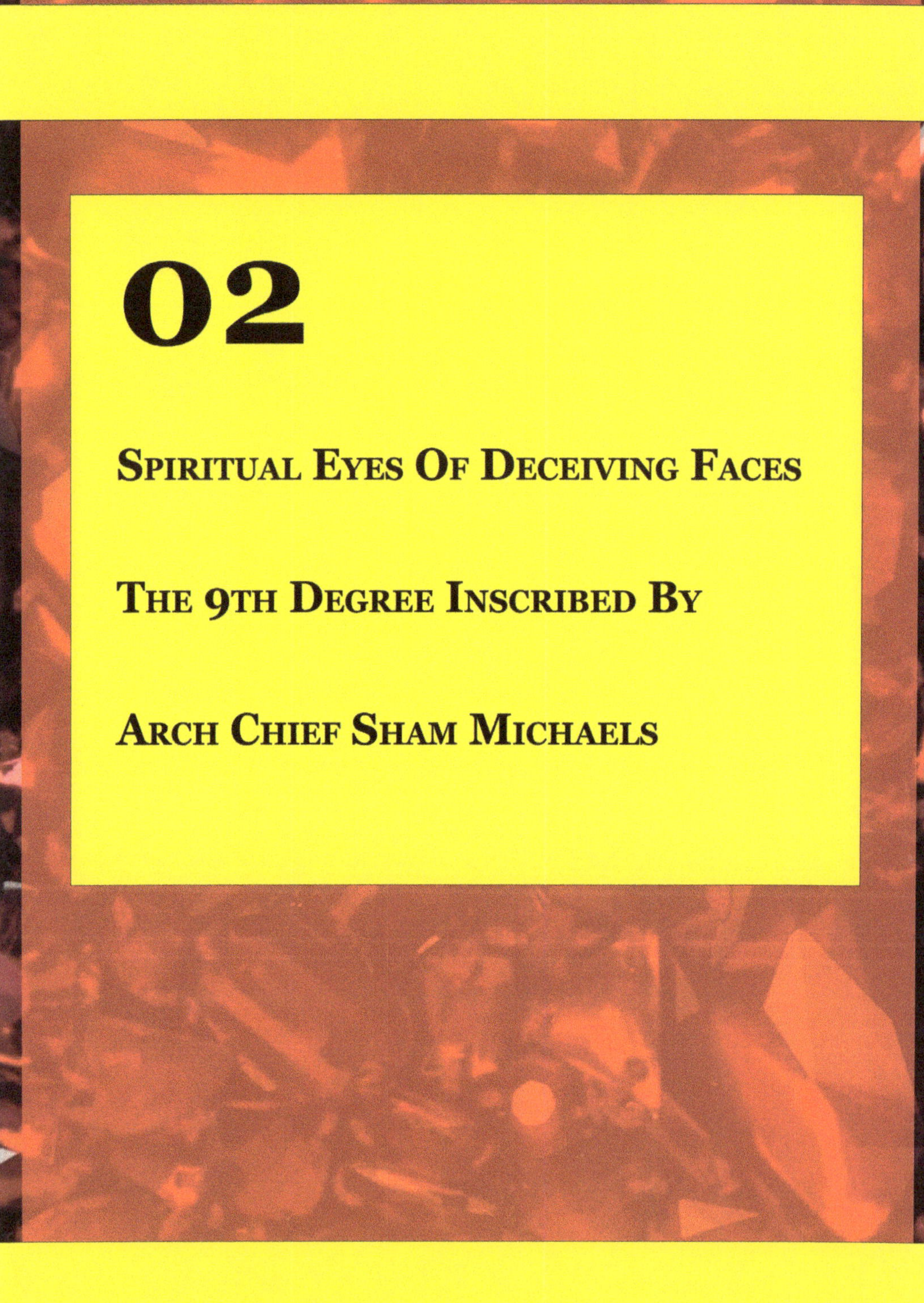
02

SPIRITUAL EYES OF DECEIVING FACES

THE 9TH DEGREE INSCRIBED BY

ARCH CHIEF SHAM MICHAELS

In The Year 2027 D.A.,

It Is Wednesday, September 18TH, In The Year 2027 D.A.At 9:45 Pm And This A Recorded Report, File Number 138-09 Arch Chief Michaels, The Recorder Wirelessly Connected To The Laptop On The Wooden Table Began Recording Michaels's Voice.

"Lo And Behold, There Came That Unholy Revengeful Cosmic Shadow Hour On 87TH Street On **Occupied Chicago**'s South Side. The B.R.L-Illiana Surveillance Focused On The Warehouse Of Stanley's Office Supplies Containing Computer Chip Technology.My Chiefs Posted On The Rooftops Across The Street. We Watched It All, Inside The Warehouse With Our Infrared Television Monitors. Just One Block And A Half Away, Under That Dim Light, Sat A Dark Blue Lincoln Continental With Tinted Windows.Inside Were Two Known Felons Scanning What Appeared To Be A Malicious Plot Unfolding. As The Thunderous Rain Hit The Pavement, The Tensions Rose." Michaels Continued To Describe **Occupied Chicago**'s Greatest Massacre Of War-Torn Spirits In All Of Its History.

"The Most Notorious Criminals And Warring Citizens Were Engaging In The Most Unconventional Civil, Interstate War-Fighting Since The Southern Invasion."

Michaels Leaned Back Slowly In The Wooden Chair That Held His Solid Frame. "The Foreign Government's Stronghold Was... No," He Paused "...It Is, An Illusion, And Playing Both Sides Of The War In An Attempt To Weaken Both Opposing Forces."

Michaels Looked Over His Right Shoulder To The Window Of The Small Apartment And Saw His Reflection Pulling Him Deeper Into His Memory. "Based On Our Plans, Members Of Da Ill-State Enforcers Were In The Dark Blue Lincoln Continental Knowing That Our Wiretaps Were In Place."

The Tall Man Turned And Stood Up From The Chair And Continued Looking At His Reflection, "Our Wire-Tapping Intercepted The Following Conversation Pick-Up Through The Cell Phone Signals Between The Individuals In The Lincoln,"

Michaels Turned Back Towards The Table And Pressed A Button On The Laptop Which Played The Conversation Between Two Men.

Cleni: Man, You See That Massive Beam Of Light Over There!

Chaos: What Light? I Don't See Anything —Oh Stress!

Cleni: You Know, I Saw That Before!

Chaos: You Scared? Man, You Better Drive This Negative Soul,

Turn Down The Alley

Cleni: Man, I Hope Castoni JR. Is Ready To Go Before It Gets Too Hot!

Chaos: Call Up "Da Drego" And Tell Big Bro Not To Smoke Up All My Stress!

Both Men Broke Into Laughter On The Recording. Arch Chief Michaels Put The Small Wireless Recorder To His Mouth As He Stopped The Recording Of The Two Men.

"As The Blue Lincoln With These Individuals Turned Down The Side Street.

My Chiefs Spotted Six Black Paddy Wagons And Three Squad Cars Moving In Fast,"

Michaels Said Putting One Hand On His Head And Ran It Over His Face To His Chin,

"And Just In Front Of Stanley's Warehouse, A Chain Reaction Was Set Off.

In No Less Than A Split Second, Officers Of The Sixty-Sixth Precinct Police Kicked In The

Front Doors."

Michaels Looked At His Laptop And Used His Cursor To Drag A Hidden Screen To The Front Of His Other Opened Documents. It Was The Recorded Footage Of That Night. The Men On The High Definition Screen Looked Like Cockroaches That Were Scrambling For Protection From The Light. "Renegade Mobsters Were Inside While Some Were Posted Outside With Weapons. Immediately, The Gunfire Opened Up, And Many Bodies Were Dropping In The Suicidal Raid," He Said As He Watched The Footage.

"As My Chiefs On The Ground Attempted To Apprehend The Suspects In The Lincoln, They, Unfortunately, Found The Car Running With The Doors Wide Opened And Abandoned… Then Suddenly, The Warehouse Exploded!

Flames Emerged Out Of Anger As If It Were Another Big Bang Theory But In Reverse… You Know," He Said Rubbing His Tired Red Eyes, "Not To Make Things Confusing But, The First Big Bang Is Just That… Theory, Because Someone Would Have To Witness Another Man's Creation To Record What Happened. This Was Its Reverse Because It Was Recorded.

Anyhow, The Massive Structure Burned And Distracted The Chase Of The Two Suspects Lorenzo "Chaos" Larson, 36 And Cleni JR Cleni, 39 Who Both Escaped."

Michaels Walked To The Sink That Was Adjacent To The Wooden Table And Poured Out Steaming Hot Water From A Kettle Into A Mug That Had A Tea-Bag Waiting For It. He Drank The Tea And Cleared His Throat "Ah Hem, Ah Hem... So Then, Not Too Long Afterward; My Unit Fled The Scene To Assist The Other Chiefs Who Were Attempting A Raid On One Don Marquis Castoni Warehouse On The West Side," He Said.

He Then Drank More Of The Hot Liquid While Absorbing The Heat From The Mug Into His Palms. "Now To Prevent Any More Possible Passing Away Of My Chiefs, And Placing Them In Harm's Way, The Raid Was Delayed. We Lost The Two Suspects Cell Phone Signals After The Explosion…The Connection Was Lost," Then Michaels Remembered Something, "Chief Ezra's Elite Team Did Say They Noticed Massive Beams Of Light From An Object Hovering Above Castoni's Property…Yeah, What Was That?" Michaels Threw His Head Back And Poured The Rest Of The Tea Down His Throat. He Threw Out The Tea Bag, Placed His Mug In The Sink, Then Pulled Up The Chair To The Table And Continued Speaking, This Time With More Energy.

"There Were Two Unknown Women, Referred To As Anunnaqis…

One Of Them Was Tall With Silvery Hair, Wavy And Long, The Other Woman Apparently Younger With Sandy Brown Hair In Twists; Renegade Henchman Was Surrounding Them.

My Chiefs, Out Of Great Fear, Refused To Intervene With The Confrontation Based On What They Saw Around These Women," Michaels Said As He Watched Other Video Footage.

"My Chiefs Stated That They Saw Bright Flashes Of Light Of What Appeared To Be Lightning Bolts. Being Emitted From Somewhere In The Vicinity Where The Women Were Located. The

Lightning Flashes… That's How They Were Described… It Was So Bright It Caused Some Temporary Blindness To My Men." The Flashes Were So Bright On Michaels's Laptop That The Entire Screen Turned White.

"My Chiefs Continued To Observe Several More Flashes Of The Now Confirmed Lightning Bolts, Striking Individual People…De-Materializing Them Like A Judgment Upon Its Victims!" Michaels Shouted, Unaware Of His Excitement.

"Now, Shortly After This Dynamic Phenomenal Wrath Of An Unknown Power. It Was Released At The Renegade Men That Were Merging In Towards The Women. A Massive Beam Of Green Light Shone Out Of The Clouds Upon The Anunnaqi Women And They Vanished,"

Michaels Said Shaking His Head In Disbelief While Pressing Stop, Rewind And Play On His Laptop Repeatedly. "And Like I Said, The Lightning Bolts Had Already Stopped…And They Just Disappeared!" Michaels Repeated The Footage Over And Over, And The Women Were Gone.

As He Sat Rewinding The Footage, He Forgot About The Recorder, And It Stopped Automatically As His Voice Went Quiet. He Could Not Give Any Valid Explanation For The Disappearance Of The Women.

"The Chiefs Hesitated To Move Towards Their Assigned Target," He Said As The Recorder Began Recording At The Sound Of His Voice.

"The Chiefs At First Could Barely Recognize What Was Left Of The Six Bodies. There Was No Need For Ambulance Assistance Because The Only Remains Were Of Blood And Dust. The Winds Of **Occupied Chicago** *Blew What Was Left Of Them Into None Existence."*

As Arch Chief Michaels's Voice Began Drying Out From His Excitement, He Took The Same Mug From The Sink And Rinsed It Out With Cold Water From The Tap. He Poured More Water From The Kettle And Mixed In Some Honey And Drank The Mixture. "Okay," He Said,

"Director Jentson Is **Occupied Chicago**'s B.R.L-Illiana Director In-Charge Of Both Operations. Although He Lost Contact With His Informant, The Second Pre-Dawn Raid At 10:09 PM At Castoni's Warehouse Was A Success."

"Soon After, They Discovered More Bodies Of Blood And Dust. They Entered Through The Back Of The Building To Find Mr. Marquis Castoni Watching His Renegade Entourage Pleading For Their Lives…I Mean So Many Things Were Happening At Once," He Said Pausing The Footage.

"On The Balcony, There Was Another Anunnaqi…With A Silhouette As A Woman I Think, Camouflaged Within The Shadows, Sparking Lightning From Her Hands Or Something… Choosing Her Victims Carefree, So They Had To Find Cover In The Oddest Places!"

Michaels Said Closing His Eyes. "By The Time The Other Chiefs Stormed The House Of Judgment. They Were Caught Up In The Lightning Trance. The Anunnaqi Woman Then Spun Her Back To Them And She Jumped Over The Balcony. They Ran Towards The Handrail And Saw Her Feet Below, Casually Walking Away From The Scene,"

Michaels Said Laughing To Himself, "I Mean Where Is The Logic? Why Didn't She Beam Into The Green Light Like The Other Two? And Finally To Our Surprise, We Found The Person Who BRAZOS Hierarchy Assumed Played Out The Role Of The Enforcer Da Larcenni."

Arch Chief Michaels Looked At The Time On His Laptop; It Was 1:25 AM.

"Just 30 Minutes And I'm Done." He Picked Up His Sweater Off The Table And Pulled It Over His Head And In A Snake Like A Twist, Stretched His Long, Lean Arms Through The Sleeves. He Sat Back In The Same Position And Continued Thinking Out Loud, Recording What He Remembered.

"Now After, The Anunnaqi Sighting, There Standing In The Midst Of All The Chaos, Gunfire And Lightning Smoke, Was Mr. ChristOn M Larson…At Least, We Thought It Was Him. I Could Swear That From Where I Was Standing, I Saw The Two Rings That He Is Well Known For, Da 9Ruby Ring And Da Emerald Lion Of Judah Ring."

Michaels Scrolled Through Various Surveillance Footages And Finally Found His Confirmation; Larson Was Captured Standing A Few Feet Away From The Anunnaqi When She Jumped The Balcony. Right In That Same Corner Was A Hidden Camera, Allowing Michaels To Pause It And Zoom Into Larson So That He Could Verbalize His Observations.

"Larson Was Crowned With Silky Black Kippah, Wearing A Long Black Silk Gucci Hooded Robe Which Pressed Against His White And Black Ethiopian Wardrobe."

As Michaels Watched The Paused Screen, He Could See The Power In Larson' Eyes.

"I Was Later Told That Larson Was Found Standing Unarmed In A Bodyguard Position, Somehow Protecting Marquis Castoni, As If He Wanted Him Unharmed. Both Subjects Were Captured. The Other Suspects At Stanley's Warehouse Had Eluded The Authorities Of BRAZOS Because There Were No Microchips Implanted In Their System." Michaels's Voice Went Silent.

In The Year 2027 D.A.,

The Brown Hand Picked Up The Remote And Turned Up The Volume On The Television Screen. The Voice Of A White Woman With A Tanned Complexion, Blue Eyes, And Jet-Black Hair Began To Speak. Her Name Was Jan Lysalot A Wgn News Reporter.

"We Would Like To Interrupt Your Regularly Scheduled Programming To Bring You This Special Report. Reporting Live From Wgn Studios, Here Is News Anchor Lilith Fox".

A Black Woman Appeared Immediately On The Screen. "Thanks, Jan,"

Lilith Says While Hypnotically, Penetrating Her Dark Brown Eyes Into The Camera. "Tonight Tragedy Strikes In The Heart Of **Occupied Chicago** Land, With The Passing Away Of The Late Mayor Donald James Finley"; Lilith Said Expressionless Blinking Only Once, "B.R.L-Illiana Chiefs Discovered Our Mayor Elite Brutally Murdered Around 4 Am With Dismantled Robot Soldiers Surrounding His Body". Lilith Suddenly Pauses In Her Seat And Stared Blankly Through Her Screen, "I Am Now Receiving An Update…That The Body Was All Machinery Parts,"

She Tilted Her Head An Inch To The Left And Squinted Her Eyebrows And Blinked Twice.

"Yes, It Is Apparent That Mayor Elite Donal James Finley…

He Was An Artificial Robot With Human Organs," She Said.

"This Brings Up The Question, What Happened In The Assassination Of Former Mayor Donald James Finley So Many Years Ago. And Is This Connected To Mayor Elite Donal James Finley So Many Months Ago When The Meteorite Hit? When BRAZOS Chancellor Elite, Madame Helena Ishtar, Was Appointed As Head Of BRAZOS Rule Of Law, Which Was The Same As This Morning. As We Know, If There Are Any Emergencies With The Mayor Elite, Madame Ishtar Takes His Place Temporarily."

Lilith Twisted Her Chair 45 Degrees Left, Making Visual Contact With The Second Camera,

"Nine Months Ago, Chancellor Elite Ishtar Was Severely Scared In The Face When She Attacked During The Second Civil War That Lasted Sixty-Six Days. Following That Event Three, Thirty-Six Ton, Iron Meteorites Smashed Into The State Leaving Countless Passed Away, While Sixteen More Iron Meteorites Brought Destruction All Over The World. After Being Treated By Facial, Reconstructive Laser Surgery, The Chancellor Elite Returned To Her Place Of Business Wearing A Mask Giving No Information Leading To Her Attempted Assassination."

Lilith Turned Back To Her Original Position And Put Her Right Hand On Her Chest,

"We Brought **Occupied Chicago** The Story Of How Our Mayor Elite Donal James Finley. He Survived The Three Meteorites That Smashed Into His City-State Office Building. Which Had Engulfed Nineteen City Blocks Nine Months Ago," She Said Putting Her Hand On The Desk.

"After The Devastation, No One Could Have Imagined Any Survivors Of The Thousands Of Citizens Who Died, And Remarkably Mayor Elite Did!" The Woman Shuffled The Paper On Her Desk Without Taking A Glance Off The Screen.

"He Was Almost Worshiped And People Marveled Him Around The Globe As If He Were A World Mayor Elite!" Lilith Said As Her Voice Rose. "When Questioned About The Robotic Body Presumed To Be That Of The Mayor Donald James Finley," Finding Her Composure, "The B.R.L-Illiana Chiefs Refused To Discuss Any Details."

As The Commercials On The Television Ended, The Face Of Lilith Fox Immediately Appeared. In Another Related Story Tonight," She Said,

"The City Has Seen Its Worst Massacre In History. Since The St. Valentine's Day Massacre That Happened Eighty-Four Years Ago In 1929 A.D. BRAZOS Officials' Report That An Explosion At Stanley's Warehouse On 87TH Street, In The City's South Side, Caused The Immense Magnitude Of Devastation Within That Area. A Massive Amount Of Burnt Cocaine Smoke From The Explosion Saturates The Air As Firefighters Struggle To Gain Control Of The Fire... And Of Themselves."

The Woman Paused And Twisted Her Seat Again To Get The Attention Of The Second Camera To The Left Side Of The Spacious Shaped Room.

"Reports Of The Explosion Left Six Hundred People Passed Away; Sixty-Six Of The Passed Away Were Brave Police Officers From The 66TH Precinct Who Were Heroes That Were Participating In A Drug Raid That Turned Sour. No More Than Twenty Minutes Later, Across Town On The West Side, More Bodies Were Found. B.R.L-Illiana Chiefs Carried Out Another Raid, This One Ending With Two Arrests Tonight."

"One Arrest Was Of Don Marquis Castoni From One Of The Elite Families And His Arch Rival ChristOn M Larson. Whose Reappearance Is Somehow Puzzling And Bizarre, Because He Was Declared So-Called Passed Away On December 5, 2026, D.A. Of Last Year."

"Authorities Even Found Out That He Was The Mysterious Enforcer Called Da Larcenni. Officials Said They Had Sawed Larson In A Dark Red Lincoln Continental Before Everything Occurred. Larson Was A Well-Known Celebrity In The Entertainment Business And Won Many Awards. While Larson Was Under Arrest, He Was Disarmed Of His Semi-Automatic Handgun And Other Weapons. We Are Being Told That He Was Taken Down By BRAZOS Chiefs In An Extended Shoot-out Where No One Was Harmed." "And That Is All The Current Development We Have On The Latest Events," Lilith Said As She Swung To Her Right To Face Camera One.

"Wgn News Will Keep The Citizens Of **Occupied Chicago** Informed As These Stories Develop. We Will Now Return To The Regularly Scheduled Programming."

Suddenly The Television Screen Went Black."

Sayings Of The 1ST Elder Akatri̇̈el, Here…Lies The Truth And Hearing Lie With No Truth. Cleni And Lorenzo Were Seen At Stanley's Warehouse In A Dark Blue Lincoln Continental. Larson Was Later Found Protecting Castoni And Was Not In A Red Lincoln. Here In Lies, There Is No Truth…But In Time There Will Be."

Who Is This Spiritual Soul Known As ChristOn M Larson?

It Was Thursday, September 19TH, 2027 D.A. At Markham Courthouse In **Occupied Chicago**. The Courtroom Was Filled With Curious Minds, Gossiping Tongues And Creative Liars. The Courtroom Door Swung Open, And Everyone Turned To Them And Gazed Upon The Young Man Who Was With Two BRAZOS Police Escorts. There Was Extreme Fascination As Everyone Turned And Glanced At Each Other.

They Were Watching A So-Called Passed Away Man Walk Before Them, And All They Saw Was A Mystery, But They Were All Filled With Nervousness. To These People, The Man Somehow Just Didn't Fit The Description Of A Dangerous Man Or As An Enforcer. Some Of Them Wondered Why He Was There And Others Thought He Must Be The Victim. The Handsome, Healthy Looking Young Man Was ChristOn M Larson. He Walked Through The Courtroom, And Everyone Watched Him In Astonishment And Silence.

Many Of Them Had To Drop Their Heads Because His Aura Overpowered Their Spiritually Beaten Down Bodies And Programmed Minds. He Walked By The Micro-Chipped People Into The Room And Disturbed Many Of Their Bestial Spirits. *It Was Only The Abyssinians That Were In Support Of The Once Presumed So-Called Passed Away Man Who Was Now Mysteriously Alive Again. They Felt It Was Some Sort Of Resurrection…But Of What?*

The Announcement Of Larson' Return Instantly Overwhelmed All Of His Mockers. As He Strolled To The Front Of The Courtroom With The Spirit Of Grace, His Light Brown Eyes

Overshadowed By Thick Brows, Sent Sharp And Abrupt Strikes Into The Eyes Of Spectators Catching Them Off Guard.

He Knew That By Doing This, They Would Turn Their Heads Away As If The Stars In His Eyes Didn't Mesmerize Them. Those Who Were Secretly Not Implanted By Microchips Smiled As If They Knew His Secrets, And In Return, He Raised His Right Arm Precisely Pointing His Pinky Towards His Sternum With Confidence And Smiled Back At Them. He Realized They Saw No Evil In Him.

"Damn Right," He Thought To Himself And Began To Feel Better. Now He Wanted To Be There, And He Started Feeling More Comfortable When He Noticed Someone Else In The Audience…A Particular Woman Of Brownish Gold Complexion, Sandy Brown Hair In Twists. Who Was Wearing A Light Brown, Silk Gucci Robe With A Pair Of Gucci Sunglasses.

She Lifted Both Hands To Adjust Her Shades To Reveal Her *Da 9Ruby Princess* Ring On Her Right Hand And The *Da 9Sapphire Falasha Ring* Ring On The Other. Also Seated In The Court Was Mary Larson, And Daveed *Da 9Scholar*.

Larson Stepped In Between The Table And His Seat Giving Everyone In The Room A Better View Of His Neatly Pressed Black Gucci Suit With A Silky Black Kippah To Match. It Hung Loosely Against His Slender, Muscular, 180 Lb. Body. His Shiny Gold Chain Sporting An Ankh With A Man Displayed On It Lit Up The Room As It Dangled Around His Neck And Bounced Off His Cotton, Button-Up Collared Shirt As He Adjusted Himself.

He Looked Like A CEO And A Model Ready To Market His Own Line Larson 9Wear Clothing. But Everyone Knew Who He Really Was; A Well-Spoken Spiritual Man That Caused Everyone To Hold Their Breath, Because Whatever He Had To Say Inflicted Uproar On A Massive Scale.

Larson, With His Tight Skin Fade And Unevenly Trimmed Beard, Stood At The Desk Alone With No Lawyer Or Representative Present; Yet, He Didn't Care And Just Looked At The Courtroom As A Theater With Him As The Highest Power.

He Touched His Dark Suit And Patted His Tie Made Of Ethiopian Silk. It Was Red And Purple And Looked As If It Had Been Stitched With A Touch Of Royalty. His Fancy Gold Cuff Links Hung Over His Ruby Watch And His Black Onyx Rolex That Covered Each Wrist.

On His Left Pinky Finger Was Da Emerald Lion Of Judah Ring And On His Right Pinky Finger Was His Da 9Ruby Prince Ring. His Size Twelve Shoes Were Polished Military Style, And They Reflected The Florescent Lights.

He Was Five Feet, Nine Inches In Height, But He Stood Confidently As Though He Were Nine Feet Tall While Emitting A Powerful Presence Gearing Up To Enter The Playing Field.

He Was Ready, And Everyone In The Courtroom Who Knew Him Knew He Was The Celebrity That Gave Life To The Mentally Passed Away As If He Were The Master Who Returned.

The Bailiff Began The Proceedings,

"All Rise, Presiding For The Pre-Trial Hearing, The Honorable Judge Julian Kharnas.

Case Document Number 8471-11A, The City Of **Occupied Chicago** Versus Mr. ChristOn M Larson. You May Be Seated." Judge Kharnas Entered The Room Swiftly From A Door Located Behind His Podium And Found His Seat And Began Reading A Document He Brought To His Desk. Larson Took His Seat And Instantly Fell Into A Slump As If All His Bones Had Just Given In On Him.

Judge Kharnas Stared At The Document In Front Of Him Quietly For A Moment Then Slowly Peered His Blue Eyes At Larson. The Jebusite Man Lifted His Head And Noticed That Everyone In The Room Was Visually Captivated By Larson And Could Not Take Their Eyes Off Of Him.

The Judge Was Jealous Of This Attention, Instantly Decided He Didn't Like The Young Man At All. Larson, Picking Up On The Judge's Vibration, As He Glanced Over To The District Attorneys. As If He Wanted To Beat The Meaningless Lives Out Of Their Wicked Bodies, But Quickly Found Mental Composure.

After All, He Was Putting On The Performance Of A Lifetime And This Moment Of His Fame And Celebrity Status Was At Its Highest Peak.

He Looked Deceivingly Calm, But He Was Nervous With Stage Freight. He Returned His Gaze To Judge Kharnas Who Was In His Pulpit Hissing With Jealousy.

Larson Could Hear The Thoughts Of This Man, Placing Judgment On Him And Wanted To Slam The Corrupted Book That Wasn't Even A Bible, At The Judge Before The Trial Began.

"Where's The Separation Of Church And State?" Larson Thought To Himself.

"And If I Plead The Fifth, It's Automatic Guilt," He Continued Thinking Shaking His Head, "And The Lawyers Are All Friends With Each Other…It's Just The Way The Game Is Played."

Larson Declined To Neither Swear Nor Plead Against The BRAZOS Hierarchy. Defendants Were Forced To Place Their Hands On A Book That Contradicted The Authority Of Da Most High, Causing Sinners Of All Walks Of Life To Swear While Telling Lies.

One Plays The All Mighty Judger With The Sword While The Other Plays The Good Or Bad Angel. Larson Did Not Have The Face Of A De-Materializer, The People Said To Each Other Quietly. He Did Not Care Nor Have Concern Against The BRAZOS Regime So They Doubted He Would Be Violent About It.

Judge Kharnas Looked Over His Courtroom, "Mr. Larson Do You Understand The Charges Being Brought Against You?" Larson Responded In Disbelief, "I Rebuke You."

Judge Kharnas Stared At The Young Man Intently, "You Are Being Charged With Your Symbolic So-Called Passing Away Certificate. Eleven Counts Of Conspiracy To Commit Illegal Tyranny Assembly As A Spiritual Leader… One Count Of Attempted High-Minded Teachings, And Three Counts Of Extortion. Now, How Do You Find Yourself Of These Charges?" The Judge Asked Crossing His Fingers Onto His Desk And Leaning Back Into His Oversized Leather Chair."

"I Rebuke You," Larson Repeated Sharply.

Judge Kharnas' Tone Deepened With Anger, "Understand Mr. Larson, You Will Be Turned Over To The Authorities Of The BRAZOS Rule Of Law's Investigation." The Judge Pushed Forward Onto His Desk And Looked Over Larson' Charges.

He Took A Deep Breath And Looked At Larson Mischievously, "It Seems You Are Considered A Threat To Society!" He Shouted Angrily.

Everyone In The Court Erupted In Loud Conversations Amongst Themselves. Suddenly, The Courtroom Doors Swung Open Disrupting The Courts' Chatter.

"Excuse Me, Judge! Excuse Me!" A Female Shouted. Larson Turned To Face The Woman Advancing Down The Aisle. The Voice Was Of Marla Carter. She Paused To Catch Her Breath When She Approached Larson' Desk.

"High Honor, I'm Sorry I'm Late. I'm Mr. Larson' Attorney, Marla Carter," The Tall Woman Said Staring At Larson. She Placed Her Briefcase On The Desk And Continued,

"High Honor I Request A Decent Bond For My Client." Judge Kharnas Became Annoyed And Bit His Bottom Lip To Contain His Anger,

"Ms. Carter..." He Said Roughly, "You Come Into My Courtroom Late, And Now You Want To Request A Bond For Your Client?" He Said Slamming His Hand On His Desk.

"Yes, High Honor That's Correct," Marla Carter, Answered With Confidence Resisting The Judges' Negativity.

"Excuse Me, High Honor," The District Attorney Interrupted Standing From His Seat, "We Requested The Defendant Not To Be Given Bail," He Said Throwing An Angry Glare At Marla Carter For Entering The Courtroom.

"I Object To That High Honor!" Marla Carter Responded Rolling Her Eyes Towards The Prosecutor. "I Mean, After All, He Is Considered Very Dangerous," The District Attorney Interrupted Sarcastically. Marla Carter Became Impatient With The Disagreeable Man And Turned Toward The Judge. She Spoke With Authority, "Yes, Yes, We Already Heard That Part High Honor," She Said Sternly Staring At The District Attorney Then Back To The Judge,

"But Regardless Of The Charges Against Mr. Larson, He Was Forced To Go Into Hiding For Months For His Protection."

"Yes, She Is Correct," Judge Kharnas, Mumbled Painfully Not Wanting To Admit The Truth.

"High Honor," She Continued, "For My Client To Be Accused Of Being The Larcenni The Enforcer Is Just Plain Crazy." Marla Carter Looked At Larson Who Had His Eyes Closed As Though He Were Meditating. "High Honor, When The B.R.L-Illiana Chiefs Arrested My Client They Had Not Seen Him Electro-Lightning Striking Anyone, And They Have No Proof That He Did," Marla Carter Said Holding Up A Document From Her Desk. "Still At This Time, The B.R.L-Illiana Chiefs Cannot Identify This So-Called Da Larcenni...Da Anunnaqi,"

Marla Carter Said Sarcastically Looking At The District Attorney. "I Also Wanted To Add That, Upon His Arrest, There Was Another Person Who Had Eluded The Scene...We Have Documents And Footage To Prove This!" The Courtroom Erupted Again In Loud Murmuring.

The District Attorney Dropped Into His Seat And Began Searched Through His Paperwork,

"Okay, But High Honor, We Are Starting An Investigation In Connection With His Arrest At Stanley's Warehouse Explosion...Why Was He There?"

"Oh Please Belying, Come On!" Marla Carter Shouted Towards The District Attorney,

"High Honor, There Is No Way My Client Could Have Been At Both Locations At The Same Time! The Travel Time Between The Two Sites Is Approximately An Hour Drive. My Client Was Reported To Be At Castoni's Warehouse Twenty Minutes After Stanley's Warehouse Explosion—Impossible," Marla Carter Said Laughing Out Loud While She Pulled Out The Seat Beside Larson And Made Herself Comfortable.

"Now Are There Any Objections To Her Arguments?" Judge Kharnas Asked Belying Disappointingly. "No High Honor," Belying Replied, "Not At The Moment."

"Well Then," The Judge Said, "I'm Setting A Requested Bond For One Million. Are There Any Objections To The Bond Ms. Carter?"

"No, High Honor," She Replied. The Judge Tapped His Fingers On His Desk, "District Attorney, And Do You Have Any Objections?" "No, High Honor," Belying, Said.

"Okay, Let's See. I'll Set This Trial For Friday, September 27, 2027, D.A., At 9 AM. BRAZOS Rule Of Law Adjourned,"

Judge Kharnas Said Hitting His Sound Block With His Gavel. "All Rise…"

BRAZOS Police Carrying Electro-Taser Guns Quickly Escorted Marla Carter And Larson Out Of The Courtroom. Camera Flashing Android Paparazzi Waited Patiently Outside The Courtroom; And Clogged The Court Hallway Slowing Down In Desperation; To Capture A Photo Of ChristOn M Larson. The BRAZOS Guards Began Using Electro-Taser Guns To Fight Off The Swarm Of Android Reporters And Photographers. Larson Was Still A Celebrity In Their Eyes, Not Only Because He Was Mysteriously Alive, But Also Because He Stood Up Against BRAZOS With No Fear. He Was Always Cautious About Any Remarks He Made About BRAZOS In The Media Because He Knew His Words Would Be Altered Negatively. As Larson Made His Way Through The Crowded Hallway, He Found Himself Lost In His Thoughts.

"My Life Was Placed In The Hands Of BRAZOS Rule Of Law…The Greatest Illusionists Of All!" He Thought Frustratingly. He And Carter Continued To Push Through The Bodies That Barricaded Them So They Could Get A Shot Of Larson.

"Look At Them," He Thought, "They Believe That They Know Me.

Who Is ChristOn M Larson?"

He Says In His Mind, As His Body Got Closer To The Exit, A Man Caught Up In This World Of BRAZOS When I Only Wanted Out!" He Pressed His Hand On His Head While Still Being Escorted By The Police Who Were Somehow Protecting Him From The Surrounding Frenzy.

"Rumors About Me Are Spreading…About Me Being A Mystery Enforcer; Yet, There Was Never Any Mystery About Me In The First Place. I Am Only That Voice They Fought To Keep Silent," He Thought As He Felt His Anger Rising In His Chest.

"Did I Fake My So-Called Passing Away Or Are They Denying That They Were Trying To De-Materialize Me? Apparently, Their Persecution Did Not Go The Way They Planned."

Larson Pushed The Existing Door Of The Building Open And Kept Walking Towards A Vehicle With Carter. The Reporters And The Paparazzi On His Tail. He Jumped Into The Black

Tinted Escalade Truck. Reporters And Paparazzi Pasted Themselves To The Vehicle Like Ants On An Apple. Larson Smiled To The Cameras That Were Pressed Against The Window.

"So What Is The Truth To This Story?" He Thought To Himself. "We Pulled Off The Ultimate Double-Cross, By Denying Who We Really Are…So We'll Wait Until That Final Hour…To Let The Ultimate War Of Enforcers Begin!" Larson Shouted In His Head As His Truck Pulled Away From In Front Of The Courtroom. He Turned To Look Out The Back Window And Saw The Crowd Beginning To Chase His Vehicle Moving Slowly Towards The Red Light A Few Feet Ahead At The Intersection.

Marquis Castoni's Charges Were Presented Next By The Prosecution To The BRAZOS Hierarchy…They No Longer Needed Him, Castoni, Because He Betrayed Their Trust For The Very Last Time Making Him An Enemy To The BRAZOS Rule. Therefore, Friends Become Enemies And Enemies Become Friends For Survival… That One Man They Assumed Was Destroyed, Is Now Staring Them In The Face. As It Was Recorded In The Scriptures, 'Judge And You Will Be Judged,'" The Elders Nodded In Agreement A Second Time.

"Tua, Tua," They Said In Unison.

"For That Great And Dreadful Day Is Here, Now. In The World Of Spiritual Eyes Of Deceiving Faces, There Is No Such Thing As Good And Evil…Why? Because The Evil Man Is Good At Being Evil, And The Good Man Is Evil At Being Good. These Events Will Spark The Last War For Universal Rulership Because Both Sides Are Trying To Prove Their Greatness Of Free Will… With Only A Few Wanting To Please Da Most High."

****

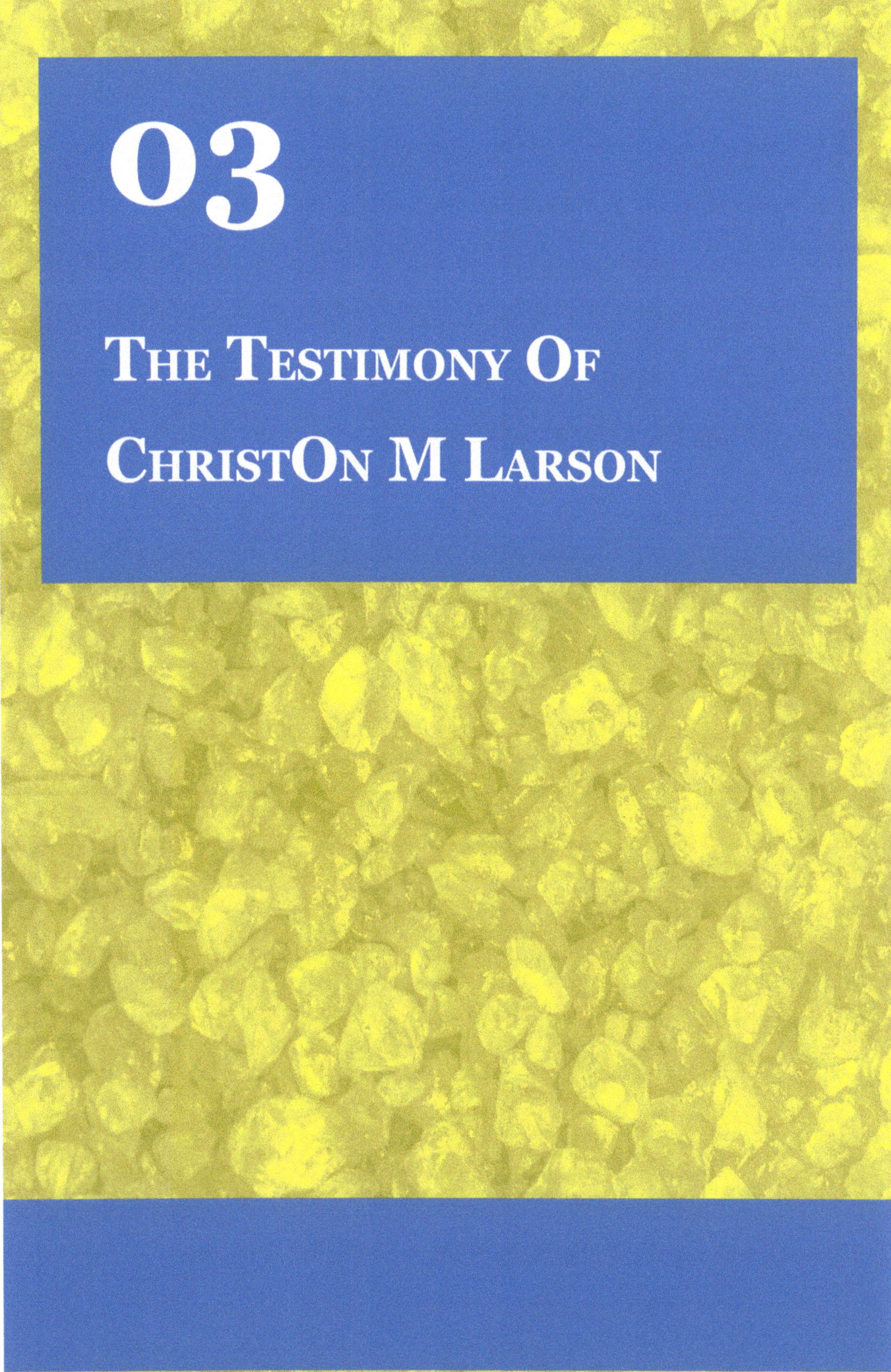

03

THE TESTIMONY OF CHRISTON M LARSON

After The Hearing, Larson Was Escorted To The B.R.L-Illiana Office In The BRAZOS Rule Of Law Building Downtown. He Was Placed In A Small Air-Conditioned Room Where The Walls Were Covered With Wanted Pictures, Some Of The Photos Dated As Far Back As The 1930s. There Were Also Photos Of Illinois State Chiefs Receiving Awards. One Particular Photo Was Of Mayor Elite Abraham Musa; He Was With Then City Attorney Francis Aurelius And The Illinois Head State Director Paul Romajinn.

"Excuse Me," Larson Said Slightly Stressed Out By The Day.

"Yes, Mr. Larson?" Ms. Marla Carter Answered As She Pulled Out Her Seat At The Table Where Larson Was Sitting. She Removed Her Glasses From Her Face And Placed Them On The Table. As She Turned To Larson And Looked At Him Seriously. She Was A Gorgeous Woman With A Honey Brown Complexion. If It Weren't For Her Silver Colored Hair, You Would Think She Was In Her Late Twenties Or Early Thirties; She Looked Very Young.

Her Attire Was Of Abyssinian Origin; It Was An Ivory Colored Dress With The Royal Purple And Red Colors Streaking Through It. Carter Also Sported Da Supreme 9Ruby, And Da Grand Emerald Lioness Of Judah Rings On Each Pinky Finger Like Larson Wore His.

She Looked Away From Larson Quickly, Then Glanced Back While She Began Searching Through Paperwork, "You Know," She Said Squinting Her Eyes At Larson, "I Just Love Those Rings. I See We Have A Similar Style," She Said And Smiled Softly. Suddenly, Both Larson And Carter Paused And Quickly Looked Towards The Turning Doorknob. As The Door Pushed Open, Carter Reached For Her Glasses And Stood Up Quickly.

It Was B.R.L-Illiana Chief Ragu'el, A Tall Abyssinian Man Approximately 5'11" With A Muscular Frame. He Had A Short Hair Cut About And Inch Away From His Scalp And A Freshly Cut Goatee. Chief Ragu'el Walked Into The Room And Offered Larson And Carter

Coffee. Larson Hesitated To Say Yes Because He Preferred Drinking The Expensive Brands And Considered Any Other Kinds.

"Cheap Tasting Coffee. It's Been A Long Day, Why Not?" He And Carter Accepted A Cup.

Carter Placed Her Briefcase On The Table, And She Pulled Out A Notepad And Began Searching For Her Pen In The Side Pocket. Chief Ragu'el Handed Them The Cups And Walked Out Of The Room Without Saying Another Word.

"That's Strange," Larson Said Taking A Sip Of His Coffee, "But Anyways, As I Was Saying…" He Began Since Both Carter And Ragu'el Interrupted Him Earlier.

"I'm Sorry, But I Don't Remember Hiring An Attorney," He Said Calmly Letting His Guard Down With A Sigh Of Relief Since He Left The Courthouse.

"Oh Yes, That!" She Said Looking Down At Her Documents. "Listen, Do You Trust And Have Faith In Father EGZIABHER Is Controlling Your Destiny?"

She Asks Without Glancing Towards Him And Continued Writing. "Of Course. Why?" He Asked Going On Guard Again.

"Well Mr. Larson," Carter Said With Her Head Tilted Down And Her Eyes Are Peering Over The Rims Over Glasses Staring At Larson Across The Table, "I'm…Your Guardian Angel."

"Whaaa…?" Larson Said Surprised By The Woman's Comment. "Wow…I Mean Okay? I Wasn't Expecting That Answer. So What…Father EGZIABHER Sent You To Me?"

He Asks Looking At The Woman With A Puzzling Expression On His Face. "I Mean…Come On Now Larson. You Don't Fit The Usual Description Of A Hardened Criminal. And I Know You Don't Feel Like Talking To Anyone About What Happened That Night."

Larson Paid No Attention To The Woman, "Guardian Angel?" He Thought While He Sat Staring At The Wall With A Confused Look On His Face.

"Did You Hear What I Just Said Larson?" She Asked.

"Yeah, Yeah, Of Course," He Said Shaking His Head And Putting His Hands On His Temples As Though He Had A Headache. "Listen Ms. Carter; It's Just I Don't Trust Anybody That's All."

"Why Is That?" She Asked Still Peering At Him Over The Rims Of Her Glasses.

"Well, I'm Scared I Might Get Put In Jail, Get Tortured Or Mistreated. I Mean If There's Anybody I Do Trust It Would Be Arch Chief Michaels And My Private Psychologist Dr. Addis W. Gondar…There The Only Two I Trust," Larson Said As He Stood Up From His Seat With Ms. Carter Following Him With Her Eyes.

"If You Want Answers, They'll Have To Be Present," He Said With Back Turned To Her As He Stared At The Photos On The Wall. "If You Want Answers, Then Please Call My Doctor."

"Okay," Ms. Carter Replied As She Pushed Her Glasses Up On Her Face Looking Through Them Better. "I'll Make The Call. You Got A Number For The Both Of Them?" She Asked.

Larson Wrote It Down For Her, And She Walked Out Of The Room. An Hour And Thirty-Seven Minutes Later The Doctor, Followed By Arch Chief Sham Michaels, Entered The Room Where Marla Carter Had Been Waiting.

"Hello, You Must Be Ms. Carter?" Dr. Addis W. Gondar Said Stretching Out His Hand To Carter. "Yes, I Am," She Said Accepting His Hand And Shook It Firmly.

"How Are You Doing? I'm His Psychiatrist Dr. Addis W. Gondar, And From What I Was Told, You've Already Met Arch Chief Sham Michaels Of The B.R.L-Illiana Police Department?" He Asked Facing Arch Chief Michaels. "Yes, We've Met," She Said Nodding Her Head To Arch Chief Michaels, "How Do You Do?"

Arch Chief Michaels Nodded In Return, "I'm Well Thank You." Dr. Addis Faced Carter, "So Ms. Carter, I Was Told That One Of My Patients Requested My Service."

"Yes, A Mutual Client By The Name Of ChristOn M Larson." Dr. Gondar's Neck Stuck Out In Astonishment, "What! Mr. Larson' Alive?" He Looked At Arch Chief Michaels With Wide Eyes. "They Said It Was Only A Rumor…Well, This Will Be Fascinating," Dr. Gondar Said Removing His Khaki Trench Coat To Reveal A Black Suit With A Mustard Colored Tie. The Man Was About Six Feet Tall With A Bald Head And A Neatly Trimmed Mustache.

"Where Is He Now?" His Voice Was Raspy And Seemed To Command Attention Naturally.

"He Is In The Other Room," Ms. Carter Said Nodding Signaling Towards The Door Down The Short Hallway. "He Is Willing To Talk, But Only To You Two. I Need You To Get Full Details," She Said To Him.

"I Believe We Can Put Him Under Hypnosis," Dr. Gondar Said As The Other Two Agreed. The Three People Walked Into The Room Where ChristOn M Larson Was Seated With His Back To The Door.

"Mr. Larson," Arch Chief Michaels's Voice Thundered Through The Room As He Leaned Against A Wall Staring At The Young Man, "We've Been Looking For You For Quite Some Time Now. I Can Arrange For Your Relocation To BRAZOS Concentration Camps If You Like," Michaels Said Annoyingly, "Oh And Your Psychiatrist, Is Standing Behind You."

Larson Turned To See Dr. Gondar Who Was Still In Shocked From The News. "You Look Great ChristOn!" Dr. Gondar Shouted. Larson Stood, And Both Men Greeted Each Other Warmly. "The News Of Your Passing Shocked Many Of Us ChristOn…The Performances… Your Music…Your Film Production…It Was Greatly Missed. It Has Been A While Since We've Last Had A Session, Are You Ready?"

"Yes Doc," Larson Replied And Noticed Two Chiefs Wheeling A Recliner Chair Into The Room. "So What Will The Session Consist Of?" He Asked.

"I'm Going To Put You Under Hypnosis ChristOn, Have A Seat," Dr. Gondar Directs Him Towards The Chair. Larson Sat In The Chair And Adjusted Himself To Be Comfortable.

Well, Where Do We Begin?" Larson Asked As He Gathered His Thoughts On What He Might Say Or What He Might Choose To Remember.

"This Will Be Recorded In My Files," Arch Chief Michaels Said Pulling Out A Small Recorder From His Pocket. He Pulled Up One Of The Chairs Beside Larson.

"Anytime You're Ready Dr. Gondar". The Doctor Began The Procedure, "For Now Lie Back And Close Your Eyes, I Want You To Feel Relaxed… Take A Long Deep Breath…. Take Another Deep Breath And Just Relax."

Larson Closed His Eyes And Could Hear Dr. Gondar's Voice Counting Backward From 10, As He Fell Further And Further Into A Deep Sleep. His Mind Drifted Back Down Memory Lane To His Senior Year In High School. At That Time, He Was Trying To Make Money And Wrote Rap Lyrics During English Class, Which He Felt Was Often A Boring Class.

"I'm On The Street Corner…Yeah, I Remember It's Thursday At 9:30 PM, The Year Is 1995 A.D. …" Larson Said In His Hypnotic State.

In The Year 1995 A.D.,

For As Long As I Can Remember, I've Always Wanted To Be A Rap Star. I Grew Up In A Conservative Vice Lord Neighborhood, Just Four Blocks From Our Arch Rivals. Observing Amnesia Negus Getting They Hustle On, Always Looking For A Dice Game. I Picked Up On That From My Older Cousin, Joe Da Posey. We Used To Ride Around In His Gold Color 84 Bonneville Passing That Hot Water Around, Early In The Morning… Everyday. Joe Da Posey Was One Of My Favorite Cousins, And He Honestly Didn't Give A Damn About Anybody's Feelings Or Excuses, But He Was Always Cool With Me, Making Sure That Nobody Messed With Me. His Reputation Was Harsh, Known For Slappin' Negative Souls As Amnesia Negus.

I Learned Profanity From Him As If He Was The Master Of It. And The Females…Wow… He Talked The Worst Stress To Them, And They Loved Him For It Because It Was All Flattery Attention The Women Loved About Him. Joe Had A Long Paper Trail.

He'd Drive Around In Defiance To The Law And Would Talk Stress To The Police Without A Drivers' License. He Had Cookouts Almost Every Day, And He Was A Mean Cook On The Grill… And He Bragged About It Too, Causing Everyone To Come On The Scene; From South Bend, Indiana And The Rest Of Da Ill-State Enforcers From East Bellefontaine Street. Joe Gave Me Respect Because I Gave Him Knowledge About The Creator And Ancient History. He Taught Me The Ways Of Surviving The Streets, And He Knew I Would Always Have His Back. Later On, He Went To Jail During The Time I First Got Deployed To The Middle East As An Infantryman Soldier.

You Know, I've Always Wondered Where The Middle West, Middle South, And The Middle North Were? Rumor Has It That The Ancient Abyssinian Empire, Once Stretched As Far Being Rulers Of Jerusalem, Controlled By The Abyssinian Falasha Tribe Before The Pale Arabs. Who Originally Are The Persian And Hindu Tribes Invaded And Infiltrated And Introduced Their Version Of Islam And Called Theirs Dina Islam. The Pale Arabs Sanctioned Slavery On The Nubians After They Defeated The Romans. These Original Nubians Resided In Iraq, Saudi Arabian, Yemen, Syria, Palestine And Northern Territories Of Continent Ethiopia, Africa.

This Truth Was The Kind Of Knowledge We Shared While Keeping In Contact Through Letters After He Was Incarcerated And Moved Down To Champaign. He Would Play His Biggest Role To Me. In My Eyes, He Was Of The Most Honorable… He Was Da Enforcer Jo Da Posey, With A Personality Great Enough To Be Written In Books Made To Become Movies Entitled, "Jo Da Posey, Slappin' Negative Souls As Amnesia Negus For No Damn Reason!"

Larson Laughed To Himself In His Hypnotic State…."Okay…Okay…My Mind Is Somewhere Else Now," Larson Said As His Eyes Began Blinking Rapidly Although They Were Closed. "My Life Has Always Been A Simple Routine, But For Some Reason One Particular Night, I Started Seeing My Life From A Different Angle. Here I Am Losing Money, While The Nine Million Warring Angels Known As Former Gang Members Talking Stress On The Side.

Especially Cochise Russell Aka Big X, The Hood Leader, Who Is Really Rubbing It In. See, Big X Fell Out With My Best Friend Chaos Because We Didn't Buy Cush From Him Anymore, But I'll Get To Chaos Later. Anyway, Big X Was The Biggest Demon And Instigator, But He Was Untouchable In The Hood. We Always Wondered Where His Cush Came From? But I Found Out Later… But Anyway, Back To The Story. See It Was 10:13 PM, And We Were On The Block. A Red Car Pulled Up. At First, I Don't Recognize Whom It Is Right, Until T-Slick Yelled Out, 'What's The Demonstration, Amnesia Negus?' And Suddenly The Dice Game Stopped!

Everybody Jumped Into Defensive Mode. The Wrong Word Can Mean Somebody's Life Or Life Behind Bars. But We Were Motivated Superficial, Invincible; None Of Us Cared About Dying…Only Getting Robbed.

Big X Yelled Out With An Attitude, 'T-Slick Man…Amnesia Negus Shut The Hell Up! They Apostles From Magog Park! Ya'll Amnesia Negus Stand Down; Anyways, What's Up Reno And K-Man?' Big X And Karo Approached The Car. I Mean…This Stress Was Odd Because I Wasn't Strapped. I Moved To The Back Of All Them Amnesia Negus Still Staring Cuz I Noticed Big X And Karo Whispering To The Amnesia Negus In The Car… Some Funny Business So I Cuffed My Money And Some Other People's Money Quick From The Pavement And Moved Over To The Corner Of The Alley And Watched From The Side.

Suddenly Another Car Pulled Up. Pow! Pow! Brains And Pieces Of Skull Explode Everywhere From Karo's Head…And It's Like I Saw Him Falling In Slow Motion And Time Stopped Like A Wounded Animal Under A Cloud Of Smoke. Pow! Pow! Pow! Pow! More Gunfire Erupted From Both Sides. I Was Scared As Hell, Dippin' Through The Small Alleyway, Hearing Bullets Popping Off In The Background Feeling Like Every Last Bullet Was Screaming For The Passing Aways! I Hear Other Feet Behind Me As I Run South Towards My Street. The Red Car Must Have Swung Around A Corner Real Quick.

Cuz, I Saw It In A Reflection Behind Me. I Saw A Glimpse Of The Other Guys Running Behind Me Too…We're All Runnin' Fast. We Dipped Into Another Alley, Ran Into The Street And Saw The Car Speeding Down Another Street Parallel Tryin' To Cut Us Off. T-Slick Pulls Out His Strap; The Car Spun Around The Corner And Headed Straight At Us As We Ran Across The Street To Get To The Other Side. He Sent Six Slugs Straight From Hell At The Speedin' Car And Hit The Windshield. The Whole Scene Was Like A Movie, But No One Yells 'Cut!' And For The Ones Getting Shot, There Were No Stunt Men To Take Their Place Changing Scenes. We Keep Running As Fast As We Could. Most People Would Try To Get Revenge On These Amnesia Negus, But From My Point Of View, I Didn't Care.

Fear Was There Until I Felt Like Something Was Keeping Me From Getting Shot. As I Continue Running, I Was Dodging And Jumping Over Crazy Ass Animals Not Knowing Where It Came From? We Kept Running And Saw The Car That Was Driving Parallel To Us, Spun Wildly Onto Another Street And Drove Away In The Opposite Direction As Police Sirens Closed In On Them.

I Ran In A Dark Corner Breathing Hard, My Heart Beating Out Of My Chest And T-Slick Dismantled The Gun With My Sweaty Hands. He Threw It In Pieces Down Some Holes In The Cement. I Wiped The Sweat From My Forehead And Began Walking Down The Sidewalk.

I Don't Know If Someone's Life Was Lost And Big X, If He's Still Alive, He's Got Some Explaining To Do. I Made My Way To My Bedroom Without Waking My Mom. I Don't Even Bother To Turn On The News; I Just Counted My Cash. It Was Just Under Fourteen Hundred Dollars…Not Bad! I Fell To My Bed Staring At The Ceiling, Looking At All The Famous Rap Artist Posters, Saying To Myself, 'I Need To Be Doing Just That.' I Was Tired Of All The Bullstress, Always Getting Caught Up In Other People's Drama.

I Hear My Mother Call Me…Her Voice Was So Comforting, She Always Worrying About Me. Can't Let Her Know About Tonight That's For Sure. I Hear Her Call Me Again. I Don't Need Her Walking In My Room, So I Replied To Her, 'Yeah!' 'ChristOn I Was Just Checking To See If You're All Right. My Mother Was Always Doing Her Random Checks, 'Don't You Have School Tomorrow? I Hope You Weren't In Some Stress Tonight Young Man…You Know, I Don't Play That!' 'No Mama I'm Fine, Just Getting Ready For School Tomorrow. Sorry, I Came In So Late … Sorry!' 'Night Baby,' My Mother Said, And I Heard Her Door Close. I Changed My Clothes, Took A Shower, Threw On A Pair Of Pants And Closed My Eyes Tired As Hell.

The Next Morning

'ChristOn Larson, ChristOn Larson, Boy Get Your Behind Up!' Damn, It Was Daytime Already. I Looked At My Clock And Saw That I Slept For Seven Hours, But It Felt Like Fifteen

Minutes. I Have To Remember To Take My Freshly Pressed Outfit Down From The Door Cuz She Never Fails, To Slam The Door Open And It Falls To The Ground. 'ChristOn!'

'Mama…What Man!' My Mouth Slips And Only Makes The Situation Worse. I Threw The Sheets Over My Head Like They Were Sound Proof But Her Voice Penetrates It. 'First Of All,' She Pushed The Door Open And Down Went My Outfit, "I Am Not Your Goddamn Man. Second, I'm Sick Of Coming In Here For The Third Time To Get Your Ass Up For School.'

She Issued Her Drill Sergeant Commands And Walked Out My Room With My Outfit Crushed Behind The Door. Mrs. Mary Larson, A Strong Spirited Mother, Without A Doubt, Does Not Take Stress From Anybody, But She Remains A Good Person. Luckily For Me, I'm The Only Child She Was Raising In Occupied Chicago. We Lived In Salsara Park On The West Side, Of East Bellefontaine Street. I Don't Remember My Father That Much…Just Stories; He Was A Scholar And Citizen In Abyssinia. My Parents Separated When I Was Nine.

She Said My Dad Was Forced To Go Back To Abyssinia Because Of Political Views. However, My Best Friend C. Andrew Linzy Was That Father Figure In My Life. He Helped Influenced Me To Join The Military. He Had Another Family, Who Were My Half Brothers In Champaign, Illinois. Mama Often Said That Being A Scholar Was Very Controversial; He Traveled Too Much, Plus He Was Too Secretive. I Know He's Still Alive. I Know Because I Receive Nine Hundred Dollars A Month And We Own Our House.

Mom Used To Be A Secretary For This Law Firm Until Donald James Finley Was Selected Pro-Tem Mayor Elite In 2023 D.A. She Was Furious That The Organization Called BRAZOS Had Taken Over The City. She Said That All The Lawyers Who Wouldn't Work For BRAZOS Were Being Forced Out Of Practice And All Local Unions Were Abolished.

At Least Work Wages Went Up, So Mama Quickly Changed Her Mind About BRAZOS. After A Week Of Being Laid Off, She Received Money For Not Working—A Check In Her Usual Full Amount. It Wasn't Unemployment Money; It Was From The BRAZOS Administration Offering Mama Three Weeks To Work For Them, An Offer No One Could Refuse…With Double Pay.

But Back To 1995 A.D., My Mama Cooks The Best Food So Waking Up Wasn't So Bad Just Cuz Of The Breakfast. In Just A Couple Of Minutes My Ride Was Coming So I Had To Eat Quick… Then The News Came On About The Shoot Out!

'ChristOn Larson, You Wouldn't Know Anything About That Shoot Out, Would You Now?' I Got So Nervous I Couldn't Swallow. I Mean What Do I Say? If I Say No, She Will Know I'm Told The Greatest Story Ever Told. Cuz I Didn't Know How To Lie To The Woman. And If I Say Yes…Damn, I Was Screwed. 'Mama, I Only Heard Shots!'

'What! So You Were There?'

'Not Really... Kind Of Mama But I Got Out Of There!' 'Boy, You're My Only Son! My Only Child! I Don't Need To Loose My Only Child ChristOn! Do Not Bring Them People To My House Tellin' Me Your Passed Away! Stay Away From That Stress!' Thank Goodness The Doorbell Rang; It Was Haweyah. 'You Better Get Your Rear-End Back Home After School! You Hear Me ChristOn!'

'Yeah, Ma! Love You', So I Ran Out The House And Into The Car. This Was The Way My Day Started Every Morning Before School. I Greeted My Girlfriend, Haweyah By Kissing Her On The Cheek When I Jumped In The Car. 'What's Going On Girl?' '

Nothin', Haweyah Turned Up The Volume On The Songs That I Made And Began Giving Feedback On Them." I Had Been Anticipating Her Presence Since The Day Before—Just Trying To Imagine What Outfit She Would Wear. The Girl Had An Aura Of Deception; She Tried So Hard To Be Good, But I Was Turned On By Her Seduction.

All I Could Do Was Stare At Her While She Drove And Spoke. Intrigued By Her Dark Scorched Copper Tone Skin And Blue Eyes That Were Touched With Eyeliner And Mascara. While She Looked At The Car In Front Of Her And Checked Her Rear View Mirror With The Light Reflecting Off Her Glossed Lips. Yeah…I Noticed Everything Except For What She Was Saying Because Of How Beautiful She Was. She Was About 5'10"; Medium Built With Thickness In The Right Places…A Healthy Girl, Less Than Perfection. She Always Wore Her Hair Relaxed

Straight, Either In Weaves, Tracks On The Side Showing The Length Of Her Artificial Hair That Sat Almost To The Middle Of Her Back. But Today, Her Hair Was In A Ponytail With Her 'Press Hanging Down In An Oval Shape. She Turned Her Face To Me, And I Saw Her Lips Move… And All I Could Think Was 'She's So Maybelline.'

'ChristOn…Hello…Are You Listening To Me?' She Said To Me Then She Looked Back At The Road, 'Where's Chaos, I Thought You Would Be With Him? And Why Were You Looking At Me Like That?' 'Oh Yeah,' I Looked Back At The Road Quickly And Pulled Myself Out Of Haweyah's Trance, 'Can We Pick Him Up?'

'Yeah, Of Course, Why Not,' She Said And Turned Into A Few Back Roads Towards Chaos' Girlfriend's House. We Pulled Up To See Chaos Waiting On The Sidewalk Like He Was Waiting For The Magic School Bus To Show Up. 'What's Happenin' My Amnesia Negus'?' Chaos Said As He Jumped In The Car With A Huge Grin On His Face. He Sat In The Middle Back Passenger Seat, And As Usual, He Left His Backpack On His Back So His Body Could Lean Forward And Be Pressed Up In The Midst Of Haweyah's Seat And Me So He Could Be A Part Of Our Conversation.

'Man, Why Don't You Take Your Bag Off And Lean Your Ass Back? I Can't See The Cars Behind Me Cuz Of Yo' Big Head!' Haweyah Said, And We Couldn't Help Cracking Up. 'I'm Not Leanin' Back Girl Cuz When Ya'll Talk The Music's Too Loud Back Here, And I Can't Hear Stress!' Chaos Said Still Grinning His White Teeth. 'So I'll Turn It Down,' I Said To Chaos, But He Was Still Persistent As Always. 'Nuh Uh! I'm Comfortable Right Here,' He Said.

'Okay Fine, Take Your Bag Off Your Back Then, And Crouch Down A Little Cause I Got To See Behind Me And You're Blocking My View,' So Chaos Did Just That. 'Thank You, Big Head,' Haweyah Said And Kept On Driving Safely Like She Always Did. 'So I Got Something To Tell You Guys,' I Turned And Looked At Them, 'I Was Out With Castoni JR. Last Night.' Chaos And Haweyah Looked Passed Away At Me With Their Mouths Dropped Open. 'Castoni JR! Were You With That Thieving-Ass Gangsta? You Know Your Mom Don't Like You Hanging Around

Him!' Haweyah Reminded Me Sounding Disappointed. I Know, But Listen, You Know That Fancy Club On Bridgeview Avenue, Castonis Bar? 'Yeah, I've Been There,' She Replied. 'Okay, I Got An Interview With The Boss, And Chaos, You Too!' I Told Him Excitedly. 'What? Are You Serious?' Chaos Leaned In Towards Me. 'We Plugged ChristOn?' He Asked. 'Yeah That's Right Chaos, And We Got To Rehearse Too!'

I Explained Everything To Them About The Interview, And They Were Both Excited, And I Felt Great…Like A Hero Because I Was Changing Our Foundations; We Were All Very Talented. Lorenzo Aka Chaos, My First Cousin, Was A Vicious Emcee. You See, I Knew Chaos Since We Were Infants And He And I Are One In The Same; We Did Everything Together. If He Had A Problem, It Became My Problem… And Trust Me; He Had A Lot Of Challenges. He Also Had An Uncontrollable Temper. One Time He Got A Speeding Ticket. On The Day Of The Trial, Instead Of Just Paying The Ticket, He Slapped The Officer Who Gave It To Him, And Then He Spit In The Judge's Face!

Being A Minor, He Got Seven Months In Saint Charles' Correctional Center. He Then Quickly Gained The Reputation Of Being A Brutal, Chaotic Violator…Someone Who Just Didn't Give A Damn! I Told Chaos About The Dice Game And The Chase, And He Didn't Say Much, But I Knew What He Was Thinking. Haweyah Didn't Say Much Either, But She Always Kept Quiet And Never Gave Her Opinion. She Knew Things Happened The Way They Were Supposed To And Left It Alone. We Had Bad Habits, But We Never Gave A Stress; However, We Were Young And Ignorant, Not Knowing Self At The Time.

Most Of The Amnesia Negus On My Block Didn't Make It Past The Age Of Thirty Years Old. 'ChristOn, What Time Are You Meeting With Castoni JR.?' Chaos Asked Me Leaning Back In His Seat. 'Right After School,' I Turned My Head To Look Out The Window And Saw Some Of My Classmates Drinking While Walking Towards School. Those Kids Always Got Drunk Before Class. I Don't Know How They Did It. 'Damn! The Alcohol, I Got The Cush,' Chaos

Said And Pulled Out A Rolled Blunt And Lit It.' No Hangovers Here; Only High Thinking, For Greater Minds And Higher Learning!'

The Car Filled Up With Smoke, But The Road Was Still Visible Because We Rolled The Windows Down. We All Took Turns, And Haweyah Just Continued To Drive Safely On The Speed Limit. 'We Got A Little Time Haweyah, At Least 15 Minutes. Let's Dip Around A Few Blocks.' Chaos Said So Haweyah Drove Through The Neighborhood Around The School Slowly.

While We Finished Up The Last Few Tokes. About A Few Minutes Later, Haweyah Pulled Into The School Parking Lot, And We All Jumped Out The Car. We Took Advantage Of The Wind And Walked Slowly To Air Ourselves Out.

We Spoke To A Few People As We Made Our Way To The School Door And Headed To Our Separate Homerooms After The Smell Had Gone From Our Clothing, But Like Every Morning, We Were Each Late. I Didn't Care Though Because All I Could Think About Was For Three O'clock To Hit So I Could Meet Castoni JR.. When The Bell Rang, I Made My Way Down To My First-Period Class, And There She Was, Haweyah E. Nekaybaw…The Love Of My Life, Sitting In The Front Row With Her Sweater On The Seat Saving It For Me. I Sat Down Beside Her, 'Thanks,' I Said To Her And She Smiled Back, Then Class Began.

Honestly, Haweyah Was The Only Girl For Me She Would Take Many Visits To America From Haiti. Last Two Years She Decided To Stay In America To Finish High School. We've Known Each Other For Just Over Three Years Now But Began Dating A Year Ago. Before We Dated, Chaos And I Had Different Girls Every Week…And That's The Truth! It Was Fun; We Were Players Of All Players, But It Got Boring. The Girls Were All The Same, None Of Them Gave Me What I Wanted Mentally, And Spiritually There Was No Stimulation And No Growth.

I Had To Find Out The Hard Way When I Lost Trust In Haweyah For Keeping Secrets. She Always Claimed On Another Man To Touch Her Either, Yeah Right! She Was Far-Reaching In Her Voodoo Studies And Traveled In Between Haiti And The States A Lot.

During Those Days She Practices Black Magic Something I Didn't Understand, Yet I Never Acknowledge Or Participated In Her Practices. She Was Gone During The Summers; We Would Always Anticipate Seeing Her During School Days; Mind You This Was Before We Were Together. At Times, I Really Didn't Think She Had Emotions Until One Day She Beat The Hell Out Of This Girl That I Was In A Relationship With? This Female Abused My Kindness Because I Was Trying To Put My Player Ways Behind Me, But Haweyah Made The Girl Pay The Ultimate Price, And The Girl Never Came Around Again.

Haweyah Told Me That Black Girls Were Never Taught To Be Loyal Due To The Fact They Are Not On Her Black Man's Side. If I Mention To Her The Woman's Fault She Would Get Infuriated And Did Not Want To Talk Much About That Touchy Subject. She Was Still Upset That I Didn't Protect My Heart And Pay Attention To The Manipulation That Was Happening To Me. One Day She Said To Me, 'These Women Out Here, Are Not For You; They Are Only Distractions. Now Promise Me You're Going To Maintain Your Focus!' But I Wanted To Be With Her; Confused If It Was A Lustful Feeling Or A Godly One.

I Knew Being With Her; I Could Not Be As Mannish As I Wanted To Be And Show Her My Sexual Side Like I Showed Those Other Chicks. So Yeah I Guess I Wasn't Ready For Her Yet. I Felt She Was Too Smart For High School. I Even Thought Maybe She Was Here To Watch Over Me Because She Stuck With Me Through The Roughest Times. As Sweet As She Smiled Looked Was As Deceiving As Her Grin Below The Surface Was.

After School, I Met Up With Castoni JR. He And I Have A Bit Of A Past. Castoni JR. Dropped Out Of School And Is A Few Years Older Than Me. He's A Thief, Just Like My Mama Always Lectured Me On Him. He Was Simply The Craziest Somalian I've Ever Met. I Remember Hearing The Rumors, As I Was Riding Around With Him. I Robbed That Liquor Store Off 23rd Street. All I Remember Was That He Was In The Store, As He Started Snooping Around, Then Ran Up To The Cash Register, Kicked In The Side Door And Pulled Out A Gun To The Man Behind The Till.

'Freeze! Negative Soul! Hands Up!' He Shouted. Castoni JR. Shot The Gun Twice, And The Cashier Went Into Shock. The Cashier Was Never Shot Or Injured Before He Grabbed The Cash And Ran Out The Store. As He Ran, He Turned Around And Said To The Man, 'This Is A Message From Rob Greene.' Of All The Stupid Things He Could Have Said, Why Rob Greene?

Greene Was Kingpin On The North Side—A Real Monster. The Joint We Hit Belonged To Marcus Doaker, His So-Called Partner Who Owed Him Money. Well After That, Greene And Doaker Went To War. Doaker Was De-Materialized, All Because Of Castoni JR's Bullstress. As Far As I Know, Castoni JR. Could Have Been De-Materialized, Too…I Mean The $7500 Was Not Worth The War, And He Could Have Been De-Materialized.

Okay, So Back To Me Meeting With Castoni JR After School…There He Stood In The School Parking Lot. He Threw His Cigarette On The Ground, Stepped On It And Walked Towards Me. He Was A Tall Guy About 5'11" And Very Skinny. Causing Him To Wear Layers Of Clothing To Make Himself Seem Bigger.

Like Today, He Was Dressed In A Blue Suede Jacket, With A Thick Sweater Underneath And The Collar Of His Black T-Shirt Sticking Out Through The Top. His Jet Black, Curly Hair Was Brushed Back, And His Mustache Was Thinly Shaved. He Never Wore Jeans Only Dickies…Just Because It Made His Legs Look A Little Fatter. He Pulled Out A Cigarette From His Pocket And Lit It.

'Hey, ChristOn!' He Said To Me Drawing A Breath In With His Head Leaning To The Side. 'How Are You Feeling?' 'I'm Cool. Are You Ready To Go?'

'Oh Yeah,' Castoni JR. Said Taking A Few Tokes Of His Cigarette.

'Castoni JR. What's Up?' Chaos Said While He And Haweyah Walked Up Behind Him. Castoni JR. Turned Around To Face Them, 'Chaos What's Going On? What's Up Haweyah, You Looking Good.'

'Hey Castoni JR.,' Haweyah Murmured And Walked Over To Give Me A Hug.

'So, ChristOn, You Ready To Go?' Asked Castoni JR..

'Yeah, Let's Bounce,' I Gave Haweyah A Kiss On The Cheek. 'Listen, Call Me When You Ready Later,' Chaos Said, Giving Me A Serious Look—As If He Had A Mission Elsewhere.

'Alright,' I Walked Away With Castoni JR. As He Walked Towards A Drop Top, Candy Red 1995 Mustang Sitting On Wishbones. 'Damn, This Is Your Ride?' I Jumped Into The Car, And Castoni JR. Began To Drive. It Took Us About A Half-Hour To Get To Where We Were Going But Felt Like Fifteen Minutes Because Of How Much We Were Talking.

Castoni's Bar Was Located Off Of Bridgeview Avenue, And It Was A Very Spectacular Club Internally And Externally Architecturally And Because Of The Famous Recording Artists That Came Through. The Bar, Which Was Actually A Club, Was Always A Full House Every Night And Was A Place Where Big Timers Came To Get Peace Because Of Its Low-Key Profile.

It Was A True Moneymaking Machine, And I Was Invited To Perform There... Owned By The Don, Marquis Castoni, Castoni JR.'s "So-Called" Father. Castoni JR. Had His Doubts About The Old Don, But That's Another Story. I Walked Through The Large Sliding Glass Doors Of The Bar And Entered Into The Seating Area.

The Bar Was Huge And Was Designed With Glass And Mirrors All Over. The Staircase That Led To The Second Floor Was Also See-Through Like A Glass Substance As Well. The Second-Floor Balcony That Over Looked The Stage Was Also Glass With A Ledge Where Spectators Could Set Their Drinks Down. Castoni JR. Led Me To The Third Floor Of The Club Where I Had Never Been Before. We Stepped Out Of The Glass Elevator And Into A Hallway That Over Looked The Club.

The Walls And Floors Were Also Glassed And It Was Freaky As Hell Because I Thought I Would Fall Through It. We Walked Down The Long Hall And Turned A Corner Into Two Red Doors. It Was The Lavish Office Of Don Marquis Castoni I Assumed Because I Saw Him Sitting At A Large Wooden Desk Talking On A Cell Phone With Two Large Body Guards Relaxing In Some Leather Recliner Seats. He Greeted His Son And Me With A Nod And Gestured With His

Hand To Sit Down In The Leather Seats Across From His Desk. His Walls Were Filled Pictures And Paintings Of Famous Artists Who Came To Castoni's Bar; They Were Mainly Rap Artists.

'Yes, Yes, Come Tonight I'll Be Here,' Marquis Castoni Said To The Person On The Phone. 'Johnny, Johnny Listen, You Don't Have To Worry About Doing Work Here Because My Office Is About 90% Sound Proof You Understand?' Castoni Shook His Head. 'Okay, Well I Can't Talk Right Now About This I Have A Client In Front Of Me. Alright.' Castoni Hung Up The Phone. 'Castoni JR., You Don't Offer Your Friend A Drink?' The Man's Voice Was Husky And Cumbersome Like His Body.

'Oh Yeah, ChristOn You Want Something To Drink?' Castoni JR. Asked As Walked To The Mini Bar Across The Room. 'Water Is Fine Thanks,' I Told Castoni JR. 'Water? We Have Every Kind Of Alcohol Here, And You Want Water?' Castoni Asked Jokingly. 'I Don't Like Alcohol,' I Said.

'Ahhh,' Castoni Said Rubbing His Chin. 'So You're The Young Man My Son Spoke About? The Talented Freestyler?' The Man Asked. Don Marquis Castoni Was A Strong Black Somalian Man With Truckloads Of Wealth…The Man Was Wealthy Beyond His Means And Spent And Invested His Money Wisely, Which Later Affected His Political Status Positively In **Occupied Chicago**. Like Many East Africans, Castoni's Hair Was Wavy, Which He Wore In A Ponytail Often. His Skin Complexion Was As Dark As His Black Hair And Dark Eyes.

He Was About 6'3", The Same Height As His Son Except He Was Much Larger, In A Muscular, Medium Built And Chubby Way Because He Used To Be A Local Boxer. Later He Became A Manager In The Music Industry Along With His Older Brother, Who Was Shot And De-Materialized Twenty Years Ago. After His Passing Away. Don Marquis Married His Brother's Girlfriend. The Man Was So Godly In The Eyes Of Many That Castoni JR., His Son, Wanted To Be So Much Like Him To The Point That He Did Everything To Please Him. When Castoni Shook My Hand, I Couldn't Help Notice His Illuminating Dangerous Grin. In His Eyes There Was Power. 'Yeah, My Name Was ChristOn Larson. I Make Rap Music.'

I Paused Feeling A Bit Nervous Because I Had Seen This Man Many Times And This Was Our First Real Direct Conversation. 'So You Ready To Show Me What You Got?' Castoni Asked Me. I Handed Castoni Bodyguard Bruno My CD. 'Get Him A Mic,' Castoni Said To Bruno. 'Hey, Kid, This Is Just A Run Through So Give It Your Best, Okay?'

'Yeah…I Will…Sure!' I Tell Him, 'I'm Ready.' I Was Excited As Hell And Waited Until I Heard The Beat Coming Through The Surround Sound Speaker System In The Office. 'Cadillac Jumpin…Beats Be Bumpin'…Players Stay Fronting…All For Nothing…Foxhole Rubbing!'

I Checked The Mic And Began Spitting Lyrics And Brought The Rain. After Five Minutes Of Performing, I Got The Job. Castoni Introduced Me To His Friends. I First Met Bruno And Thanney, His Bodyguards. They Said They Would Keep Me From Getting Roughed Up When I Entered The Club Through The Back. Then I Met Castoni's Attorney Francis Aurelius, A Fine Well-Dressed Man, But Seemed Like A Wimp To Me.

I Just Couldn't Believe It, Don Castoni… I Was Going To Work For This Legend. It Was Like The Greatest Moment Of My Life, And Also Meant Ties With The Mafia… Okay, Not Really, But Hey; At Least I Got To Live Out My Dreams For Now. Who Knows, Someday They Might Call Me 'Larson Da Elite Father' Or 'Jimmy Jones Da Great Polo.'

In The Year 2027 D.A.

Dr. Gondar's Voice Began To Penetrate Larson' Memories. Larson Tossed And Turned In His Chair, Trying To Ignore The Voice Calling His Name. He Opened His Eyes, And The Bright Lights Quickly Brought Him From A Time Of Innocence Back Into His Present-Day Nightmare. Lifting His Body Into An Upright Position, He Found Himself Staring At The Three Strange Faces. In A Moment Of Silence, He Thought That Possibly He Had Said Too Much, Or Maybe Not Enough. "What Happened Next Larson?" Dr. Gondar Asked. Larson Stared At The Doctor Strangely. "Did He Forget I Was Under Hypnosis?

Why Is He Speaking To Me Normally As Though There Is An Answer To What My Mind Was Saying Even Though I Was Supposedly Hypnotized?" Larson Thought To Himself Still Looking At The Doctor. "Well Larson, What Happened Next?" The Doctor Asked Again.

"Okay, Then I Paged Chaos." "Okay, Mr. Larson, Let's Take A Break," Dr. Gondar Said. Larson' Memories Were Very Convincing And Maybe He Was The Enforcer. But He Only Gave Information On Him Trying To Be A Rap Star, And Under Hypnosis, He Didn't Place Himself At The Crime Scene. Arch Chief Michaels Turned Off His Recorder, But The Room Was Under Constant Monitoring. Aside From The Wanted Pictures On Two Walls.

There Was A Two-Way Mirror And Larson Knew People Were Observing From The Other Side. The Room Door Swung Open, And BRAZOS Director Jentson Rushed In Without Acknowledging The Four People Inside. He Walked Urgently Over To Arch Chief Michaels And Whispered In His Ear; Then Both Men Quickly Walked Out Of The Room Together.

Everyone Could Sense Something Was Not Going According To Plan. Arch Chief Michaels Closed The Door Behind Him. When They Were Out Of Earshot Of The Others, Director Jentson Said To Michaels Quietly, "I Need A Minute With You." "Yeah, What Is It?" "That Suspect In There—Well Somebody Made His Bond!" Director Jentson Growled. "You're Kidding Me!" Arch Chief Michaels Said In Shock. "Well Did You Find Out Who It Was?" "Yes, But Get Ready…It Was Lorenzo Larson, Your First Suspect.

Of Course, We Detained Him." "I Tell You, This Is A Very Unusual Situation," Arch Chief Michaels Began, "Finally We've Gotten A Hold Of Larson. After The Explosion At The Warehouse, He Was Gone From The Car." But Understand This Jentson, We Don't Have Enough To Hold Him, But We'll Get Something Out Of Him." Arch Chief Michaels Thought To Himself, "Why Would Larson Even Show His Face Around Here, How Stupid!" Director Jentson Began Grinding His Teeth And Couldn't Hide His Animosity Any Longer. But He Had To Be Professional About His Tasks.

"My Informant Hasn't Contacted Me Yet. Let's Just Hope He Isn't Passed Away! Oh, One Other Thing, Marquis Castoni's Bond Has Been Made By His Chancellor Attorney, Francis Aurelius." Arch Chief Michaels Paused, Knowing That Jentson Was Ready For A Short And Gruesome Exchange Of Words With Larson. Regardless If He Was On Bond Or Not. Jentson Took Pleasure In Violating People's Rights.

"Give Me A Few Minutes With Mr. Larson. Oh, And Jentson, Don't Start Larson' Interrogation Without Me." Arch Chief Michaels Said. Larson Started To Brace His Nerves For What Was Going To Happen Next In His Life. He Had Been Presumed Passed Away For Nine Months Now. In A Sense, There Was No Need To Catch Up With The Past. How Much Did They Know About Da Ill-State Enforcers? Larson Just Wanted To See His Mother Again So He Could Tell Her Everything. He Also Needed To See Alesha, Chaos, And Everybody Else—The Ones He Actually Cared About Us! This Was Where The Son Really Needed His Father The Most!

****

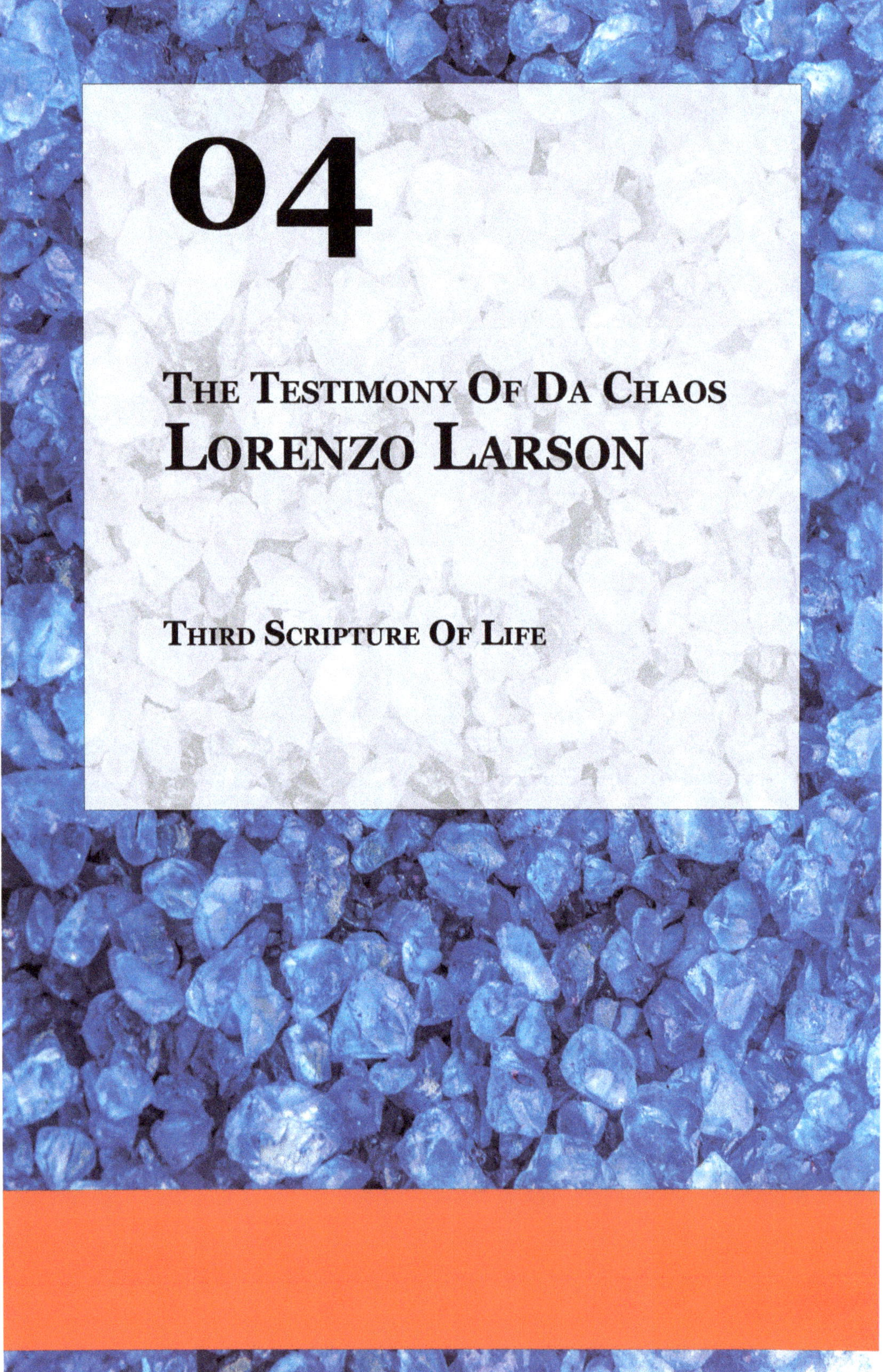
04
THE TESTIMONY OF DA CHAOS
LORENZO LARSON

THIRD SCRIPTURE OF LIFE

Arch Chief Michaels Opened The Door To The Room Where Larson, Carter, And Dr. Gondar Were Waiting, And Stood In The Doorway. Something Had Just Come Up.

"So, Ms. Carter, I'll Be Leaving Shortly," He Said, "Oh, And Dr. Gondar, Thank You For Your Time. Your Services Are No Longer Required, And You Can Go Anytime." As Michaels Shut The Door, He And Jentson Walked Down The Hallway To Another Interrogation Room, Where Lorenzo Larson A.K.A. Chaos Was Being Held.

It Was 2:35 PM.

"Let Me See His File," Michaels Said, Taking The Paperwork From Jentson. "Okay, His Full Name Is Lorenzo "Chaos" Larson; Alias Name Chaos. Last Known Address Listed As 1404 West Central Avenue. Let's See; His Mother Is Brenda Larson, Son Of Disco Larson. He Has Known Relatives Andre Da Drego, Jo Da Posey And ChristOn M Larson, Cousins, And God-Brothers."

Michaels Flipped Through The Documents So More, "Okay, This Is What I Want To See… Prior Convictions For Assaults, But None As An Adult. Remember, Jentson, No Information About The Informant."

"Sure, Whatever You Say," Jentson Said Shaking His Head Marching Alongside Michaels.

"Let's Go Down And Confront Him." Both Chiefs Stepped Through A Small Staircase And Entered The Room Where Chaos Sat At A Table. "Lorenzo Larson, So How Are We Doing Today?" Michaels Said Slamming The Door Behind Him. "Or Should I Call You Chaos?"

Michaels Turned To A Small Corner Table, "Coffee?" "Yes, Thank You," Answered Chaos. "May I Get Some Cream And Sugar For My Cup Of Joe?" Chaos Was Cool And Collected, Used To Having His Rights Violated Since His Teen Years. He Was 5'8" Tall And Weighed In At 220 Pounds, Broad Shouldered With A Football Player's Frame. His Black Hair Was Cut Real Low Like His Neatly Trimmed Mustache. Which He Didn't Have Much Of Since He Didn't Have

Much Facial Hair. He Wore A Pair Of Baggy Jeans That Sat Fitted Around His Waist Because He Never Liked His Pants To Sag, And His White Nike Low-Tops Matched His White Polo Shirt.

"Let Me Introduce Myself," Jentson Interrupted, "I Am Head Director In Chief Greg Jentson."

Instead Of Shaking Chaos' Hand, Jentson Loosened His Tie And Unzipped His Gray Sports Jacket, Then Adjusted His Belt Enough For Chaos To See His Sidearm. Jentson Was A Pale White Man With Very Blond Hair And So-Called Blue Eyes. The 6'6 Inched Man Was 206 Pounds And Stocky. One Time He Was A Good Cop, But Not Anymore.

"Oh Wow," Chaos Said Sarcastically, "What A Pleasure. And Who Is The Other Chief?" Chaos Asked Looking At Michaels. "This Punk Is Really Asking For It," Chief Jentson Thought To Himself. Michaels Began Reading Into Chief Jentson's Angry Expression And Replied To Chaos' Question, "My Name Is Arch Chief Sham Michaels." As He Stood Holding The Cup Of Coffee Staring At Both Men, He Began Feeling The Intense, Confrontational Heat Rising Between Them. Jentson Knew He Had To Be Very Cautious With This One They Called Chaos.

"Well, We've Got Quite A Few Questions To Ask You Lorenzo," He Said Putting His Hands On His Hips. "So What He Hasn't Read My Profile? He Doesn't Know I'm Chaos, The Man Who Tells Society To Kiss My Black Ass?" Chaos Thought To Himself. In His World, Law And Respect Were Words That Were Not Supposed To Be Associated Together In The Same Sentence.

"Listen, Am I Being Charged Here For Something?" "Did I Commit A Crime?" He Asked Cautiously. Director Jentson Felt He Had Met His Match…He Felt Chaos Was Some Arch Rival Due To His Silent Flamboyant Nature. "Didn't I Say We're Asking The Questions Around Here Lorenzo?" He Asked Chaos Angrily. "Well…Am I?" Chaos Asked Impatiently Crossing His Fingers Together On The Desk In Front Of Him. Chief Jentson Stared At Chaos As Though He Owed Him No Answer. "At This Time Lorenzo…No."

"Does This Negative Soul Know My Name Is Chaos From Salsara Park Lords? Okay, I Got Something For This Pissy Sissy," He Thought Angrily With No Expression On His Face. He Then Began Grinning Mischievously With Amusement,

"Well, I Have Nothing To Talk About Then Chiefs." Jentson Erupted Slamming His Fist On The Desk, *"Cut The Stress! We Can Place You At Stanley's Warehouse."* Chaos' Temper Rose, And His Grin Disappeared, "First Of All, I Can Put You At The Warehouse Die…Rectum Jentson!"

Chaos Shouted Pointing His Finger At The Cop. "What!" Jentson Yelled Turning Red And Began Losing Control Of His Mind And Emotions. *"Listen Here You Amnesia Negus Bastard, Don't Get Smart With Me! I Can Assure You 1,000 Years In Menard Correctional Center,"* Jentson Shouted Red-Faced Through His Clenched Teeth With His Veins Bulging From His Neck.

"You Better Start Talking To Save Your Rear End! And If You Try To Slap Me Like You Did Those Other Negative Soul Ass Cops And Judges, Amnesia Negus I'll De-Materialize You Right Here! Right Now!" Arch Chief Michaels Set The Cup Of Coffee Down In Front Of Chaos Calmly And Grabbed Jentson By The Arm Directing Him Out Of The Room. "Excuse Me, Larson," He Said And Closed The Door Behind Him.

As They Walked Out Into The Hallway. Chaos Could Tell They Did Not Get Along But Felt Relieved Once They Left. He Knew That As BRAZOS Chiefs; They Knew About Everything Going On In The City…Nothing Was Hidden. Chaos Figured If He Filled In The Blanks, It Would Get Off The Case Clean. He Knew They Had Something On Him, But He'd Be Damned To Inform On Himself. The Door Opened Again, And Chiefs Jentson And Michaels Walked Back Into The Room. Chaos Began To Calm His Temper Because He Didn't Feel It Necessary To Have It Blazing.

And It Was His Psychological Way Of Breaking The Ice And Keeping Everything Cool. He Almost Forgot Why He Was There In The First Place. "Listen, Before I Start Talking Can I At Least See Larson?" He Calmly Asked. Jentson Sensed A Change In Chaos' Attitude And Thoughts, "Maybe My Ego Was Overbearing But I'll Let Arch Chief Michaels Do The Talking Until You Get Out Of Line Again," Jentson In Trying To Back Down Slowly. "No, Because We've Got To Make Sure Your Story Checks Out. We Wouldn't Want You Two Giving Off Any Signals To Each Other," Arch Chief Michaels Said Calmly Sipping His Coffee.

"Damn Man! I Can't Believe This Stress! My Best Friend Passes Away And Comes Back To Life, And He Didn't Tell An Amnesia Negus…He Didn't Even Call An Amnesia Negus!" Chaos Thought Confused. "Anyways, It Felt Good To See Him Again On The TV…On The News And Stress. Damn, That Son Of A Negative Soul Fooled Everyone. The Strangest Thing Is, I've Always Felt Him Around Us, Just Watching And Somehow Protecting Us,"

Chaos Continued Thinking To Himself. "We Did What They Said Couldn't Be Done. They Were Exposed, And We Dismantled The BRAZOS Goons Completely…That Stress Felt Good," Chaos Laughed To Himself While Both Men Stared At Him In Silence. What Chaos Still Couldn't Understand, Was How Long BRAZOS Had Been Involved And How Much They Were Involved. Here He Was In An Interrogation Room With BRAZOS Cops And BRAZOS Agents And The Media Were Lined Up And Ready To Drill Him With All Kinds Of Questions. They Talked About A Conspiracy, Racketeering, Drug Dealing, And Electro-Lightning Striking… But The Electro-Lightning Striking Was The Worst!

He Knew He Had Not De-Materialized Anyone In The Warehouse, But He Was Glad They Never Asked For The Money. He Just Made Sure To Tell Them He Didn't Work For Castoni, Only ChristOn Did. Arch Chief Sham Michaels's Primary Concern With Chaos Was To Cut A Deal With Him In Exchange For Valuable Information. Because Arch Chief Michaels Had Suspicions About Cleni JR Cleni And Castoni JR. Chaos Decided He Should Tell Them How It All Went Down Including Him Not Knowing About ChristOn Faking His Passing, But Where Should He Start? *ChristOn Had Been His Best Friend And Bailing Him Out For A Hundred Thousand Dollars. Was Worth It Because After ChristOn Suddenly Disappeared, Chaos Had Taken Over Da Ill-State Enforcers?*

He Knew That BRAZOS Tried To Break Up The Organization, But They Failed And Couldn't Break Them. But If They Did Chaos Knew That As Far As Chief Jentson And Other Suspect Cops Were Concerned; The Whole Crew Would Have Gotten Life In Prison. Before Chaos Spoke Of Anything He Knew, He Observed Both Chiefs Intently And Drew In Their Energy As He

Studied Their Body Language. Oddly, It Seemed Like Arch Chief Michaels Wasn't Really After Chaos And His Friends He Thought. He Felt That Michaels Was Just Too Calm In Some Way Compared To Jentson. And That Maybe Michaels Was Also In The Race To Try And Bring Down BRAZOS' Reign. Chaos Continued To Observe That Behind Michaels's Rude, Take-No-Stress, Just Ready-To-De-Materialize-Anybody-For-The-Slightest-Reason Exterior, He Actually Cared For Chaos And His Friends' Well Being. Chaos Then Looked At Jentson And All He Could Feel For Some Reason Or The Other That Michaels Didn't Get Along With His Boss Jentson...

Who Was Also **Occupied Chicago**'s *B.R.L-Illiana Director?*

Chief Jentson Was A Real Lost Soul!, And He Didn't Want To Compromise For Anything; Yet, He Had Taken Very Particular Interest In This Case. He Was Just Trying To Figure How To End It All By Implicating ChristOn So That Da Ill-State Enforcers Would Make The Wrap Under The Rico Act, Which Stood For Racketeer Influenced And Corrupt Organization.

Arch Chief Michaels Set His Cup Down On The Table, "So Tell Me, Mr. Larson, How Did Larson Get Involved With Castoni?" "Okay, It Started When I Picked Up ChristOn From The Club." "What Club?" "Castoni's Bar Located On Bridgeview Avenue. Well, Anyway When I Went To Pick Him Up I Started Telling Him About…Uh, What Was It Again…Oh Yeah, We Had A Situation In The Hood."

Jentson Interrupted, "Like What? What Situation In The Hood?" He Wanted To Make Sure Not One Part Was Skipped Over. "You Know…Things!" Chaos Said Trying To Avoid The Man Because He Was Aware That Anything Jentson Said Wouldn't Be Positive. "What Things?" Jentson Asked Hoping Chaos Would Mention Drugs Or Electro-Lightning Striking. "Well, Many Things, For One, The Shootout The Night Before I Picked Him Up From The Bar." Chief Jentson Insisted Again Turning Red And Impatient, "So Tell Me!" Apparently He Was Hoping That Chaos Was Somehow Involved With The Shootout Just To Add More Fuel To The Fire.

"Well, ChristOn Happened To Be At The Scene When Those Magog Park Apostles Amnesia Negus Showed Up Talking Stress. And Then They Started Shooting." *"Where Were You?"* Jentson Asked Hoping Chaos Would Place Himself At The Scene. "At My Girl's House On Clock Street," Chaos Said Shrugging His Shoulders. *"What's Her Name?"* Jentson Pushed Persistently Trying To Find A Hole Somewhere. "Her Name Is Judea." *"And Does This Judea Have The Last Name?"*

"Of Course, Everyone Got The Last Name…Jentson," Chaos Said Peering At The Man. "It's Warnley…Judea Warnley," Chaos Said Shaking His Head Annoyingly And Turning His Face Away. *"Alright, Alright, Now You Picked Him Up…"* Jentson Said Rotating His Hand For Him To Continue. Chaos Leaned Back In His Chair. He Closed His Eyes And Went Back In Time To A Place He Remembered So Well. He Saw All The Faces, Some Of Them Alive. He Remembered What Outfit He Was Wearing Back Then And Even The Weather.

He Even Remembered How Much Money He Had Back Then Compared To What He Had Now. His Mind Traveled Back To His Former Girlfriend Judea. When He Used To Do Homework With Her And All The Drama That Came With Her Older Brother, Who Was A Member Of The Magog Park Apostles. Even After The Warnley Family Moved Far Across Town Months Before The War…Then He Opened His Eyes, Looked Directly At Chief Jentson, And Began His Story.

"Okay, Before ChristOn Could Tell Me That He Got The Job At Castoni's Bar, We Started Talking About The Dice Game. You See, After School, I Had Gone To Find Out For Myself What Happened. Big X Said He Was Upset With ChristOn, Blaming That Stress On Him. Big X Stated That ChristOn Got Into An Altercation At The Liquor Store With The MPAS, The Magog Park Apostles. The Night Before The Dice Game. He Said The MPAS Came Over To The Dice Game To Squash The Drama, But ChristOn Had To Run His Damn Mouth At Them.

He Also Stated That ChristOn Was Bogus For That And Had To Be Violated. So I Told Him That Was Bullstress! ChristOn Wasn't Over At The Liquor Store Because He Was With Me That Night. Big X Looked Boggled After I Said That Stress! Later We Found Out That Big

X Was Copping Cush From Them MPAS Amnesia Negus And Owed Them Money, So They Sent A Message To Him.

Big X Was A Real Negative Soul As Amnesia Negus! Anyway, He Claimed That I Was In On That Owing Money Stress Too. He Was A Straight Negative Soul As Amnesia Negus Man, Just Covering His Ass Because The Main Heads Wanted Answers. Then He Got The Nerve To Say I Was Going To Be Violated Too!" The Chiefs Were Now Thrown Off With This Discovery Of Big X Owing The Mpgs. However, They Had To Act As If They Had Not Known About The Other Half Of The Story Since Larson Had Already Told Them About It.

"All Right, All Right," Jentson Said Backing Off Away From The Table Where Chaos Was Sitting, "Before We Go On Lorenzo, You Wouldn't Be Lying For Larson Would You?" Chaos Looked At The Man In Disbelief, "Man, Hell No! You Asked Me What Happened, Didn't You… What Went Down, Right? So Just Let Me Finish My Damned Story, You Negative Soul!"

"Go Ahead," Replied Jentson Turning Red With Embarrassment By The Comment, But Still Wondering If Chaos Was Lying. "I Told Big X, 'Damn You With That Violation Stress.' Then He Walked Up To Me And Said, 'Man I Don't Give A Damn What Went Down, That's Your Problem.

So What Are You Are Trying To Say, Amnesia Negus? What You Were Gonna Do To Me, Amnesia Negus? Say What You Gonna Do, Stick To Your Guns And Don't Play Innocent.'" Chaos Said Screwing Up His Face Mimicking Big X. "Before I Could Even Answer, One Of The Heads Of The Vice Lord Nation Pulled Up In His Truck Giving Us An Order." Chief Michaels Quickly Interrupted, "What Order Are You Talking About?"

Chaos Responded Calmly, "It Was An Order To Ride Up On Those Magog Park Apostles Amnesia Negus. I Got Nervous Then Because If I Had Said No, I Might Have Gotten Dealt With, Right There. After Doing Some Negotiations, I Was Given More Time To Plan Things Out. A Week Later Larson And I Performed At Castoni's Club. We Pulled In About Two Hundred A Piece For One Hour. You Know, We Were Doing A Hell Of A Job, And We Were Meeting Famous Entertainers And Another Local Talent. It Was At The Club That I First Talked To Don

Castoni. We All Hit It Off Pretty Well... You Know Good Chemistry. He Had Us Stay Over Until The Club Was Closed That Night, And Later We Rode In His Limousine."

Suddenly An Officer Entered The Room To Tell Jentson He Had A Phone Call. Both Officers Quickly Walked Out Of The Chamber. Michaels Continued To Ask Questions Where Jentson Left Off. "Exactly Who Is This 'We' You Refer To?" "It Was Me, ChristOn, The Don, And Some Geek-Ass Lawyer, Mr. Aurelius," Chaos Replied Smirking A Little At His Joke. "So Where Did You Guys Go?" Michaels Asked Sipping More Of His Coffee.

Chaos Started Shaking His Head, "Man That Was So Long Ago. As Far As I Could Remember, We Went Cruising. Oh Yeah...Actually, He Showed Us A Building Where He Was Setting Up A Recording Studio. Then I Remember Going Back To The Club." The Room Door Swung Open, And Jentson Rushed Into The Room With Some Papers In His Left Hand, "So Tell Me Something, Mr. Larson, Why The Hell Are You Holding Out On Us?" He Said Leaning Over Chaos.

Chaos Looked Up At The Man In Shock. He Just Couldn›T Understand Why The Man Was Always So Furious. Everything Chaos Said, He Thought To Himself, Just Wasn›T Good Enough For The Man. Chaos Began To Feel That Jentson Was Aiming For Only Individual Confessions.

He Felt Himself Starting To Boil With Anger, But He Controlled Himself And Said What Was On His Mind.

"I Don't Understand What You're Talking About Man!" He Replied Pushing His Chair Back From Underneath The Man Hovering Over Him. "Oh Don't Give Me That Bullstress, Mother, Damn!" Jentson Shouted Walking Slowly Towards Chaos Who Was Still Sitting In His Chair.

"Man What The Damn, You Talking About?" Chaos Cried Rising To His Feet Knocking His Navy Blue Blazer Off The Back Of His Seat. Michaels Stepped In To Defuse The Situation, "Mr. Larson, Please Control Yourself!" Michaels Wondered To Himself How Two Hot-Tempered Individuals Who Hated Each Other's Guts Could Find Some Common Ground.

"Man Talk To That Lost Soul!" Chaos Said Pointing His Finger Over Michaels›S Back That Was Facing Jentson. "I Said Cool It, Larson!" Michaels Said Raising His Hands To Chaos' Chest Signaling Him To Back Down. Chaos Then Realized His Temper Was Going Nowhere Fast And That Jentson Was Relentless On Gang Criminal Activity.

He Also Felt That Jentson Wanted To Arrest Him For Multiple Gang Electro-Lightning Strikings And Throw Away The Key, So He Calmed Down To Not Give The Man The Benefit Of The Doubt. "All Right Chief Michaels, I'm Sorry," He Said And Tugged At His Polo Shirt To Straighten It Out. Jentson Lifted His Left Hand And Showed The Documents To Chaos, "Let Me Tell You What Was Left Out," Jentson Said Standing His Ground, "You Never Admitted That You Worked For Castoni."

Chaos Paused And Stared At Jentson, "Listen, The Only Money I Received From Him Was For Performing... That's It. I Never Sold Any Cush For Him." "On That Night, Mr. Larson Was Involved In A Shootout In Which You Later Got Yourself Involved With A Few Weeks Later!" Jentson Added Staring At The Document. Chaos Insisted, "No, No, I Never Had Anything To Do With That Shoot Out!" He Looked At Michaels Confused As If He Was In Need Of His Help.

"Is That So?" Jentson Said Beginning To Smile While His Face Remained Red With Anger In His Eyes. "Chief Jentson, Where Are You Going With This?" Michaels Asked Somewhat Surprised About The Information. Chief Jentson Began To Draw Up Assumptions On What Happened...Trying To Place Chaos' Role And His Involvement. "That Night, Two People Were Passed Away After The Shoot-Out," He Said Staring At Chaos As Though He Wanted Him To Break In Half.

"The First Person Was Roy Brown Alias Brownz Of The Salsara Park Lords...One Of Your Friends, And The Second Was Mitch Roberson From Magog Park Apostles. Mark Henry An Innocent Bystander, Was Wounded From The Attack, But He Survived After Being Treated At The Hospital." Chaos' Mind Started Withdrawing From Jentson's Tired Speeches, "Yeah And So What?" "And Then, There Is Cochise Russell," Continued Jentson, "Alias 'Big X' Another

Salsara Park Lords. He Was Found Passed Away At The Liquor Store, Exactly Three Weeks Later. That Night His Passing Away Made The News. And That Was Because There Was The Broken Glass At The Piccadilly Liquor Store. The News Caught Looters Going After Unguarded Bottles." Chaos Did Not Fear This Information Because He Knew There Was No Footage Of Him Committing A Crime.

"Listen, We Didn't De-Materialize That Negative Soul!" Chaos Shouted Pointing His Finger Again At Jentson. "You Admit You Were There At The Liquor Store?" Jentson Became Severe. He Was Taking Pleasure In Trying To Make Lorenzo Sweat; Just Hoping He Would Break. However, Lorenzo Remained Cool. "Yeah But …" Jentson Interrupted, "Frankie Lamose Became The Next Leader In Salsara Park Lords. He Was De-Materialized Just Two Days Later, Making, You The New Leader In Salsara Park Lords.

In The Weeks That Followed Four Electro-Lightning Strikings Occurred In Magog Park Apostle Chaos' Temper Rose, "Listen, You Amnesia Negus! I'm Telling You We Didn't De-Materialize Them!"

Jentson Continued To Instigate, "Now Is It True...Yes Or No…That The Gang Was Divided And You Conquered, And Those Who Opposed You Were Later De-Materialized Or Cast Out Of Their Neighborhood...And Their Homes...Family And All?" "What? No!" Chaos Became Confused Beyond What His Mind Could Comprehend. Chief Jentson Was Making Him Out To Be Bigger Than He Really Was!

"Okay," Taunted Jentson, "With This Information, I Reassure You That You Won›T Get Off. And, Yes, You Lost Soul!, I Even Have Proof! I Even Want To See Alesha Go Down, Too." Now Chaos Thought That Was A Low Blow; Jentson Should Have Never Mentioned Alesha. Chaos Felt That She Had Already Been Through Enough.

He Took A Deep Breath, "Yes, Yes, I Became The Hood Leader, But Only In Title," Chaos Said Trying To Remain Calm And Not Give The Man His Energy. "Okay, So Let Me Guess, Would You Say It Was Castoni's People Who Made The Passing Aways?" Chaos Shrugged His

Shoulders, "They Just Backed Us Up Whenever We Needed Help," He Looked At Both Men Mischievously. "So You Did Work For Him?" Michaels Said Turning Towards Chaos With A Look Of Disappointment. Chaos Replied, Pleading For His Innocence, "No, Man, I Keep Telling You, ChristOn Ran The Whole Show. He Was The Mastermind Behind All Of It. I'm Telling You The Truth!"

After Two Long Of Hours Psychological And Verbal Tug Of War, They Let Chaos Go... Just Like That. He Knew He Was Going To Be Watched. They Showed Chaos Into A Dark Room, And In The Corner, There Was A Large Hd Television. Jentson Turned On The Screen, And Chaos Gasped In Astonishment; It Was Larson...His Best Friend That He Had Not Seen For So Many Months, Alive And Well Sitting At A Table With A Woman Beside Him Shuffling Paper Around.

Jentson Switched The Screen Off When He Saw The Expression On Chaos Face Then Quickly Escorted Him Out Of The Building. Chaos Was Only Hoping That He Had Helped Larson By Bringing The Bail Money, But He Was More Concerned For Alesha Now. When Chaos Was Gone, Jentson Turned To Michaels. "Well, I Can't Believe These Tough Guys Are Ratting Each Other Out," Jentson Said Putting One Hand On His Hip And Using The Other Hand To Wipe Away The Remaining Sweat From His Forehead.

"Listen, Michaels; I'm Gonna Drill Larson Some More." "How Much Longer Before We Release Him? Larson Took Care Of His Bail, So We Have To Let Him Go." "Oh, About Forty-Five Minutes From Now," Jentson Said Walking Towards The Room Where Larson Was Being Held. "Excuse Me, Ms. Carter; I Need To Speak To Mr. Larson Alone." Carter Blinked At The Man With A Confused Expression Then Squinted Her Eyes Angrily, "No I Will Remain Here And Advise My Client," The Woman Said Rising From Her Seat.

Larson Responded To His Lawyer, "It's Okay Ms. Carter," He Turned To The Man, "What Is It Now, Mr. Jentson?" "You Don't Have To Say Anything Else!" Carter Shouted As She Slammed Her Hand Down Onto The Desk And Glared Back Towards Jentson Who Was Smiling Devilishly.

"She's Absolutely Right, But Don't You Want To Know What Lorenzo Larson Told Us?" "Chaos Is Here?" Exclaimed Larson, "Where Is He? Can I Speak To Him?" "Mr. Larson…" Carter Interrupted. "Oh, Don't Worry, Ms. Carter, I'll Be Alright, Trust Me!"

Carter Stared At Her Client And Pointed Her Finger Towards Him As If She Were Putting A Spell On Him, "If He Curses You Over, It›S Your Fault Larson!" She Grabbed Her Briefcase And Stormed Out Of The Room Angrily Slamming The Door Behind Her. Jentson Walked Over To Larson Happily And Dropped A Little Pile Of Photos On The Table.

"All Right," He Said, "We Know About The Night You Performed For The First Time At Castoni's Bar And About The Big Hit After You Left The Bar. You Know… The Electro-Lightning Striking Of Cochise Russell, Alias Big X. We Also Know That You Are The Ringleader Of Da Ill-State Enforcers, Which Is Backed By Castoni Himself.

Also, After Your Own Alleged So-Called Passing Away, A String Of Electro-Lightning Strikings Occurred, Which Have Been Blamed On The So-Called Mysterious Enforcer, Da Larcenni." Larson Looked At The Man As Though He Had Something On His Face, "Is That All You Have?" He Asked Sarcastically. "No."

"Yeah, Right, Lost Soul!," Larson Sneered, "The Big Hit'? Come On! What Gives You The Right To Entitle Someone's Passing Away As 'The Big Hit'?" He Shook His Head Quizzing The Man Knowing That He Was Igniting The Man's Ego. Jentson's Temper Began To Rise, "What Are You Trying To Say?" "First Off, If You Spoke To Chaos," Larson Said Jabbing His Finger To The Man Who Stood A Few Feet Away,

"I Know That He Would Have Told You Just About Enough Information For You To See That He Was Considered An Outcast, All Because He Wouldn't De-Materialize For Those Big Shots. During That Time We Did A Lot Of Things, But Electro-Lightning Strikings Weren't One Of Them. After A Few Weeks Of Open Mic Performances That We Got Paid For, We Used The Club As A Hangout. I Just Happened To Be In The Kitchen One Night When A Drug Deal Went Awry. I Mean These Guys Were Real Butchers. I Was Pretty Much Done For Before

Castoni Walked In. I Had Never Been So Scared In My Life Seeing That Stress, So I Convinced Him... That's Allllllll," Larson Said Smoothing The Air Out With His Hands, Then Laid Them On The Table.

Jentson Said In Shock Wondering What Larson Was Referring To, "Convinced Him How?" "You Know...Truth Is, I Was Not A BRAZOS Street Dealer. Marquis Castoni And Lorenzo Would Have Never Allowed That! My Neighborhood Was Full Of BRAZOS Street Dealer, And If They Dealt With Castoni's People, They Would Have Had Protection From That Stress. I Am Not A Supporter Of Drug Dealing, But Those Dealers Were Getting Their Supplies From BRAZOS Mob Bosses. I Watched My Neighborhood Suffer From That Sickness. Once Castoni Got Involved Nobody Was Allowed To Sell In The Neighborhood, The Room Fell Silent From The Revelation.

Jentson's Words Were Caught In His Throat. He Was Not Expecting That Response Causing His Anger To Rise And Disregard The Comment, Which He Then Accepted As A Negative Hidden Response. "So What, You Swapped Out One Drug Supplier For Another Like That's Something Good?" Larson Rolled His Eyes At Jentson As If He Were The Biggest Idiot In The World, "Well If You Must Know, Castoni Only Supplied Cush. The Other Kingpins Were Heavy In Coke, Cocaine, Shrooms, Pills And All That Spellbinding Rituals.

Castoni Is Not All That Evil As You May Have Been Led To Believe...But If You Had Done Your Research, You Would Know That...Chief." Jentson's Spirit Jumped In Discernment, "Keep Trying Me If You Want To But I'll Mess You Up Real Bad, And This Time I'll De-Materialize You For Real!" "Jentson!" Michaels Shouted Stepping Into His Boss' Face, "That's Enough!" Jentson Stared Blankly At Michaels And Then He Realized His Authority Was Being Questioned.

"Is There Something I Am Missing Here Chief Jentson?" Michaels Asked. Jentson Paused Sharply As He Felt The Heat Rush From His Face. Michaels's Bloodshot Eyes Beamed Into The Man›S Soul And Made It Clear That He Struck The Wrong Nerve Within Him. Jentson Felt A Fear Run Up His Spine And Saw That Michaels Was Ready To Pound The Life Right Out His Frightened Body, And He Felt The Room Become A Heated Oven.

Jentson Sensed That If He Uttered Another Word, There Would Be A Fight...Possibly To The Passing Away. This Was The Kind Of Fear That Traveled Through His Body Now, And He Knew It Was Not In His Favor. He Did Not Know What To Say And How To Release It From His Trembling Body, But Somehow Found The Courage And Cleared His Throat, "Arch Chief Sham Michaels, I Need A Word With You Outside Please!"

Michaels Tiptoed Out The Room With Jentson Following Behind Him. Thirty Seconds Later, They Re-Entered The Room Expressionless As If Nothing Had Just Happened. Larson Examined The Both Men's Odd Behavior. He Did Not Understand What Had Just Occurred And How. He Played Ignorantly And Humbly Began To Speak, "I Wanted To Be Here In This Room, Giving My Testimony On Something That I Have Control Over," He Said To Both Men Who Were Still Silent.

Larson Shook His Head And Shrugged His Shoulders, "What Was I Suppose To Do? I Did Not Choose My Destiny; I Only Accepted It." Jentson And Michaels Continued To Listen. "I Had No Idea That A Powerful Organization Saw Me As The Threat! BRAZOS, Similar To The Leaders Of The Babylonian Empire I Feel, Gave Birth In **Occupied Chicago** And Created A Monster! I Only Met The Mayor Elite Donald Finley...May He Rest In Peace...Twice In My Life.

I Mean He Was Not Even In Charge, He Was More Like A Front Man," Larson Said Pulling His Seat Towards The Table And Crossing His Arms Over His Chest. The Comment Sparked Jentson, And He Shifted Out Of His Strange Silence, "So Who Do You Think Is In Charge Then?" He Said Putting His Hands Again On His Hips. "That's Something I'd Love To Know Myself!"

Jentson Remarked In Disbelief As His Stress Levels Began To Rise. Larson Responded Sharply, "Well Hell; We Already Know It's Not You!" He Said Reassuring Jentson Who Seemed Offended By The Remark. "You Don't Have Enough Brain Cells To Lead Sir, And You're Bad At Following Orders Which Are Great For Them! It's Not Your Fault Though Director Jentson; They Gave You A Bone!" Jentson Screwed His Face And Grimaced Painfully Trying To Control His Temper. He Showed His Yellow Teeth, Stained By Harsh Tobacco And Ground Them

Together As He Began To Growl Deep In His Chest As He Raised His Fist To His Red Face And Closed His Eyes. "Jentson..."

"I'm In Control Michaels," He Said Lowering His Tightly Clenched Fists In Front Of His Stomach As If In A Fighter Position. Larson Continued His Story Boldly Acting As Though He Did Not Notice The Man's Reaction, "Then You Have All Of The Big Drug Kingpins. Let's Face It Drugs Is Big Business. Sometimes I Wonder Why Everything In This World Is Backward? We're Oblivious To Their Tricks! DEA Is The Acronym For Drug Enforcement Agency Or The Agency That Enforces Drugs, Right? Well Put The Chosen People In There, And You Got The Agency That Literally Enforces Drugs Around Here," Larson Said Pointing His Index Finger Upward And Spinning It In The Circular Motion.

"For The Ones In Charge, It›S Good Money. You Just Have To Have The Right People Controlling It, You Know?" He Said With His Finger Still Pointing Upward As If He Just Figured Something Out. *"Okay, Now Let's Back Up A Little Bit," Jentson Said Calmly Then Slowly Placed His Hands On His Hips Spreading The Bottom Of His Jacket Open To The Side. "Let's Talk About The Passing Away Of Cochise Russell." "Big X? You Know Even Though I Didn't Like The Guy, I Felt Sorry For What Happened To Him. Lorenzo And I Were Leaving The Club. We Were Tipsy As Hell And Heading To The Liquor Store. As We Stepped Out Of The Store Big X Pulled Into The Parking Lot."*

It Was As He Came Out Of Nowhere, Talking A Load Of Stress. You See The Piccadilly's Liquor Store. That Was On The Borderline Of Our Rivals' Territory. Right At The Intersection Of Bellefontaine And Maywood Street With Dogon Street Running Right In The Midpoint Of The Two…We Call That The Star's Point Because Of The Layout. Anyways, We Had To Hurry And Leave. That's When Big X Started Pulling Rank On Us And Stress. I Could Tell He Was Drunk Because I Mean All The Loud Talk He Was Talking Was Going Nowhere And He Was Steadily Trying To Prove Something. We Didn't Have Any Guns On Us, So We Ignored Him And Walked Away Slowly. But Big X Had To Keep Running His Damn Mouth About Some

Stupid Stress Swinging His Weapon Around In The Air And Shouting Like A Maniac. A Few Minutes Later Those Damn Amnesia Negus Pulled Up At An Odd Location And Distance From Us. Then Shots Fired Off In Big X's Direction."

Larson Cleared His Throat, "Can I Get Some Water Please?" Michaels Poured Him A Glass, And He Downed It. "Thanks," He Said And Put The Empty Cup On The Table And Continued His Story. "There Was Actually A Hit Put Out On Big X, He Owed Money Or Beat Them Amnesia Negus Out On A Dice Game Or Something Like That, And They Were Looking For Him." "It Had Nothing To Do With Us, But He Was The Type To Get Innocent People Involved, But Over The Years, Your Deeds, Good And Bad, Will Come Back To You Like A Boomerang."

Larson Leaned Back Into His Seat, "So Bullets Were Sent In His Direction Right, And A Shot Hit The Store Window. Big X Jumped Forward To Shelter Himself Behind His Truck. We Were Sheltered In The Store Doorway, Close To The Back Of His Truck A Little And His Gun Flew Out His Hand Towards Us." "A Sent Bullet Must Have Hit Big X Because He Fell To The Ground And Blood Was Pouring From His Body Man. Where The Gun Flew Wasn't To Far From Us."

"So Chaos Picked Up The Gun, Dipped Into Big X's Car And Started Shooting Back At Those Amnesia Negus Through The Truck Window. The Other Side Stopped Shooting For A Second, So I Pull Big X Into The Back Seat." Chaos Sped Off Quick! We Could Tell That Big X Was Passed Away, And A Bullet Grazed Chaos' Leg. We Rushed To The Hospital, And I Called Castoni, So He Sent His People.

The Police Were Questioning Castoni's Attorney, And We Came In Shortly After The Report Was Made. We Left The Hospital With The Francis Public Prosecutor Aurelius. We Never Hated Big X; He Just Talked A Lot Of Stress. He Was Just Himself That's All." Once Again The Room Fell Silent, And Larson Observed Both Men's Facial Expression. Jentson Refused To Accept Larson' Story. His Arrogance Made Him Feel That By Instilling Fear Into Larson Some Way Would Get Him To Say What He Wanted To Hear. After All, They Suspected Him Of Being Da Larcenni And Yet This Mysterious Anunnaqi's Reputation Was Powerful. The Entire City Feared

Da Larcenni. No Witnesses Wanted To Describe This Person, And Out Of Fear And Ignorance, They Claimed It Was A Man. Jentson And Michaels Walked Back Outside, Leaving Larson Alone. Jentson Picked Up Another Document That Sat On The Table Outside Of The Room.

He Wanted The Pleasure Of Dropping Some More Information On Larson To Try To Force Him To Admit To His Wrongdoings. Jentson Waived The Envelope In The Air And Smiled To Michaels, *"I Want The Pleasure All To Myself. I Want Him To Choke Up On This!"*

Jentson Said Proudly With No Thoughts Of Giving Up And Gave The Envelope To Michaels Who Then Looked Inside Of It. Both Men Walked Back Into The Room, And Michaels Handed Back The Envelope To Jentson. Michaels Whispered In Jentson's Ear And Suddenly Turned To Walk Back Out Of The Room. But, Before He Reached The Door, He Paused As If Something Had Come To His Attention; Then He Continued On His Way Out The Door And Back To His Office. Jentson Opened The Envelope And Started Reading The Papers.

"Now I'll Tell You A Little More Of What I Know. Dr. Cinnatto, A 14th Precinct Coroner, Made A Statement That You Paid Him An Extra Four Thousand Dollars To Stage The Symbolic Funeral. That Was Pretty Damn Talented!" The Man Said Smiling. "We Also Know You Were Doing Hits For Mr. Castoni…The North Side De-Materializings. In Fact, Da Ill-State Enforcers Were A Group Of Contract De-Materializers'…Assassins For Hire. But Your Operations, For A While, Were Shut Down When Foreign Assassins Came On The Scene."

Michaels Opened The Door To The Room, "Director Jentson, I Need A Word With You." "Okay I'll Be Right There," Jentson Left The Room. "Guess Who Just Showed Up?" Asked Michaels As They Stood In The Hallway. "Two People…One Is Our Informant And The Other One's Alesha." Finally, The Moment The Director Had Been Waiting For! "Our Informant And Alesha Franacia Would Set The Ultimate Breaking Point," Jentson Thought To Himself. His Palms Began To Sweat As He Closed His Fists Again Tightly. Michaels Observed The Director Carefully While He Was Trapped In His Egotistical And Mental Prison. He Started To Believe That Director Jentson Had A Personal Vendetta Against Larson.

"Okay Great!" Jentson Jumped Out Of His Contemplation, "Let's Deal With The Girl First." "And We've Got To Let Larson Go," Michaels Added. "Listen, I Just Need A Few More Minutes, …" Jentson Pleaded As He Transformed Into A Fiend. Michaels Observed His Boss' Actions.

"Directors Usually Don't Get Directly Involved With Interrogations," Michaels Wondered. "And Why Wasn't Marquis Castoni Interrogated In The Same Manner As Larson. Castoni's Lawyer Quietly Walked In And Took The Godfather Out Of The Building." Michaels's Mind Raced With Unanswered Questions." *"Alesha Franacia Was Already Traumatized Enough. Michaels Doubted Her Direct Involvement With Da Ill-State Enforcers. Jentson Could Care Less About Da Ill-State Enforcers, But Everyone Wanted To Know Who This Da Larcenni Person Really Was?"* Jentson And Michaels Went Back Into The Interrogation Room."

"Mr. Larson, I Want You To Confess. I Want You To Name All The People And All The Places Involved," Jentson Dropped More Papers On The Table And Began To Pace Back And Forth Looking Larson Directly In The Eyes. "Thought You Had That Already," Larson Responded Calmly Eyeballing The Man. Jentson Chuckled, Secretly Wanting To Harm The Young Man Physically, But He Wanted To Surprise Him First! "Please, Let's Not Have Any More Rude Interruptions And Sarcastic Remarks. We Also Want To Know More About Mr. Francis Aurelius," He Asked Still Pacing To Settle His Nerves. "Could You Imagine The World With No Influence From The Evil One?" Larson Closed His Eyes, "Life Without Seeking For Forgiveness Would Be A Meaningless One! After All, Who Knew Of Sin, Before Reading Holy Books…You Know, Like Da Bible? When A Man Says 'What You Should Not Do' He Is Also Saying, What You Can Do!

"A Wise Man Once Said, Everything In This World Was Already Written. And All Of This Has Already Happened. And I Feel This Is An Accurate Statement. Then You Have Already Read This Life…Then You Have Already Tasted Life, And So You Have Already Read This Book; Therefore, It Was Already Written. To Deny What You Are Truly Witnessing Is Denying That You Happen To Exist," Larson Then Opened His Eyes And Looked At Jentson Who Stared At Him Dumbfounded. It Was As If The Man's Mind Was Put To Sleep In The Moon Cycle. Every

Last Brain Cell Jentson Owned Was Fried, And Larson Needed To Snap The Man He Thought Was An Idiot Back To Reality. "I'm Not Finished With You Chief Big Dummy," Larson Thoughts Are Glaring At Jentson Who Was Still Disturbed By The Comment. "I'm Not The So-Called Enforcer Known As Da Larcenni!" He Shouted Sternly.

"Just Because I Reappeared After Nine Months Doesn't Prove Anything. I Only Had Something Personal With Castoni And Came To Talk With Him…That's All!" He Snapped Causing A Jolt To Jentson Bringing Him Back To Life. The Director Blinked His Eyes And Stood Straight As Though He Weren't Affected, "So Then, Where Were You Hiding Out?" Larson Slumped Back In His Chair And Covered His Face With His Right Hand Pretending He Was Bored. When In Fact He Was Really Shining His 9Ruby Ring In Jentson's View.

"I Was Up There," He Said Then Turning His Hand Down To Look At His 9Ruby Watch, "You Know About Fort Benning, Georgia Right?" "Fort Benning? You Were Down In Fort Benning?" Larson Smiled, "I Said Up There! And Yes I Was At Fort Benning." Jentson Did Not Understand His Statement And Repeated His Question A Second Time, "You Were In Fort Benning?"

Jentson Began Pacing Again Without Noticing, To Calm His Rising Nerves."Yes, Fort Benning, Georgia…Home Of The Infantryman!" Larson Answered Knowing He Was Igniting The Director's Anger. Jentson Looked Towards Michaels With Confusion In His Expression Realizing He Came Unprepared Without This Information. And Before He Could Open His Mouth, Larson Jumped In. "Yup, I Was In Fort Benning, Georgia 15 Years Ago", Larson Laughed Continuing To Ruffle The Man's Feathers. Jentson Never Liked The Unexpected And Never Liked Games. He Realized That The Young Man Was Just Too Calm And Relaxed. Indeed, His So-Called Passing Away Had Been Real Until He Decided To Show Up For Some Reason Or Another And Caused More Disruptions In BRAZOS' Plans.

"Oh, You Lying Son A Negative Soul!" Larson Responded, "Now, Why Would I Need To Lie About That? Listen, I Have My Military Id Card… I Mean It's Expired Now," He Said Shrugging His Body And Smiling. "Chief Jentson, Why In The Hell Would I Confess To A Life Of Crime?"

"I Cannot Think Of Anybody Who Would Risk His Freedom To Life In Prison. Let Me Tell You Why…" "Do You Really Want To Know Why?" Larson Pushed His Chair Away From The Desk And Placed His Palms On His Lap. "I Am Wisdom, Knowledge, And Overstanding!"

"I'm Going To Beat This Case With No Problem. So Ask Me Anything You Want To Know… Ask Me Jentson!" Larson Triggered Jentson's Pressure Point By Phrasing His Question…"Do You Really Want To Know?" Which Echoed Through Jentson's Head As He Wondered How Much Larson Really Knew. He Then Regained His Composure.

"Okay, No Time For Games. I'll Just Tell You," Jentson Said As He Put His Hands Into His Jacket Pocket And Flapped His Elbows Twice With Excitement As Though He Were Going To Fly Away. *"One Of Your Friends Was An Informant And Has Been Working For Us For The Last Three Years During His Drug Case. And Guess Who Else Came To Pay You A Visit?"*

Jentson Leaned His Head To The Right And Placed A Half Smile On His Face, *"Alesha Franacia!"* He Watched As Larson' Countenance Began To Change And Fed Off The Energy The Young Man Emitted. *"Yes, Alesha's Gonna Be Serving Time, Too! We Have Everything We Need On Da Ill-State Enforcers Now."* "You Know, The Only Reason You Want Information Is For Reassurance," Larson Jabbed.

"What Do You Mean By That?" The Director's Neck Snapped Back Vertically. "Oh, Come On, Chief Jentson, You're Just Holding A Deep Breath Hoping Your Name Doesn't Get Mentioned."

"Oh…You…Son Of A Negative Soul!" Jentson's Arms Flew Out Of His Pocket And Hung Stiffly At His Side. *"I Could Just De-Materialize You Here… Right Now!"* He Said As He Pointed To The Ground And Stomped Forward.

"You Want To, But You Can't. Admit It…" "BRAZOS Is Bigger Than All Of Us. We Have All Been Deceived. I Am Who I Am, And That Is Who I Will Be. As For You, Time Is Running Out!" Larson Was Suddenly Knocked To The Ground, And Felt The Man's Weight On Top Of Him; His Knee Stabbed His Rib And The Cold Gun Barrel To His Temple; Pressed Against His Skull With Extreme Force. *"Watch Your Damning Mouth, You Bastard,"* Jentson Said As Spit Dripped

Down Larson' Forehead. And Then There Was A Great Force Of Energy That Surged Through The Room Coming From Within Larson' Frame. As His Etheric Body Hovered Above The Commotion. And Saw Jentson Lower His Weapon Faster Than He Pulled It Out And Stepped Backward And Upright Into His Original Position.

The Etheric Being Hovered Over Larson' Carcass On The Floor And Flew Into His Nostrils. Larson' Chest Rose As He Took A Deep Breath And Opened His Eyes. Jentson Never Even Pulled The Gun Up To His Temple. Larson Read The Man's Mind 9 Seconds Before The Man Could Even Think It. So He Raised His Palms Up Towards Jentson. Who Stood A Few Feet Away And Began Releasing Energy Into The Man's Mind To Completely Destroy The Man's Psyche.

So That He Could Not Think Any Longer And Receive The Thought. Michaels Sensed The Energy And Immediately Intervened For The Sake Of Saving His Boss Life. As He Stood Between Larson And His Boss To Offset The Science. Jentson Fell To His Knees Breathing Hard And Loud, Speechless And Could Not Explain What He Was Feeling. All He Saw Was His Weapon In His Hand, And Felt Like He Was Going To Make A Horrible Decision Of Terminating His Own Existence! "Jentson, What The Hell Are You Doing?" Michaels Said As He Dropped To The Floor Grabbing At Jentson's Shoulders, Restraining Him.

"Put That Gun Away, Now!" Michaels Could Clearly See Larson Was Too Much For This Middle-Aged Man. All Of Director Jentson's Years Of Training Became A Complete Waste When It Came To Larson. Who Seemed For That Moment, Was In Charge. Larson Breathed Heavily As He Sat Slumped In His Chair With Arms Resting Loosely On His Lap. "I'm Going To Get Off This Case Clean, You Negative Soul! I Chose To Be Here You Negative Soul… It Was My Decision!" Larson' Mouth Never Opened Up; He Was Sending Those Thoughts Into Jentson's Brain. "Believe Me On This," Larson Said, But This Time Aloud, "Alesha Franacia Ain't Gonna Serve Nothing!" Michaels Stood And Turned Away From Jentson Who Was Still Kneeling On The Floor, And Directed His Attention Towards Larson, "Well Listen, Son, Everyone Who Is A Part Of Da Ill-State Enforcers Falls Under The Rico Laws Of Conspiracy."

Jentson Slowly Rose To His Feet And Walked Towards The Table Where He Placed His Gun While Still Trying To Control His Heavy Breathing. He Pressed Both Hands On Top Of The Table For Balancing Support And Lowered His Head. "So Please Do Yourself A Favor And Tell Us How Da Ill-State Enforcers Started And When The Conflict With Mr. Castoni Began. And Let's Talk About Your Narcotics Case," Jentson Tried Standing Up Straight Still Staggering, "About How Your Fantastic Attorney Francis Aurelius Got You A Sweet Deal And, By The Way…It's Funny How He No Longer Represents You," Jentson Chuckled.

"Well, I Guess He Cannot Correctly Represent A Passed Away Man. Of Course, A Man Like That Can Do Almost Anything…The City's Greatest Officer Of The Courtroom." The Director Staggered Over To A Seat Sitting In The Corner Of The Room And Sat Down Slow. "So Are You Ready To Talk About Your War With Castoni?" "Okay, Okay. Listen, One Night I Was At The Club. It Was The Don And I Sitting At The Table." "Later Mr. Aurelius, Sometimes Called "The Arrogant One," Came To Join Us. We All Got To Talking And Laughing For A Few Minutes Before Castoni Had To Leave."

Larson's Mind Drew Him Back. He Heard R&B Music Played In The Background And The Place Was Crowded. Dim Lights Hit The Walls That Were Dressed With Painted Art And Photos Of Famous Performers. Who Had Entertained On The Lit Stage. Bartenders Paced Back And Forth Trying To Meet The Demands Of High-Class People. Who Were Celebrating The Weekend Off, Wearing Fancy Outfits. This Place Housed **Occupied Chicago**'s Finest. Waiters And Waitress Maneuvered Through The Traffic With Foods And Drinks; It Was Like Rush Hour On The Dan Ryan Expressway.

People Even Went Out Of Their Way To Greet The Owner, Don Castoni Who Sat Comfortably Among Them. Jentson Asked, "Where Did Castoni Go When He Left Your Table?" Larson Replied, "Oh He Didn't Exit The Bar, But Being The Boss He Stayed Busy. So Mr. Aurelius And I Started Talking." "About What?" "About My Future Career." "In What—Major Drug Dealing?" Jentson This Time Began The Sarcasm. "Man, Hell No! My Future Career In Music."

Larson Paused And Looked At The Man Who Could Not Keep His Eyes Open, Still Affected By The Blast Of Energy. He Knew Jentson Did Not Want To Believe A Word He Said, But He Continued Anyway, *"Aurelius Said He'd Seen Me Quite A Few Times On Stage, And He Said I Put On A Damn Good Show. I Was Surprised That He Even Paid Attention To Me." I Said, 'Thank You, Mr. Aurelius,' And He Asked Me To Call Him Francis. He Said 'He'd Seen Dozens Of Acts Come And Go.' He Asked Me How Serious I Was About My Music."*

"When I Told Him 'Far-Reaching' He Asked If I Was Making Enough Money To Survive. I Guess He Had Noticed My Hard Work. I Knew He Had A Lot Of Money, So I Told Him, 'I Do Okay, I Suppose.' He Said Mr. Castoni Was Finishing Up His Recording Studio And That There Would Be A Lot Of Artists Going There. He Said Maybe They Could Squeeze Me In Sometimes. He Continued Saying That If He Had His Own Personal Studio, He'd Make It Available For My Friends And Me. Was The Man Trying To Cut A Deal And Leave Castoni Out? I Was Not Comfortable With The Conversation When It Came To Excluding Castoni. But His Actions Would Have To Speak Louder Than Words Then I Would Have Decided. I Felt It Wouldn't Be Right To Jump The Gun Directly, But Still, I Was Interested And Kept My Eyes Open."

Larson Began Growing Impatient Answering The Long Drawn Out Questions. Jentson Interrupted Larson' Flashback, *"So What Else Did He Say?* Larson Answered, "That Was Pretty Much It." "He Looked At His Watch And Said He Had Other Business To Attend To!" "So About Twenty Minutes Later; I Got Ready To Leave. Then I Said Good-Bye To Castoni." "The Host Gave Me My Coat, And I Left. And Then, Just As I Was Walking To My Car." "Two Police Officers Grabbed Me, Searched My Jacket, And Pulled Out About Two Ounces Of Cush—Just Like That!" Jentson Couldn't Figure This Out...This Information Was Nowhere In The Files... There Was No Narcotics Case.

Was Larson Just Outright Lying To Everybody? Larson Continued His Story, "So After They Brought Me Down To The Station; The Two Officers Got A Little Impatient With Me, And Things Got Rough... I Mean Bad. Then, All Of A Sudden, The Captain Came In And Got

Angry With The Officers. He Apologized To Me For Their Rudeness. That's When Mr. Aurelius Showed Up And Asked Me How I Was Doing. *He Said He'd Paid My Bond And I Was Free To Go.*" Jentson And Michaels Were Silent With The Same Thoughts, *"Records?"* So, Michaels Went Along With The Story. "So, Mr. Aurelius Came Out Of His Way To Help You?" "Yeah, You Know, I Just Couldn't Figure Out!" "How He Got Me Off So Fast! Then Again, I'm Still Confused As To How I Got In The Situation In The First Place."

Michaels Became Puzzled, "What Are You Trying To Say?" Jentson Took To Look Through The New Information. Again He Thought Is There Might Be Someone Helping Him Out. "I'm Saying That Wasn't My Cush!" Larson Exclaimed. "And Somehow It Was Just Planted On You, Right?" Jentson Became Frustrated. Larson Looked Him In The Eyes And Quickly Turned To Stare At The Wall. He Tried To Draw Himself Back To The Incident. "Man, I'm Telling You The Whole Situation Was Odd." "In The Courtroom, Only A Few People Were There.

It Was Very Quick And Easy Just That Judge, The District Attorney, And Frances Aurelius." Michaels Asked, "So, Tell Me What Happened During The Arraignment." Larson Thought Back, "Well, I Remember Going In Front Of The Judge…Wait A Minute…That Was The Same Judge! I Got It Now! What's His Name? Ummm…" Larson Saw The Picture Of The Man In His Mind, And It Was The Same Judge, But This Was A New Situation." "Francis Aurelius Had Not Been There For Larson This Time Around Because This Period He Came In With Don Castoni."

"Judge Julian Kharnas?" Jentson Shouted Refreshing Larson' Memory. "Yeah!" Larson Snapped His Finger In The Air, "That's Him Alright!" Larson Began Feeling Confident. "Well, Anyway, Now All This Time I Had Pleaded Not Guilty To The Drug Charge. Then All Of A Sudden Mr. Aurelius Said I Had To Cop Out Of A Charge Of Resisting Arrest."

Both Chiefs Were Baffled. *Had A Charge Of Resisting Arrest Later Been Dropped? Arch Chief Michaels Was Trying To Grip The Pattern Of Aurelius' Involvement. This Lawyer Seemed To Have Much More Influence Than Michaels Would Have Thought. Jentson Dared Not To Respond?*

Michaels Commented, *"Resisting Arrest? So What Was Your Sentencing?"*

There Was Knock On The Door, And Marla Carter Entered The Room. *"He Is No Longer Available For Questioning. It's Time To Go!"* Jentson Lifted His Right Arm In Silence Signaling Permission For Larson To Leave. He Suddenly Felt A Silence Come Over Him As If He Was Feeling Alesha Nearby. Oh How Much He Missed Her He Thought To Himself. He Wondered How Alesha Felt About His Sudden Departure.

However, He Always Felt There Was A Child Out There For Him That He Was Longing To Find Or Maybe From Another Life He Was Living Before. Larson Got Up From His Chair And Walked Towards The Door. Before He Got There, He Turned Around And Said To Both Men,

"Six Months…But I Never Served A Day. The Day Of Left Court Mr. Aurelius Gave Me A Ride In His Jaguar." Larson And His Attorney Marla Carter Walked Out Of The Room. Jentson Didn't Know What To Think About Da Ill-State Enforcers. He Needed Something More Than Files And His Informant To Make Anything Stick. Of Course, Larson Would Be Under Massive Surveillance.

Jentson Could Care Less If He Happened To Be De-Materialized On The Streets But He Really Wanted Larson. Then There Was Alesha, Who Had Just Volunteered To Be Questioned Even Though She Could Have Left Along With Larson. "So, What's Her Story?" Jentson Thought, *"What's Her Reason For Wanting To Talk To Us?"* Michaels Looked At The Files And Was Ready To Proceed, "Okay, Now That He's Out Of Here, Let's Bring In The Girl." *"Don't Worry, I Got Guys On His Trail Soon As He Leaves This Building,"* Jentson Said. *"It's Funny Don't You Think?"* "What's That Again?" Jentson Continued, *"How Everyone Is Confessing About Their Roles. You Know He Said To Me That He Was Going To Get Off This Case With No Problem. And There's Something He's Not Telling Us."*

Michaels Began To Think Out Loud, "Somehow He Is Looking At A Much Bigger Picture Than We Are." For The First Time, Jentson Admitted To Himself That He Might Be Confused. All The Information He Had Gathered To Break Larson Was Beginning To Crumble. In A Very Swift Two And A Half Hours, His Twenty Years Of Technique Was Going Down The Drain.

First, His Number One Suspect Acted On Principles Of Knowing His Personal Dealings. Perhaps His Faults Were Being Monitored. Is He The B.R.L-Illiana Director, He Wondered, "Am I Giving Orders Or Following Someone Else's? Where Does Arch Chief Michaels's Loyalty Remain? Is He With Me The Director Or With That Higher Power?" Indeed Chief Jentson's Work Was Getting Sloppy, And He Was Somehow Losing Hope. *"Oh, By The Way, Michaels, Call Down To Fort Benning, Georgia, And See If Larson Was Ever There."*

As Michaels Left The Room, Jentson Pressed The Intercom And Requested That Alesha Is Brought In. The Average Gang Member's Lifestyle Was Too Simple For Him To Be Able To Mastermind Events Such As These. This Very Great Hostility Had Taken Place In **Occupied Chicago**. For Someone To Fake His Own Symbolic So-Called Passing Away Was Not Unusual, But Larson Had A Higher Level Of Intelligence Than Most. The Reason For His Relaxed Behavior Had Not Yet Surfaced.

Who Dares To Be Like Larcenni Da Anunnaqi?

Where Did That Name Come From? Maybe This Anunnaqi Was An Angel Of Judgment? Only The Evil People Had A Problem With This Threat. Larson Could Take Care Of Himself And He Had All The Reasons To Strike Back At Them. How Could A Man Like Larson Be In The Way? On That Designated Night, They Choose To Eliminate This Man Of Peace. Da Larcenni Brought Havoc On Them, So What The Hell Was They Complaining About? BRAZOS Truly Exercised An Eye For An Eye. Reports Were Made That Night About A Huge Beam Of Light Over The City. Perhaps Larson Was No Longer Left To Be Found On This Earth. He Had Been Described As Five-Foot-Nine, 180 Pounds, With Light Sandy Brown Wooly Hair And Light Brown Eyes. He Was Da Sarge With Da Staff, A Rap Singer, With Two Rings On Each Pinky, Da Emerald Lion Of Judah Ring And Da 9Ruby Ring Of Royalty, Like Unto The Ancient Spirit Of Destineye And His Fathers Before Him.

****

05

WAR IN THE CITY OF CHAOS
BRAZOS RULE OF LAW

THE 6TH DEGREE OF SIX-ETHER

In The Year 2024 D.A.

Nineteen Great Balls Of Fire Casted Down On **Occupied Chicago**. And A Second Civil War Will Break Loose. Larson Was Invited To Sit At The Table With His Mentor Don Marquis Castoni At The Same Meeting. Apparently, Castoni Was Approached With Disrespect, Due To The Increase Of Violence On The Westside Of **Occupied Chicago**. Castoni Was Accused Of Cleaning The Neighborhood Of BRAZOS Street Dealer. Before BRAZOS' System Was Put In Place In 2023 D.A.,

However, Castoni Was Known For Doing Illegal Underground Business. And Now, Seven Years Later, Everyone Was Wondering Why The Change In Heart, And When Did He Start The Change. The Elite Families Viewed Larson' Mentor As An Outcast For Suddenly Staying Away From The BRAZOS Regime. So, BRAZOS Chancellor Elite Attorney Francis Aurelius Held The Meeting Accompanied By Mayor Elite Donald Finley And BRAZOS Chancellor Elite Madame Helena Ishtar.

Castoni Was Given An Offer Of Joining The Elite Families With An Ultimate Choice, And That Choice Would Obviously Be The War Against Him! Castoni Conceded To The Pressuring Demands. However, Larson, Who Was Also At The Meeting, Strongly Opposed The Notice Of Having Da Ill-State Enforcers Siding With BRAZOS. Mayor Elite Donald Finley Smiled At Castoni Who Was Now His New Alliance, *"How Can You Allow Such A Weak Person To Attend This Meeting?"* He Said Referring To Larson. Offended By The Remark, Larson Asked Francis Aurelius Permission To Speak His Mind; However, Castoni Slammed His Right Hand Into The Glass Table.

"Silence, Larson I Gave You No Permission To Speak!" Larson Was Shocked And Protested Castoni's Remarks. "What The Hell Do You Mean By Silence!?" Larson Was Furious But Kept Himself Calm. "You Don't Run Me. How Can You Trust BRAZOS?" "Everything They Stand For Is A Lie." "They Are Trying To Enslave All Of Us!"

Mayor Elite Donald Finley Stared At Larson With A Smirk On His Face. *"BRAZOS Does Not Care About The People." "Look At How Many People Died," "Believing In This Illusion Of Hope That In Return Made Them Suffer!"* The Entire Room Went Silent Because Of What Was Said. Mayor Elite Donald Finley Stood From His Seat Evidently Upset. He Waved To His Bodyguards To Stay In Place And Walked Fearlessly Towards Larson. *"You Have Been A Problem For Me..." "Calling Yourself An Artist And Making Songs About That Deception Stress!"*

Mayor Elite Donald Finley Stood Close To ChristOn's Face. *"Why Don't You Do Like All The Other Kids And Talk About Parties And Girls, Sex And Alcohol, Money And Fancy Cars?" "Now That's Artistry...Because Then You'll Be A Serious Star All Over The World And Have So Much Of A Bigger Fan Base, To Make More Money."* Larson Felt Uneasy About The Man's Spirit. In Fact, Larson Didn't Even Feel A Spirit, Only Coldness. *"Mr. Larson, You Don't Think I Know You Were Talking About Me In Your Music?"*

"Mr. Mayor Elite, I Request Politely, That You May Not Just Walk Up Into My Face, And Begin To Instigate Unnecessary Wars And Possible Assumptions," ChristOn Said Slyly And Calmed, Stepping Out Of The Mayor's Presence. Mayor Elite Donald Finley Laughed Conceitedly, Turning 360 Degrees Around The Room Laughing With His Followers. He Then Turned Back To Face Larson Who Had Stepped A Few Feet Away From The Man. So He Could Control The Anger Inside Of Him. Larson's Body Was Beginning To Shake With Anger From His Core.

He Could Not Think And Felt His Body Vibrating With A Fierce Trembling. *"What Larson? Why Are You Shaking? Are You Crying?"* The Mayor Elite Still Laughing, Slid His Body Towards Larson, And Pointed His Finger Towards Larson's Left Eye; And The Unimaginable Happened. Larson' Hand Slid Out Of Nowhere And Grabbed The Mayor's Left Wrist, Twisting It 45 Degrees Towards The Mayor Elite's Chest, Quickly Punishing The Man.

"Break Yo' Damn Wrist!" ChristOn Whispered Loudly In The Screaming Man's Ear At The Moment Was Sending A Piercing Squeal Throughout The Room Freezing Everyone In Their Tracks. *"Aahhhhh! Secuuuuu....Rity!"* Immediately Security Guards That Rushed Towards The

Injured Mayor Elite. They Drew Guns Towards Larson And Castoni Who Were Nine Feet From Each Other. "Let Go Of The Mayor Elite!" "Let Go Of The Mayor Elite Or We Shoot!"

All The Voices Surrounding Larson Screamed Frantically To Him. As Their Hands Pointed Straight At Different Parts Of His Body. All Of A Sudden, A Blue Light Penetrated Out Of Larson's Skin. Glowing Close To The Surface. The Radiation Went To His Hands And Burned The Mayor Elite's Sleeve As Larson Released. The Man Who Then Crumbled To The Floor. Larson Extracted The Energy From The Lights Causing Them To Flicker Uncontrollably, And All The Security Guards Froze In Astonishment! As Larson's Eyes Began Turning Black, With His Hands Holding Blue Orbs Of Electricity. Spinning Wildly Like Snakes On His Palms Casting The Blue Glow On Everyone In The Room.

"What The Damn! Fire!" A Voice Shouted, And In A Matter Of Seconds, Larson Had Already Raised His Arms 45 Degrees, Exploding Lightning From His Fingertips, Into The Barrels Of The Guns, Being Held By The Surrounding Guards, Sending Their Bodies Flying Violently Across Each Corner Of The Room. Many Guards Were Passed Away And Lost Body Parts. Because Of The Intensity Of The Electricity And Fall. Their Hands Were Blown Right Off With The Guns, As Unidentifiable Objects Beside Them.

Francis Aurelius Pressed His Body Frighteningly Against The Wall, Beside Madame Helena Ishtar, As He Witnessed The Horror. *"Coward,"* She Said, Lifting A Glass, Round Table With Incredible Strength, Tossing It Like A Boomerang With Both Arms In Larson's Direction, But In Slow Motion Which Was Actually Seconds. His Fighter Instincts Made His Body Leap, Above The Circular Table That Went Crashing Into The Wall, Shattering Instantly. Castoni Had Already Found Himself Out Of Harm's Way But Noticed Ishtar Was Heading To Lift Up Another Glass Table.

"Stop! Stop!" He Shouted Alarming The Woman. Francis Aurelius Ran Towards Mayor Elite Donald Finley Who Was Crouched On The Floor For Cover. The Mayor Elite Stood And Then Signaled To Madame Helena Ishtar And The Three Of Them Sprinted Out Of The Darkened

Ballroom. All The Other People Present In The Room Crept Out Of Their Hiding Places To See That Larson And Castoni Were Also Nowhere In Sight. The Heads Of The Elite Four Families Were Terrified By The Scene Of Burnt Passed Away Bodies, Shattered Glass, And Smoke.

Don Cleni Looked At The Other Head Elite's In Disbelief, *"What In God's Name If There Is One! What Kind Of People Are We Dealing With? Is This The Real Reason Why, Larson Is Called* **Da 9Sacred Star Child**? *And Where Did BRAZOS Chancellor Elite Ishtar, Get That Strength To Lift This Heavy Table?"* The Three Head Elite's Remained Speechless By The Unexpected Blow That Happened In The Span Of Five Minutes.

"Why Would The Mayor Elite Donald Finley, With A Broken Wrist, Now Just Run Out With Francis Aurelius And Madame Helena Ishtar?"

Don Cleni Looked At The Three Other Leaders, Waiting For Some Sort Of Explanation, But Received None. He Shook His Head And Left The Scene, Turning His Back On The BRAZOS Regime, No Longer Wanting Any Parts Of This Mysterious Organization. Later That Evening, WGN Jan Lysalot Interrupted All Scheduled Programs For The Announcement That Terror Was In The Midst, And That A Foreign Assassin Attacked Mayor Elite Donald Finley.

BRAZOS Chancellor Elite Madame Helena Ishtar Was In The Spotlight And Was In Place As The Interim Leader Of BRAZOS For The Next Six Weeks. Reporters On The Scene Grilled The BRAZOS Chancellor Elite About What Happened That Night. And The Rumors That Were Still Lingering, Regarding The Legitimacy Of The Mayor Elite.

Questions Were Swarming About His Claims Of Being African-American Descent As Opposed To Him Being Of Foreign Descent. They Presented Questions About The Terror Suspect. Responsible For The Attempted Bombing Of The John Hancock Building. Stating The Terror Suspect Matched The Description Of Mayor Elite Donald Finley, Whom They Claim Just Came Out Of Nowhere.

"The BRAZOS Chancellor Was Caught Off Guard. By The Questions And Began Fabricating Stories But Could Not Mention Larson's Involvement Because He Knows All Of Their Secrets."

In The Year 2026 D.A.

Six Weeks Later, The Mayor Elite Held A Press Conference From City Hall. Mayor Elite Donald Finley Held Up His Left Arm Stating That His Wrist Was Broken. And To Everyone's Surprise, The Mayor Elite Was Wearing Something Similar To A Turban And A Full Beard. He Described The Suspect That Broke His Wrist Was Of Persian Descent.

He Then Started Chanting In Another Language Hypnotically Followed By Calling For A Civil War Of Justice, Denouncing All Un-Loyal Citizens Of BRAZOS. The Mayor Elite Spoke Into The Microphone Glancing To His Right And Left Reading Teleprompter Screens Of Words Filled With Hate! The Unsuspecting Crowd Sat In Silence As Fear Flowed Through Their Blood Attacking Their Nervous System That Was Feeling The Ultimate Deception. The Mayor Elite Uttered His Tyranny,

"In A Time Of War, We Must Prevail. Freedom Is Not Free, And We Will Obtain The Goals For The People I Serve. Yes, I Have Been Hiding My Actual Ethnicity, And My Reasons Are Simple; I Am Who I AM," His Voice Resonated Through The Speakers And Trembled The Weak Souls That Feared Him. **"Occupied Chicago** *Needed A New Direction, And I Cleaned The Streets Of Criminals Plaguing The City. You, People, Must Obey All That I Say, Because You Must Have A Ruler, Who Knows What Is Best For You. You Are My Children,"* He Said Jabbing His Finger To The Crowd, *"And I Am Your Father, Your Messiah, Your God!*

The Entire City Was In Shock! For All The Millions Of Arrogant Citizens, That Voted For The Mayor Elite. Those Who Have Persecuted All Of Abraham Musa's Warnings. They Were Feeling The Consequences Of That Ultimate Reality! They Were Merely The Sheep Herded To Their Slaughterhouse, And To The Only Witness That All The Hope And Prosperity Was Just An Illusion! BRAZOS Infiltrated Their Lives, Losing All Of Their Rights As Human Beings, Within Two Years And Some Of Their Sons And Daughters, Were Ones That They Thought Deployed Into Many Battles As A Sacrifice To BRAZOS' New Way Of Life. However, What They Did Not Know, Was That The Children. They Thought Were Being Deployed, Were Being Tested As

Guinea Pigs To Be Robotic Soldiers For The Regime. As The Crowd Began Shouting In Rage, BRAZOS Military Forces Began Firing Tear Gas Into The Crowd, And After The Smoke Had Cleared, Hundreds Were Arrested. However, On The News That Evening, Those Who Weren't Present During His Live Speech Only Saw The Edited Version,

"In A Time Of War, We Must Prevail…Freedom Is Not Free…We Will Obtain The Goals For The People I Serve. **Occupied Chicago** *Needed A New Direction…I Cleaned The Streets Of Criminals Plaguing The City."* The News Did Not Mention The Many Arrests That Took Place At City Hall. The Second Call For Martial Law Had Taken Its Position In The State. But Many Were Trying To Get Mayor Elite Donald Finley Voted Out Of Office. Shortly After That, Martial Law Was Already Secretly In Effect Within Six Months, And Six Days After The Mayor Elite Made His Hatred Speech; The Second Civil War Had Begun Causing **Occupied Chicago**'s Elections Campaign To Be Canceled Indefinitely.

The Ultimate War Of Deception Began After The Opposition To Martial Law Was Ushered In Neighborhoods, Where Unarmed Civilians Lived, They Were Ransacked, As Soldiers Searched The Warring Angels Known As Former Gang Members And Mainly Da Ill-State Enforcer Members. BRAZOS Was, However, Unsuccessful In Apprehending Neither Da Ill-State Enforcers Nor Their Family Members. Mayor Elite Knew These Elements Needed To Be Eliminated For BRAZOS To Succeed In Total Control. When The Second Civil War Started, Both Innocent Citizens And The Warring Angels Are Known As Former Gang Members.

They Were Storming The BRAZOS Detention Centers, Breaking In And Releasing Families Members. Da Ill-State Enforcers Were Fighting With Fierce Resistance Against The Regime. But This Time They Were Not Being Supported By Don Marquis Castoni's Enforcers, Due To Larson's Rebellious Confrontation With The Mayor Elite Donald Finley And His BRAZOS Authorities. However, Don Cleni JR Cleni Broke Away From BRAZOS And Became An Aid To Da Ill-State Enforcers Because His Son Cleni JR Cleni Was A Member.

Don Marquis Castoni, On The Other Hand, Remained Neutral, But He Secretly Supplied Information To His Son Castoni JR, Who Was An Associate To Some Of The Members. After Six Months Of Unrest, Thick Clouds Were Raging In The Skies Bringing Darkness Over The Land During Daylight Hours. The Clouds Were Moving Faster, And Massive Clouds Completely Blocked Out The Sunlight, And The Ever-Raging Weather Was Just The Beginning. As They Funneled Vicious Tornados And Hurricanes, Generated By Da Igigi, Who The Anunnaqis In **9Sacred Starships**. As The Rivers Of **Occupied Chicago** Rose And Overran The Streets, With The Weather Patterns Fluctuated From Hot To Cold By The Hour. Fear Had Overtaken The Coldness Of The Lawless Citizens, But Then Everyone Began To Scream.

Aahhhhhhhh!" And The Earth Began Shaking, But Not Strong Enough To Make The Buildings Crumble. The Tremor Seemed Very Controlled Somehow. But As The Earth Shook; Hail Fell From The Sky From A Vortex That Began To Form In The Thick, Dark Gray Clouds. Creating A Swirling Three Hundred And Sixty Degrees; Black And The Blue Hole In The Sky, Followed By Lightning Strikes, Hitting Vulnerable, Unsuspecting Citizens And Foreign Enforcers.

Who Worked For The Fallen. But It Did Not End There; The Thick Dark Circular Cloud, Began To Descend Closer To The Earth Out Of Heaven Giving Birth To Another Silver, Circular Object Of About 45 Square Miles, With A Diameter Of About 7.57 Miles. Placing The State In Odd Darkness Because Buildings Were Still Lit From The Inside, And So Housed Car Lights Were Still On, And So Were The Lampposts. The Bottom Of **Da Crystal City** Held A Silver Force Field Around It, That Turned A Fiery Orange When It Passed Through The Earth's Hot Atmosphere.

Shortly After, Smaller **9Sacred Starships** Shot Out The Belly Of The Hovering City And Began Circling **Occupied Chicago**. While The Flying Mother Ship Cast Her Shadows Upon **Occupied Chicago** From 29 Miles Above. Through The Cloud, It Was The All Seeing Eye-Witnessing Everything! Nothing Was Hidden Now, And All The Wars In The City Came To A Complete Halt, Except For One, Nine Days After Da Crystal City Merged Closer To The Earth.

In The Days To Follow, They Only Selected Nine Million Warring Angels Known As Former Gang Members And BRAZOS Street Dealer Who Survived The Cataclysm Were Allowed To Carry Out Their Business. On The Streets With BRAZOS Permission. It Was Tough For Any Individual Not A Part Of This Regime To Make Money, And The Circulation Of Cash On The Streets Had Been Cut Back For Over A Year And A Half. The BRAZOS Street Dealer And Re-Up Hustlers Were Designated Only For Certain Facilities, Like Warehouses In Territories Such As Those Of The Five Elite Families. Of Course, People Still Carried Paper Money For Trade, But They Were Not Allowed To Buy Drugs With It Because Of Their Chips.

BRAZOS Street Dealers Would Scan The Palm Of The Buyer's Left Hand With Their Own, Transferring And Storing The Serial Number Into Their Own Chip That Was Street Law Number Six; Called Authorized Credit And The Dealers, At The End Of The Night Would Report Back To The Warehouse And The Accountants Would Scan The BRAZOS Street Dealer's Hands When They Turned In Their Unsold Products.The Machine Would Calculate A Percentage To Be Deducted And Printed A Receipt.

Now, If The Dealer Became Short, A High-Pitched Sound Would Blast Behind The Inside Of His Ear. Only Four Elite Families Operated Off Micro-Scan Devices. The Fifth—Don Marquis Castoni And His People... Did Not. Gambling Was Also An Enormous Money Maker. Before, There Had Been No System To Track Negative Balances, But It Was Then Created. Some Sick Gamblers Were In The Hole By The Thousands And Only Knew It When The Machine Scanned Their Eyes, And The Results Were Horrible. If One Could Not Pay From Their Balance Income, They Were De-Materialized Instantly, And Their Body Parts Would Be Used For Science.

Arch Chief Michaels Had Investigations Into BRAZOS Going As Far Back As Three Years But Told Jentson That It Was Less Than That. The Problem Was That His Home Agency Refused To Cooperate With Him. So He Began Secretly Compiling Information For His Own Safe Keeping And His Own Protection. Shortly After, The War Between The Three Fallen Elite And **Da 9Sacred Star Child**, The Robot Soldiers Began Tearing Up Neighborhoods, Seeking Out

The Destruction Of Da Ill-State Enforcers And Other Disgruntled Citizens, While The Second Civil War Had Plagued The Streets Of **Occupied Chicago**.

Many Families Stayed In Their Homes Afraid To Go Outside And Mainly Because Of The Mother Ship. Massive Passing Away Became An Everyday Scene For The **Occupied Chicago**'s. WGN News. While Da Ill-State Enforcers Became The Major Target After Alesha Released An Article. After She Posed As A News Reporter In Salsara Park. Da Ill-State Enforcers Hi-Jacked WGN, News Crews' Camera Equipment When They Was In The Area, Trying To Downplay The Citizens Living Conditions.

The Second Civil War Raged On When The Citizens' Trust And Glory With Mayor Elite Donald Finley, Was Replaced With Fury After His True Intentions Were Revealed. Mayor Elite Donald Finley For Many Years Denied His Connections With "Extremist Groups" And "Foreign Associates". That Truly Ushered Him Into Power. But Then He Announced To The City Of **Occupied Chicago** That He Was The Most Wanted Extremist! The Same Man Whom The Former Mayor Elite Abraham Musa, Was Trying To Protect His Citizens From.

He Was Not Even Of African American Descendant, But Of Hindu And Extraterrestrial. And No One Was Allowed To Criticize The Unknown Young Man. Running For **Occupied Chicago**'s Highest Authority. By The Time, The Citizens Caught On To The Well-Planned Illusion; It Was Far Too Late! No One Had Guns Except For The Armed Citizen's Army. Once The Citizen's Army Seized All Weapons From Gun Permit Holders, They Ran Off All The Loyal Patriots To Jail And Made The Weapons Their Own. Some Of The Members Of The Citizen's Army Refused To Turn In Their Weapons.

So, BRAZOS' Robot Soldiers Were Unleashed Upon Them, With No Remorse! Hundreds Of Thousands Of Plastic Coffins, Were Lined Up In Neighborhoods Filled With Passed Away Bodies, And Ground Airplanes With Chemical Trails Were Releasing Mass Amounts Of Anthrax Within Industrial Areas, Poisoning Water, Natural Life And The People Living In The Countryside.

So What Was The Real Purpose Of The Anthrax Vaccines Then? It Was A Way Of Implanting Microchips In The Citizens Along With The Virus. However, The Mix Of The Chip And Virus Together Worked As Oil And Water And Made Their Bodies Nonresistant To The Actual Virus. Much More Died In Deception!

****

06

THE TESTIMONY OF ALESHA FRANACIA

FOURTH SCRIPTURE OF LIFE

In The Year 2027 D.A.

As The Chiefs Escorted Alesha To The Interrogation Room, Jentson Asked Her, "So How Are You Today, Mrs. Larson?" "I'm All Right I Guess," She Replied. She Felt Her Heart Beating Nervously. Not Because Of Jentson, But Because Of All The Events That Had Occurred. Michaels Entered The Room And Handed Jentson A File. Jentson Glanced At Alesha As He Began To Read. *"Let Me See, Alesha Franacia, Maiden Name Alesha Franacia Age 33; Was Born September 17TH, 1986 A.D.; And God-Brother To Convicted Felon Lorenzo Larson." "And You Had A Husband - One ChristOn M Larson. I Bet You Knew Mr. Larson Faked His Passing, Right?"* Crimson Began To Rise From Jentson's Neck Onto His Chin As His Pressure Also Began To Grow. "Why Would This Man Become So Hostile Toward Me?"

Alesha Franacia Thought To Herself Staring Into The So-Called Blue Eyes Of The Crazed Man With Obvious Ill Intentions. "I Am Obviously Traumatized, And After All, I Came Here On My Own Free Will. But I Grew Up In The Hood So I Could Take Care Of Myself," She Thought With Confidence. Alesha Franacia Answered The Man's Question With Innocence,

"No, I Did Not." *"Sure You Did!"* Jentson Threw The File On The Desk As The Papers Flew To The Ground With One Landing On Alesha Franacia's Lap. She Became Infuriated, "Listen, You Asshole, I Lost The Two Most Important People In My Life Last Year! I Will Never Find Forgiveness—Never!" "Alesha, Alesha, Please Calm Down!" Michaels Said Stern As He Stood In The Shadowed Corner Of The Interrogation Room.

"I Did Not Come To Hear Your Tired Out Speech, Old Man!" She Said To Jentson. "I Wanted To See ChristOn, And Your People Would Not Let Me." Jentson Had Little Patience With Alesha Franacia. He Wondered If She Had Come To The Police For Help Or Revenge. *"Mr. Larson Is An Electro-Lightning Striker!" "A Cold-Blooded Assassin! I Bet You Even Contract For Him..." "You Knew The Most About His Intimate Business!"* "None Of That's True You Psycho!" Her Tone And Manner Changed Completely. "He's Not A Assassin," She Said Uncrossing Her Legs

And Pressing Her 4-Inch Deep Purple Pumps On The Floor Firmly As She Sat Up Straighter In Her Seat. She Knew That All Jentson Said Could Very Much Be Possible.

Although Her Eyes Had Not Witnessed These Acts. But For The Meantime, She Tried Not To Feed Into The Ideas Of These Irrational People. *"I Bet You Even Contract For Him…"* Jentson's Phrase Stuck In Michaels's Head. Michaels Started Wondering If Jentson Had Gone Too Far With His Manner Of Speaking. Jentson Became Relentless As His Ego Soared Sky-High.

"Bullstress! He's That Assassin Known As Da Larcenni; That We Are Aware Of A Fact!" But Of Course, It Was Not A Fact To Alesha Franacia. "What!?" Alesha Franacia Felt Jentson Was Jumping To Conclusions With All His Assumptions. *"Well, How The Hell Did You Figure That Out? We're B.R.L-Illiana…We Don't Have To Explain Stress! Listen If You Want To Your 15-Year-Old Daughter After You Are Released From Jail. In About Two Decades, You'd Better Start Talking."* Alesha's Anger Dominated The Atmosphere Of The Room. She Feared She'd Made A Great Mistake Coming There, Resulting In Their Illogical Threats.

It Was A Small White Brick Room With A Big, Gray Glass On The Third Wall. Behind The Glass, She Knew, People Were Hearing Her, Preparing To Record Her Confessions. She Thought Wisely Before She Replied, "So How Do You Figure That I'm Going To Jail, Chief Jentson? That's Your Name, Right?" "Yes, I See You Are The Overconfident Chief!" Alesha Franacia Waved Her Slender Hand In The Air Revealing A Beautiful, Washable, Lioness Of Judah Tattoo."

Jentson Laughed, Sounding Like A Hissing Snake, *"Sssss,"* He Held His Grin And Odd Laughter For A Few Seconds. *"Yeah, That's Correct,"* He Said Moving His Palms Together. *"But The Joke's On You! Do You Not Understand That Da Ill-State Enforcers Are Wanted For Conspiracy, And Your Name Is On The List?"*

"So Why Don't You Have A Warrant For Me Yet?" Jentson Felt He Was Losing The Upper Hand, *"Believe Me, Sweetheart, It's In The Process."* "Listen, I Came Here To See If He's Alive Because I Know He Will Be In Danger." With That Statement, Michaels Felt An Odd Feeling In His Gut. "You Mean To Tell Me, You Risked Coming Into The Snake Pit Just To Check On

Him?" Michaels Thought To Himself. "You See; A Loyal And Confidant Wife Will Always Be By Her Husband's Side No Matter What." "I Needed To See That Nobody Would Do Him Any Harm. Who Do You Think I Am?" Jentson Stared At The Young Woman Puzzlingly, Entranced By The Indigenous Beauty And Also By Her Intelligence. He Shook His Head, Interrupting His Thoughts,

"Who Cares!" He Put His Hand On His Head, *"What Difference Does It Make If We Can Trust You Or Not?"* He Was Trying To Find The Way To Get Information Out Of Her Through Threats And Intimidation. He Also Wondered How She Knew His Name Because He Didn't Tell Her. "Listen, We Know Too Much About The Corruption In The BRAZOS Organization." They Tried More Than Once To De-Materialize Us! I Even Know They Sent Men After Mr. Castoni," Alesha Stared At Michaels As She Spoke. Michaels Thought If Castoni Were Tied Into BRAZOS, Why Would They Want Him Out Of The Picture?

"So Alesha, Why Don't You Tell Us More Then On That Story?" "Only Under Certain Conditions." "If You Don't Meet Those Conditions, I'll Take What I Know To The Grave And Bury It There. Overstand? As Much As BRAZOS Hates ChristOn, He Didn't Cause All These Problems; That I Know For A Fact!" Michaels And Jentson Couldn't Turn Her Down.

Her Presence Was Too Persuasive. Her Beautiful Eyes Dominated The Atmosphere As If She Could Stare Into Your Soul. She Held Anunnaqi Large Oval Shape Pupils Of Dark Brown Settings. That Were Mesmerizing And Very Celestial Unknown Among The Human Population. Alesha Franacia Was A Very Attractive And Her Unusual Beauty With Abyssinian Perfected Blended Mixer Of Indigenous Traits Like That Of The Cherokees, Pure From Any European Features.

Her Black Liquid Liner, Mascara Eyes Were Not Very Wide As They Were Pulled Up In A Slant By Her Long, Sandy Brown, Kinky Hair, That Was Lining Perfect To The Middle Of Her Back. The Width Of Her Nose Was Of Perfection Because It Brought Considerable Attention To Her Natural Habesha Lips, Which Were Just A Shade Lighter Than Her Smooth Texture, Glowing, Brownish Gold Tan Skin That Radiated A Perfected Exotic Tone Under The Dim Yellow Light In The Room.

It Was Evident That She Was Of The Bloodline To Those Replicated Human, Abyssinian-Egiptian Statues That Were Destroyed To Hide The Maker's True Identity. Her 5-Foot 9-Inched Frames Have Always Been A Soft, And Femininely Posture Of A Masterpiece; Now Covered By A Loose Fitting Purple, Pant Suit With A White Silk Blouse That Lay Neatly On The Blazer's Collar. Around Her Neck Lay A Gold Lion Of Judah Symbol. Alesha Was Dawned In Her 9Ruby Chandelier Earrings With Her Matching 9Ruby Princess And Da 9Sapphire Falasha Rings. She Knew What She Was Up Against And She Was Very Confident And Well Poised. Truly She Was Like No Other Woman!

She Blinked Her Long, Black Lashes To Jentson Who Was Lost In Her Magnetic Field. "What If She Was There?" Jentson Asked Himself Staring At The Brown Girl With The Rings. *"Are You Willing To Testify Against Him?"* He Said To Her. Alesha Realized She Had To Play The Game. "Never," She Replied Blinking Once. "Besides, I Need Your Help," She Crossed Her Arms Over Her Chest. "I Want You Guys To End All Of This Madness!" Arch Chief Michaels Now Realized Why BRAZOS Would Make Her A Target. He Could Also Feel That Director Jentson Had Become Heartless. As He Did With ChristOn And Lorenzo. Could He Ever Trust His Own Boss?

Michaels Was Really Trying To Bring The BRAZOS Case To A Close, So He Had To Try Something New. He Was Also Trying To Seize The Opportunity Of Breaking The Case, And He Could Not Let Jentson Ruin His Investigation. He Had To Convince His Boss That Alesha Could Not Give Information About Da Ill-State Enforcers. Michaels's Plan Was To No Longer Mention BRAZOS In Any Following Conversations; So He Suggested To Jentson, To Let Alesha Go.

"Excuse Us For A Moment," Michaels Interrupted The Conversation And Turned To Jentson, "Let Me See You Outside For A Minute?" Jentson Closed The Door Behind Them, And Michaels Began To Speak, "Listen, She May Be The Key To Solving The Identity Of Our Mystery Enforcer. We've Got To Offer Her Immunity." Jentson Disagreed, *"Yeah, But Our Informant..."* "Can Only Cover So Much," Michaels Finished.

"Now If She Knows Enough—If Her Story Parallels With His Story ..." *Yeah, Yeah, I See Your Point,"* Jentson Interrupted. He Was Indeed Getting Frustrated By All Of It. "Still Having Da Larcenni Around Became A Dangerous Threat," He Thought. "Does Alesha Have Answers About The Identity Of The Assassin?" "Just The Suspicion That Larson Is Da Larcenni Just Isn't Enough!" His Mind Wondered.

Michaels Also Decided Not To Tell Jentson About Larson Going Through Basic Training At Fort Benning, Georgia. "Full Immunity!" He Said Staring At Jentson. "Listen, Her Testimony Will Give Us All Of The Ringleaders! Boom! Everybody!" Michaels's Rough Voice Sent A Jolt Through Jentson Because He Began To Like The Idea A Bit.Jentson Agreed. He Knew His Men, At His Signal, Would Make Sure Larson Never Make It Back To Court. But He Was Also Growing Impatient With Michaels's Dedication In Bringing Down The Corruption Of BRAZOS. Instead Of Being More Diligent About Going After Da Ill-State Enforcers. Plus, Jentson Had Never Planned On Holding Alesha Any Longer, After She Had Told Her Version Of The Story.

He Held His Composure; "We Can Release Alesha Only If She Can Prove The Identity Of Da Larcenni." "But What If Larson Isn't Da Larcenni, Jentson?" "We've Still Got To Find Who De-Materialized Mayor Donald James Finley." "Who Gave The Order For The Police Raid?" "Who Planted The Bomb? Whoever Is Running This BRAZOS Society Isn't Too Eager To Reveal Himself!" Michaels Placed His Hands In His Pocket And Waited For Jentson To Respond.

Jentson Finally Gave In, *"Okay, Immunity. But Somebody Will Be Held Responsible For All This Stress!"* He Said, However, This Time He Did Not Turn Red As Usual. His Actual Appearance Began To Shine Through, As He Became Agreeable With Michaels. If It Were 1507 A.D., Jentson Would Have Passed For An Older, Blonder Cesare Borgia. Most Bosses Don't Like To Admit Their Faults Out In The Open. The B.R.L-Illiana Usually Had All The Answers Within The First Twenty-Four Hours. But In This Case, Some Suspects Had Already Been Questioned, Some Were Passed Away, And One Had Just Come Back To Life. The News Reporters Continued To Call The B.R.L-Illiana Offices, But The Calls Were Not Returned. B.R.L-Illiana Chiefs Could Not

Legally Hold Larson In Their Custody. Yet They Did Not Have Da Larcenni In Custody Either. Marla Carter Had Played A Huge Part By Having Larson' Bond Paid, And There Was A Mystery Surrounding Larson' Fate. The Only Evidence Of The Existence Of This Mysterious Enforcer.

Da Larcenni Was The Name Painted On The Walls—A Reminder To All Criminals Involved With BRAZOS. Jentson And Michaels Returned To The Interrogation Room; Michaels Took A Seat Down Across From The Young Woman. "Okay, Alesha, If You Want Immunity You've Got To Tell Us All About Da Ill-State Enforcers, Right Up Until ChristOn Larson" "So-Called Passing Away."

Alesha Rolled Her Eyes And Looked Away From Both Men Amusingly. She Saw Them As Buffoons. "Okay, So Da Ill-State Enforcers…Where Do I Start?" She Crossed Her Right Leg Over Her Left While Unbuttoning Her Blazer, Removing It And Folding It Neatly Onto The Table. She Undid Both Sleeves On Her Purple, Silk Blouse And Folded Them Neatly To Her Elbows. "Well, You See ChristOn Started The Business Two Months After He Was Dismissed From Court. Some Lawyer Helped Him Start It Up." "Was The Lawyer Francis Aurelius?" Michael Inquired.

Alesha Answered, "Yeah, That's His Name." Jentson Looked At Alesha, As He Tried To Concentrate On Larson' Case, "So What Was Da Ill-State Enforcers' Order Of Business?" "A Recording Studio," She Replied. Jentson Asked, "Where Did The Money Come From?" "The Lawyer I Guess…" "I Dunno! All I Know Is That ChristOn And Mr. Castoni Had Some Argument Over The Phone." Jentson Leaned Into The Table, "What Was It About? Drugs? Or Maybe Just Drug Money?" "No, It Was Something About Backstabbing." Alesha Paused, "Now That I Think Back, The Person Who Argued With ChristOn May Not Have Been Mr. Castoni Himself—I Believe That It Was His Messenger."

"So, Later, At Around Six O'clock, We Had Dinner At Castoni's Bar. Mr. Castoni And Castoni JR, His Son, Came And Sat With Us. Mr. Castoni Went On Saying How Much ChristOn Had Embarrassed Him." "There Was Tension In The Air. I Recognized BRAZOS Associates There

As Well, Sitting As If They Were Having A Meeting. While We Were Eating, Castoni Looked At ChristOn And Said, 'Kid, I Treated You Like A Son. "How Dare You Show Me Such Disrespect? You Don't Turn Your Back On Me!' Castoni JR. Said, 'You Got A Lot Of Balls Treating My Pops Like That!' And Castoni Said, 'Sorry, But There's Nothing Else I Can Do For You Anymore! See You Around, My Friend.' But What Really Shocked Me Was That ChristOn Never Spoke A Word."

"Where Was Your God-Brother Lorenzo?" Michaels Asked. "I Don't Know." "He And ChristOn Had Spoken Earlier, But Chaos Left Before We Went To The Club." "So Where Did He Go Then?" Michaels Persisted. "Well, He Said He Had A Business Appointment." Jentson Interrupted, "With Whom?" "Don't Know." "He Just Said Something About Making An Alliance." Jentson Took A Wild Guess. *Let Me Guess, Don Cleni's Mob?*" "Oh Yeah, Your Informant's Father, Right!" Alesha Replied Nonchalantly Looking At Her Nails And Playing With Her Rings. Both Chiefs Were Stunned By Her Comment. Michaels Remained Silent While He Fumbled Through His Paperwork. "What Did You Say?"

Alesha Now Focused Her Attention Towards Director Jentson. She Knew Her Response Caused A Reaction Through His Nerves. She Smiled, "You Know…Michael Cleni Jr.? We Knew About His Drug Case." Alesha Began To Play The Game. No Longer Could Jentson Look At Alesha's Innocent Looking Face. All He Could Think Was, "Are We Playing A Passed Awayly Game?" Nevertheless, He Had Tried To Dumb Down The Situation. Now He Needed To Find Out Exactly What She Knew. "Who All Knew About This Information?" He Asked.

Alesha Confessed, "Everybody In The Da Ill-State Enforcers Knew." Michaels Looked Up From The Documents And Stared At Her, "What About Dr. Cinatto? Do You Know Him?" Alesha Thought Confusingly, "No I Don't Think So," Because, She Really Had No Idea Of Whom They Were Talking About. Michaels Leaned Closer Into The Table Towards Alesha And Explained, "He Was The Coroner Who Examined Mr. Larson' Body…"You Remember Now?" Jentson Showed Her A Picture Of The Doctor; She Refused To Recognize The Face Saying It

Wasn't Larson' Coroner. The Picture Was Of A Man She Once Saw At Castoni's Bar, And She Didn't Dare Say Anything About It Because She Knew That Face From The Club.

Jentson Added, *"Cleni Knew About Him. And That's How We Were Led To This Coroner's Arrest."* A Wave Of Sadness Suddenly Hit Alesha In Her Stomach, And She Started Sobbing, "No, No…That Can't Be Happening At All," She Began Crying Uncontrollably, Leaning Forward Onto Her Elbows, Planting Her Face In Her Hands That Covered Her Eyes, While Cupping The Flow Of Tears That Started Rolling Down Her Cheeks And Onto Her Blouse.

"He Was Paid An Extra Four Thousand Dollars For His Services…" "You Know, To Pretend ChristOn So-Called Passing Away," Jentson Continued Calmly Ignoring The Crying Female. Alesha Cried Harder, "No, No!" She Said Catching Her Breath And Waving Her Left Hand To Jentson As She Wiped Her Cheek With The Other. "Rabbi Walter Edwards Held The Services And The Mortician, Dr. Earl Miller, Did The Body." "Now Tell Me, Were You Familiar With Dr. Miller's Work From Before?" Jentson Continued. Alesha Insists, "Yes, Yes I Am!" "How?""My Step Son Baby's Symbolic Funeral," She Sobbed Harder And Wiped At Her Running Nose. Her Chest Heaved Slowly As The Memory Ran Through Her Body. She Squeezed Her Eyes Tighter From The Painful Thought.

"ChristOn So-Called Passed Away…Next Thing I Knew…Nine Days Later…My Step Son Was Founded So-Called Passed Away!" She Shouted Looking At Jentson With Red Eyes And A Wet Face. The Man's Tone Changed, *"You Lost Your Baby?"* Jentson Asked As He Began To Feel Sympathy For Her. Alesha Took Some Tissues From The Box That Jentson Placed In Front Of Her. She Fell Back Into Her Chair, Wiped Her Face And Hands, Blew Her Nose And Closed Her Eyes. She Took A Deep Breath, As More Tears Fell Her Face.

"Yeah," She Whispered, "Those Cowardly Bastards Kidnapped My Precious Child…Our Son," She Moaned With Pain As She Lifted The Tissue To Her Eyes, As Her Body Began To Jerk As A Result Of Her Trying To Stifle The Sound. "The Symbolic Assassins Were Never Identified, Were They?" Michaels Asked.

"No, He Was Later Found Him So-Called Passed Away!" Alesha Took More Tissue And Blew Her Nose Blinking Her Wet Eyelashes Wildly. "But The Strangest Thing I Did Not Recognize My Nine-Month-Old Son!" "I Was More Hurt When The DNA Was Not A Match. I Just Had To Accept It As Truth, But I Have An Idea Who Was Behind It!" Michaels Became More Curious, "Who?" Alesha Speculated, "I Think They Were The Guys Who Tried To De-Materialize Us. They Worked For Castoni. But When ChristOn Confronted Him, He Denied Taking Any Role In The Hits."

Jentson Began To Follow Her Story, "There Was Another Hit?" "That's Right. ChristOn And I Were Shot At." Michaels Took A Deep Interest In This New Evidence. He Stopped His Recorder And Placed A New Tape From His Pocket Into The Machine. He Then Restarted The Recorder, Spoke Identifying Information Onto The Tape, And Said To Alesha, "So, Tell Us About The Incident."

In The Year 2026 D.A., December 4

Alesha Took Them Back To That Night—A Scene She Remembered Vividly. Her Face Expressed The Trauma That Only A Few People Ever Experienced. She Finally Felt Safe Enough To Tell Somebody. It Didn't Matter Who Heard It; She Felt She Was Lifting A Huge Burden Off Her Shoulders, Saying About A Loss She Would Never Recover!

She Began Her Story: *"I Can Tell You This Much, It Was The Worst Two Days ChristOn Ever Lived You See This Was The Time When Our Old Neighborhood Was Under Siege. The First Day Corey Was Shot To Passed Away." "At The Time I Didn't Know What Was Going On..All This Was During Martial Law." "ChristOn Had Left Me In A Hotel Downtown By Myself." "He Said He Was Going To Be Gone For A Few Hours. But Never Said Where He Was Going.*

The Next Day He Came Back Saying How Much He Loved Me…More Than Life. I Was Pissed He Left Me There, But I Looked Into His Eyes And Saw The Most Stressed-Out Human Being In This World. He Told Me That Everything That Had Happened To Us Was Going To End Peacefully. That Night We Slept Together, And I Felt Like It Was Going To Be The Last Time."

"I Regret Not Telling Him I Was Going To Have His Second Child; That Still Haunts Me Today. Maybe If I Had Said, We Would Not Have Left The Hotel. So, What Happened After You Left The Hotel Room?" Michaels Asked.

"Adrian Called And Said To Come Back To My House…That There Was An Emergency. Somehow, I Knew Something Wasn't Right, But I Just Went Along With Everything. During That Time We Were Always Tight With Security Everywhere We Went, And I Was Concerned That ChristOn And I Had Gone Off Alone. Adrian Said There Was A Car Out In Front Waiting For Us. I Really Got Worried Then…Because ChristOn Had Never Mentioned Our Location To Anyone.

So Anyway, We Got In The Backseat Of The Car With Marty Frank Driving And Adrian In The Front Passenger Seat. Frank Started Telling ChristOn That Adrian Was Over Reacting About There Being An Emergency. That's When We Have Begun Feeling Better. He Also Mentioned That There Was To Be A Peace Agreement Proposed By Mr. Castoni. And That Mr. Aurelius Was To Bring About This Arrangement. Next Thing I Know, The Car Stopped, And Then I Saw Fire Flashes And Heard Shots. An Odd-Looking Lady Was In Distress..So She Made Us Get Into Her Car. She Drove Us To The Hospital. After A Few Hours, Ramon Came, ChristOn Had Called Him And Asked To Borrow His Car. ChristOn Left, And That Was The Last Time I Ever Saw Him!"

Alesha Also Had The Opportunity Of Reading The Poem She Read From Their Mansion Estate Cornerstone In Champaign, Illinois Of ChristOn And His Son. It Was The Ultimate Sign Of Deception To Leave Out His Very Own Wife, 9Ruby Princess. *To Deceive You Must Learn How To Manipulate The Power Of The Weak Minded Six Ether Forces Using The Power Of The Nine Ether Mind Of Truth, Justice And Right Knowledge"*, She Remembered Very Well The Words Her That Husband Taught Her In Dealing With Demonic Spiritual Forces. However; The Chiefs Were Looking At A Very Powerful Spiritual Soul, Who Was Indeed Capable Of Protecting Herself!

****

07

Testimony Of Michael Cleni, Jr.

Fifth Scripture Of Life

Report File Number 141-15 By Arch Chief Sham Michaels

Date: September 19th, 2027 D.A.

On September 19, 2027, A.D.,

After Four Hours Of Interrogation, The Third Suspect, Alesha Franacia Of Amarna , Was Released With Full Immunity. Alesha Confided Information Linking Da Ill-State Enforcers With Marquis Castoni's Mob. She Detailed Random Acts Of Violence And Indicated Several Party Links To Unsolved Symbolic So-Called Passing Away; A Connection To ChristOn M Larson' Symbolic So-Called Passing Away. 2. After Careful Consideration, We Believed Mrs. ChristOn Was Unaware Of Mr. ChristOn' Deceitful Acts. 3. Upon Discovering Enough Grounds For The Other Apprehension Of Mr. Castoni, 4. A Warrant Was Issued By Supreme Court Judge To Override Judge Julian Kharnas' Decision; 5. A Decision In Which Attorney Francis Aurelius Advised Mr. Castoni To Plead To Ninth. 6. Under The New Evidence, Mr. Aurelius' Powerful Influence Has Been Denounced. 7. Still, We Have No Proof That ChristOn Is The Mysterious Enforcer Known As Qaddisin Da Anunnaqi. 8. Our Special Operations Informant Is Also Being Detained For Questioning. 9. Currently, We Still Have No Positive Leads On The Assassination Of The Late Mayor Donald James Finley. 10. Our Investigators Are Still Clearing The Rubble. They Are Searching For Any Involvement Of The 66th Precinct Police Department. *End Of File 141-15*

Michael Cleni Jr. Was In B.R.L-Illiana Custody For Questioning. Arch Chief Michaels Stared At The Broken Young Man With Hate And Anger. *"Mr. Cleni, If I Didn't Know Any Better I'd Say You Were Playing With Us! And You Know Of Course That We Don't Like To Be Played With!"* Michaels Shouted Intimidating The Man Seated At The Table With His Hands Tightly Clasped Together. "Trust Me Chief, I'm Not Messing Around—I Swear To You!" With The Back Of His Hand, Cleni JR Wiped The Sweat Off His Forehead, Then Wiped It On His White Pants That Enclosed His Shaking Leg That Shook The Small Table.

"Boy, I Can Tell That You're Scared. You're Making Me Nervous!" Both Jentson And Michaels Laughed. "Whadah You Talkin' About Man? I'm All Right," Cleni JR Shook Harder And Wiped His Palms On His White, Sleeveless Vest Leaving A Wet Handprint. "Um...Um...Um Okay! I Dunno Know About You...Dunno Know About You." Cleni JR Smirked Nervously Clasping His Wet Hands Together.

"Eyy Cleni JR! You're Shaking The Life Out Of My Coffee Here! Ease Up On The Vibrations..." "Take It Somewhere Else!" Jentson Said Wiping The Mess Off Of The Table With The Paper Towel. "Oh Yeah...Sorry," Cleni JR Pressed His Hands To His Vest Leaving More Dirty, Sweaty, Prints. *"If This Were A Crime Scene Cleni JR, You Would Quickly Get Caught,"* Michaels Added. "I Said Sorry, I Shake When I Get Nervous." "I Thought You Told Me You Were Fine?" Jentson Interrupted. "Sounds Like A Bullstress Script You're Running," Jentson Threw The Wet Paper Towel Into The Trash. "Well I'm Not Impressed; In Fact, I'm Pretty Pissed Off At You Myself. Were You Trying To Bail Out On Us?"

Michaels Walked Over To Cleni Jr., "Why Was Our Communication Cut Off?" He Asked Pointing His Finger To The Young Man's Head. Cleni Blanks Fearfully At The Finger, "I Had No Choice At All. Chaos Knew I Was Wired, I Swear!" Michaels Continued, "Whose Idea Was It To Blow Up That Warehouse?" Cleni Was Caught Off Guard "What? Hold On; I Thought Your Guys Did It!" *"Cut The Bullstress Cleni! And If You Try Hiding Out On Us Again...This Will Be The Last Anyone Hears From You!"* Michaels Grew Impatient.

"Why Do You Think I Was Hiding Out? I Thought You Guys Were Trying To De-Materialize Us When The Warehouse Blew Up!" "So Why Did You Show Up Back Here?" Jentson Asked Taking A Sip Of His Coffee. "Cause We Had A Deal," Cleni JR Shrugged His Shoulders And Held A Distressed Look On His Face As His Mind Became Tired. Jentson Placed His Mug On The Sticky Table, "So What Were You And Chaos Planning?" Cleni JR Swallowed His Saliva Loudly, Resembling A Little Boy Who Just Got Caught Telling A Lie. "We Were Gonna Rob Them Blind In The Warehouse. Chaos Said There Was A Score Of Cocaine Money In That

Building. So He Came Up With The Idea. So We Drove There And Turned Down The Side Street To Enter Through The Back. We Got Out Of The Car, And Luckily We Caught Castoni JR Before He Went Off To His Limousine. And Then All Of A Sudden, Bamm!"

Cleni JR Raised His Arms High, Shaking The Table Again. "Out Of Nowhere The Building Blew Up. We Tried Running Back To Our Car, But The Fire Was So Severe At The Warehouse. We Had To Snatch Up Castoni JR. In His Ride." Michaels Became Curious, *"Where The Hell Did You Guys Go?"* Cleni JR Was Feeling Nervous, "All The Way To The North Side Suburbs..." "That's Where We Got Out Of The Limousine." Michaels Trying To Catch Him In A Lie, "So What Happened To Castoni JR.?"

Cleni JR Insisting For Faith In His Words Answers, "We Made Him Drop Us Off At A Hotel." *"Why Did You Let Him Go?"* Michaels Begins Turning Up The Heated Questioning.

Cleni JR Confesses In Fear Of Upsetting Michaels, "Well, For One, He Was Shaken Up By The Explosion!"Jentson Interrupted, "I Thought He Was The Enemy?" Cleni Corrected The Director, "Well, Chaos Wasn't Interested In Taking Out Castoni JR.." "He Only Wanted The Money From The Warehouse." "Besides, We Had Nothing To Gain; There Was No Purpose In De-Materializing Castoni JR.." *"So Chaos Let Him Go Just Like That!"* Michaels Squinted His Eyes At Cleni. Cleni Reassures Him, "Yeah, I Mean, After All, He Was Our Escape Route."

"Then Why Did You Get Dropped Off At The Hotel?" Jentson Asked Confusingly.

"Chaos Had Gotten Sleepy I Guess," Cleni JR Replied.

Jentson And Michaels Looked At Each Other; Both With A Confused Look On Their Faces. "After We Checked In We Went To The Diner Across The Street. I Remember Watching The TV, And That's When The Special Report Came On. We Were Like, Damn, All These Things Going On In One Night? The Warehouse Explosion, Plus The Mayor Elite's Passing Away?"

Jentson Left The Room And Came Back Carrying A Tape Recorder In His Hand. He Leaned Against The Table, "Okay, Cleni, I Want You To Hear These Tapes So You Can Fill In The Blanks!" Cleni JR Listened To The Testimony Of ChristOn And Chaos In Silence For

Forty-Five Minutes And Finally Nodded His Head, "Yeah That Sounds About Right!" He Said Nodding His Head Looking At Both Men Confidently. Jentson Gave Cleni JR A Devilish Grin, "So You See, Mr. Cleni, We Don't Need You Any Longer! So The Deal Is Off! Besides Alesha And Da Ill-State Enforcers Already Knew You Were Wired. So I Figure, Whoever Da Larcenni Is; He'll Get You Because Of The Deception…I'm Sure Of It!"

Cleni Clenched His Teeth, "You Double-Crossing Bastard! We Had A Deal!" "Correction— You Had A Deal With Arch Chief Michaels," "Not With Me. See I Make The Final Decisions," "Cause I'm The B.R.L-Illiana Director In The City Of **Occupied Chicago**." Cleni Started To Enlighten The Chiefs, "You Know, That's Fine And All Punishing Me For Helping You Guys Out But You Forget Something; Da Ill-State Enforcer Members Are De-Materializers." "Will I Be Alive To Take The Stand?" "Oh Yeah, That's Right, You Gave Alesha Franacia Immunity Leaving Me With No Protection!"

Jentson Started Laughing, "Immunity?" "Yeah Right! That Will Never Happen In This Lifetime!" Jentson Looked At Michaels Deceivingly. *"Jentson, We Made A Deal!"* Michaels Shouted. "That's Over My Passed Away Body, 'Cause, If You Didn't Know Already, I Don't Care For These Scumbags!" Michaels Became Furious But Decided To Keep His Emotions Under Wrap.

Cleni Disregarded Both Men, "Listen; They Only Mentioned Little About Business, And I Can Still Give You Everything About Da Ill-State Enforcers, Because Guess What After ChristOn Left, When Things Got Bad, Who Came To The Rescue? Yeah, That's Right… Da Larcenni, The Mysterious Enforcer. He Doesn't Even Touch Da Ill-State Enforcers." The Room Became Quiet As Cleni JR Tried Hard To Prove His Importance. "I Know Da Larcenni De-Materialized Every Last Japanese, Malaysian And Russian Assassin Throughout The State…Even Assassins Of Other Nationalities…That Was The Word In The Streets. I Mean He Did It So Coldheartedly; Still To This Day, They Can't Identify Him…He Just Left A Big "Q" Splattered On The Area With Their Blood. No Footprints, No Fingerprints…Not Even You

Guys Will Find Him!" Cleni JR Said Amusingly Mocking The Chiefs. He Began Shaking His Leg Again Out Of Excitement And Nervousness As He Smiled Thinking He Found A Solution For Them To Want To Keep Him. Jentson Answered Disgustingly, *"We Already Know Who He Is! He's ChristOn!"*

"If That's True Chief, Why's He Back On The Streets Then?" Cleni JR Shouted Screwing His Face To The Man. *"He's Being Watched Twenty-Four Hours A Day!"* He Replied. "Come On Now Chief Jentson; You Have No Proof! Let Me Drop A Colossal Hint…They Are Two, Entirely Different People, Trust Me! Da Larcenni Makes Herself Known Only When She Wants To Be Seen…Only To A Select Few In Da Ill-State Enforcers!" Cleni JR Shook His Head At Jentson And Began Smirking Loudly. Michaels Was Stunned By Cleni JR Cleni's Comment And Stopped The Conversation,

"Chief Jentson, I Need To Talk To You Outside!" And They Both Left The Room. It Was Evident That Jentson Was Excited As Blood Vessels Popped Through His Neck And Ran Up The Side Of His Temple Through His Face With An Odd Grin On His Face, "Yeah! We're Gonna Squeeze Everything Out Of Him. In Fact, He's Gonna Identify Da Larcenni!" He Said Clenching Both Fists. *"Then What About Their Immunity?"* Michaels Asked The Red, Wild Man. Jentson Ran His Hands Through His Platinum Blond Hair, Twisting His Face Annoyed By The Question. "Well, If You Haven't Figured It Out By Now Mykie, They Are All Career Electro-Lightning Strikers! Can't Trust Any Of Them! The Wacky Ones Like Cleni JR Are The Damnin' In Your Face De-Materializers…The Innocent People Like Alesha…Oh Yeah, She'll Chop Your Head Off While Smiling At You…Gut Your Insides While You're Feeling Sorry For Her And You Won't Even Know Your Passed Away. Now The 'Normal' Ones," Jentson Raised His Fingers Up Making Quotations, "Like ChristOn And His Friend Lorenzo…Those Are The Dangers To Society…Their Shadow De-Materializers! Yeah!" He Shouted Wildly Scratching His Head Unknowingly Leaving His Hair Spiked And Disheveled. *"What The Hell Jentson?"* Michaels Shouted. "Listen, Mike, If You Have A Problem With Any Of My Decisions, Let Me

Know Now; Because If You Do! I'll Have You Transferred To Montana Somewhere…Alaska Or Some Stress, Or You Can Resign!"

"No Problem At All, Mr. Boss-Man, I'm Just Trying To Do My Job. I Am Only Trying To Complete My Investigation Assignment Thoroughly." Michaels Was Not Threatened By The Man's Words Because Jentson Knew Michaels Was The Best Man In Illinois To Do The Job. "We Got More Info To Hear Mike! Let's Not Waste Time…" "We'll Have Ego Trip Later." *"If You Say So Then Mr. Big Chief,"* Michaels Replied Sarcastically. The Chiefs Returned To The Interrogation Room.

Jentson Cleared His Throat, "Listen, I Want To Apologize For My Behavior Earlier." "It's Just That So Much Has Been Going On. Anyway, Your Deal Stays The Same." Cleni Was Relieved, "Fair Enough." "You Remember About The North Side De-Materializings, Right?" "And Did You Know That Chaos Was Castoni's Number-One Enforcer?" Jentson Continued, *"Is That A Fact Now?"* "Yeah, Really Castoni Was Thinking Of Involving Chaos In The Plot To Get Rid Of Robert Greene, The North Side Drug Lord…Didn't Work, Though. Aside From That, Chaos Paved More Territory Through ChristOn For The Don; More Than Tripling His And Castoni's Profits. It's Funny How ChristOn Denied His Role As Leader." "He Was The Leader, But Only In Title 'Cause He Had The Brains." "Chaos Was The Man With The Fighting Power," Cleni JR Shook His Head. "ChristOn Only Had The Cush Connections. You Had To Give It To Him, Though, He's Always Been The Smartest." *"What Do You Mean By That?"* Asked Jentson. "For Example, He Would Tell You A Definite Plan He Was Going To Do! And Whoever Was Listening To His Plan, The One He Chose, They Ended Up Being The Ones To Carry Out The Mission; The One With The Most Expertise For That Project. ChristOn Would Sit Back, Watch From The Sidelines And Then Collect The Prize. He Wasn't Rude Or Condescending Either, So They Listened And Got The Job Done. They Liked His Negotiation Skills 'Cause They Always Got Paid Well. But Then To Show How Smart He Really Was, He Would Carry Out The Toughest Missions He Knew Would Fail, And In Doing So, He Would Accept Full

Responsibility. "He Was Aware That To Fail, It Was A Cover Up For Something Greater…The Ability To Find The Strengths And Weakness Of The Task At Hand. The Illusion Was If They Think You Failed Then You Would Give Up, So They Kept The Rhythm The Same. A Great Mastermind At Work No Doubt. He Was A Spur-Of-The-Moment Guy, But Do You Know Where The Cush Came From?"

Michaels Asked, *"Who?"* Cleni Didn't Blink, "You Know Of Him…That Mister High Power Himself, Francis Aurelius." "The Strangest Thing Happened Right Before ChristOn Received All That Cush." Jentson Became Curious, *"What's That?"* "A Big Drug Lord Was Found Passed Away In The Street." "His Name Was Frankie Montero… From The West Side," Cleni JR Pointed His Thumb Over His Back And Glanced Over His Shoulder. *"Let Me Guess; That's When ChristOn Got Too Big For Castoni?"* Cleni JR Swung His Index Finger Quickly Resembling A Needle On A Gauge. "Nope, The Fallout Came When ChristOn Found Out Castoni Was Dealing With Magog Park Apostles, Whom Sold Chronic Also." "You Know ChristOn And Chaos Are Sworn Enemies With The Magog Park Apostles." *"So That's How The Feud Began?"* Michaels Became Even More Confused. "Listen, Listen…Soon After The Shooting Happened On The West Side, Castoni Quickly Cut Off Magog Park Apostles."

"For The Sake Of ChristOn Because Of Conflict Of Interest, But It Was Chaos Who Kept The Stress Going On. See; Let Me Tell You About Chaos. I Mean; This Guy Really Lives By His Nickname. Every Time He Had To Carry Out A Mission He Would Purposely Overdo It. After Big X Was De-Materialized, The Neighborhood Became Divided, But Before Allll111 Of That, Chaos And Frankie Montero Split Salsara Park Lords In Two, Cause Frankie Had Employees Over There. I Mean Every Day On Their Streets Shootouts Occurred. It Got To The Point That Nobody Would Come Outside. Since Castoni Was Losing Money, He Spared Chaos' Life.Because He Liked That Chaos Was Creating Problems And Splitting People Up, This Gave Castoni The Chance To Find Alliances Secretly. Later Chaos Was Complaining About Why They Shouldn't Be Paying Castoni For Business. In Their Neighborhood Because

He Didn't Trust Him. So Then, Chaos Started A War With Magog Park Apostles Because He Felt Something Fishy Was Happening Between Them And Castoni. *Was He Trying To Send A Message To Castoni?"* Michaels Was Still Confused And Was Trying To Understand Where Cleni JR Was Taking Them. "Honestly, I Think He Was Just Bored With Peace. And Had Too Much Time On His Hands; That's All. He's A Wild Guy—A Street Hustler's Nightmare. I Mean He Just Loved The Opportunity To Ruin Your Day."

Jentson Grew Frustrated, *"Okay, Put Aside All That Jibber Jabber, What Happened Between ChristOn And Castoni?"* "The Don Didn't Like The Idea That ChristOn Was Making More Money. Than He Should At Such An Age And Such A Fast Rate…Plus Remember ChristOn Was Working For Castoni. Not Only That But Castoni's Son Was Also Working For ChristOn… Yeah…For Months ChristOn Started Slacking On Kickback Money. And Stopped Buying Because The Don Went Up On Purchase Price. When He Sold To Him And He Was Asking ChristOn For More Tithes. Maybe There Was A Sense Of Disrespect On Either Side Or Something I Dunno. Then The Don Sent A Strong Message Showing Who Was Really In Charge. Castoni Knew That Chaos Meant Business, So He Hired Rivals From Falasha And Magog To Intimidate Him, Plus He Had His Men. Around That Time Castoni JR. Had Already Taken His Father's Side."

"So ChristOn, Being Smart As He Was, Got My Daddy Involved. For Weeks Bodies Were Found Dropped Off On The Streets…Around The Time When Frankie Montero Got De-Materialized. So, After That, Other Drug Lords Got Involved; Like Cordelle Braylo. It Had Gotten So Bad That The Mayor Elite Called In The Chief Of Police, But Police Officers Were Caught Up In The Stress Too!" Michaels And Jentson Stared At Cleni JR Still Trying To Figure Out Where He Was Going With The Story. "Nobody Was Making Any Money Except For ChristOn…How? No One Knew; That's When Mr. Aurelius Got Involved. He Arranged Private Meetings With The Ringleaders To Make Settlements To Stop The Bloody War."

"For The First Time, ChristOn Was Recognized As An Independent Leader, And He Was Given Territory On The North Side." After Six Months Of Peace, Chaos Invaded Frankie Montero's Old Territory. And He Gave It To A Newbie From Los Angeles, California Rob Greene Who He Saw Had Big Connects...And No One Could Get Close To Him. That Was Considered The Last Straw. My Father Forced Me Out Of Da Ill-State Enforcers. I Wasn't All That Quick To Leave Until I Got So-Called 'Accidentally' Shocked! The Other Kingpins Held A Closed Meeting. This Time ChristOn Wasn't Invited Because Of What Chaos Did."

"Initially, The Company Was Dismantled, And Someone Hired Japanese Assassins. During That Period Alesha's Step Son Baby So-Called Passed Away, Then ChristOn And Alesha Narrowly Escaped A Drive-By Shooting, Then Chaos Manhandled Magog's Hood Single High-Handedly...At Least That Was The Word On The Street. Next Thing I Knew, ChristOn So-Called Passed Away!"

Arch Chief Michaels Glanced Over At Director Jentson, "Okay Cleni, You Have Permission To Leave Now." "My Check From You?" Cleni Stared At The Chief." The Young Man Stood 5'10. He Had A Light Brown Complexion And Small Tight Curly Hair That He Always Wore In An Afro, Which Held His Cap Tilted. Cleni Had The Features Of A Young Man Who Was Just Going Through Puberty. He Had Minimal Facial Hair And Little Body Weight, Yet He Did Not Look Skeletal, Just Muscularly Slender. His Light Brown Eyes Were His Real Deception, But His Ability To Control His Nerves Gave Him Away.

"Here," Michaels Handed Cleni A Check Written Out For $1000. "Whaaaaaat? That's It?" Cleni Stared At His Check As Though It Had A Stench. "We Had A Deal Chief!" *"Yes, We Had An Agreement...To Find Larcenni. But Did You Find Da Larcenni?"*

"No." Cleni Dropped His Hands To His Sides. "But What About All The Info I Gave You Just Now?"

"Still; Nothing On Larcenni." "Come Back When You Got Info On The Larcenni. Then You'll Get The Next 9 Grand." "Everything You Told Us We Knew. Including The Timelines

Which You Had Off A Bit." "This Is Bullstress Chief!" The Young Man Shouted Pounding His Fist Into The Desk. *"Tell Me About It,"* Michaels Sat Calmly By The Table And Stared At Cleni. As He Stomped Out Of The Room, Slamming The Door Closed Behind Him.

"I See We're Going To Need Surveillance On Mr. Aurelius," He Said Cross-Legged Turning His Head To Jentson. Who Was About To Pour Himself Some Coffee. Michaels Began Flipping Pages In The File On The Table, *"Let's See, I Will Need To Contact Internal Affairs About Him."* Jentson Slammed The Mug Onto The Table Beside Michaels Spilling Some Of The Beverage Onto The Documents. He Leaned Over And Grabbed The File From Him.

"No...No...No! None Of That's Going To Happen!" Michaels Stared At Jentson In Disbelief, *"I Don't Understand!"* "Let Me Put It Friendly And Straightforward," Jentson Muttered Glaring Angrily At Michaels.

"You're Beginning To Dig A Little Too Deep! You're Off The Case!" Michaels Placed His Finger In His Right Ear That Was Closest To Jentson. He Stood Up And Faced The Man Moving His Hand In A Chopping Motion Towards Jentson's Face, *"I'm Too Close To Bringing Down The BRAZOS Organization. I've Been On This Case For Over Three Years Now!"*

Jentson's Brows Jumped To His Forehead As His Eyes Popped Wider. "Really?" He Growled Exposing His Coffee Stained Teeth. "You Know, I Only Assigned You To This Case Eleven Months Ago!" "Maybe I Should Start Doing A Background Check On You!" He Jabbed His Finger In The Air. *"I'm Not Going Anywhere, You Can't Send Me Anywhere, And The Unit Needs Me More Than You,"* Michaels Responded Confidently.

"And For Your Info, I've Been Thinking About Resigning. Once This Case Has Been Solved And Over With," Michaels Turned Away From Jentson And Sat Back At The Desk Pulling At Other Files. "You Know...Stress! I'm Starting To Feel That You Know Exactly Who This Larcenni Really Is!" Jentson Held Onto The File He Grabbed From Michaels And Stomped Out Of The Room. Michaels Ignored The Man And Began Reviewing A Letter Cleni Sent Into

Michaels's Office A Few Weeks Back. About All His Observations Of What Was Occurring In The State. Cleni Labeled It "Da War Of Tribulation." Michaels Began Reading:

******

Attention: Arch Chief Michaels

These Are All My Observation Thus Far, But Before I Begin, Forgive Me Because I'm A Little Tipsy And Discombobulated. If You Got Questions About What Follows, Hit Me Up On My Cell. If Anyone's Close I Won't Answer But Will Return Your Call When No One's Around. WGN News Reporter Jan Lysalot Began Her Segment Of Surprising News That Rocked The "Sears Tower" Into Many Scandals That Would Follow An All Out "Second Civil War. That The New Mayor Elite Donald Finley Had Stirred Up. The Mayor Elite Made False Accusations Resulting In The Former State-Elite Leader's Arrest; However, State-Elite Cleophas Was The One Responsible For Placing The New Mayor Elite, Mayor Elite Donald Finley, In Office.

The New Mayor Elite Was Behind The Engineering Of The Stock Market Crash By Stealing Money, Amending The Laws And Giving The Money To "Foreigners" And Was Now Dressing In Foreign Attire That Sent Shock Waves To The Masses. They Became Worshippers Of Mayor Elite Donald Finley, And It Reminded Me Of The Twenty-Fifth Verse; Deuteronomy Seven; It Goes Like This, The Graven Images Of Their Gods Shall You Burn With Fire: You Shall Not Desire The Silver Or Gold That Is On Them, Nor Take It Unto Yours, Less You Be Snared Therein For It Is An Abomination To The ChristOn, Your Father EGZIABHER". I Mean I'm Not Religious Or Nothing Just Spiritual, But I Remember That Passage 'Cause My Grandmama Used To Read It To Us When I Was Young.

It Was Like A Foreign Invasion Of **Occupied Chicago**. *Most People Were Taking Their Daily Routes And Had Gone Home From Work. That Night The Charismatic Leader Made A Bold Statement In City Hall Saying, Any Illegal Aliens Living In The City Must Leave Now. He Said*

There Would Be Buses Going Through Neighborhoods To Round Them Up. He Said, "Your Exodus Is Now! I Mean Many People Were Stunned By His Comment Because Most Of The Individuals In The State Were Foreigners. He Did Not Mention Where People Were Going Or What Particular Group He Was Forcing Out! Now I Know Mayor Elite Donald Finley Was Not Talking About The Mexicans Or Any Middle Eastern People Because The Majority Of Them From What I Assume, Have Already Become Citizens.

It Was Mandatory Two Years Ago, For People Of Those Two Nationalities To Become Citizens If They Wanted To Stay In The State. Now Before He Did This, Mayor Elite Donald Finley Had Been Seen Wearing A Turban And Long Beard Resembling The Most Wanted Terrorist On Television, Campaigning That Every Nationality Of People In **Occupied Chicago** *Should Work In Harmony.*

There Were Questions Concerning Whether The Mayor Elite Was Of Natural Citizenship Himself... If He Were Even Born In The Us Because Of All His Foreign Attire, But Other Die Hard Followers Kept Loyal To Him. As For Other People, His Comment Really Upset Them Because The Mayor Elite Started Singing A Different Tune Once He Seized Power.

Do You Remember What Happened After He Made That Comment During His First Year In Office? All Of The Military Posts And Reserve Centers Began Closing Down. The Illinois Military Had Been Relocated... How? It Was As If It Were Planned. The New Jobs And Reserve Centers Were State Of The Art Million Dollar Facilities. Five Days Later After The Opening Of The Facilities, In The Earlier Minutes After 10 P.M., There Was A Major Blackout That Occurred And Water Systems Were Shut Off.

Do You Remember? You Got To Remember! This Was After His Crazed Comment. Multiple Loud Explosions Echoed Throughout The Entire City! Doors Were Kicked In, Not By Swat Teams Or Local Police, But By Military Foreigners, In Newly Fashioned Uniforms With Ak-47's Pointing At Scared Citizens! Families Witnessed Loved Ones Being Dragged Out Into The Streets By These

Government Gangsters, Forcing People To Lay Their Faces Down On The Pavement. Some Helicopters Appeared To Be Hovering In Silence In The Dark Sky...How?

The War Popped Off With No Warning, The Homeland Soldiers From Illinois Were Nowhere In Sight. All Because The Mayor Elite Relocated Them... Changed Them Or Something To Have The Attack On The Citizens A Complete Success, Which It Was. I Don't Know Where You Were, But I Remember That Most Of The City Was Up In Flames, Except For Certain Areas On The West Side Of The City.

There Were Rumors Of High Beams Of Light Hovering Over The Darkened Neighborhoods Such As Falasha And Magog Park... I Wasn't There, But It Could Have Been Those New Ass Helicopters. They Now Have... Or It Could Have Been Something Else Because I Was Told That The Beams Of Light. Shot Three Helicopters Out Of The Sky So That They Couldn't Have Been From The New Take Over. It Was 6 Hours Of Darkness And Hell I Was Told By Some Of My Boys. Who Were There. The Wealthy Neighborhoods Where My Family. The Castoni's And All The Other Rich Folks Live Were Left Untouched. Someone Told Me That The Foreign Soldiers Began Acting Strangely.

As They Saw The Helicopters Falling Out A Distance From Them. The Person Also Said That They Saw Other Beings In Black Robes. Standing In Shadows Close By The Foreign Soldiers, Sending The Soldiers Fleeing Mysteriously Away From Innocent People. Arch Chief Michaels, The City, Had And Has Been Taken Over! People Were Bused To The Closed Down Military Posts And Reserved Centers And That's When It All Started Making Sense To Me As To Why The Illinois Military Was So Quickly Relocated.

People Said Fires Raged In Separate Areas Through The City And Later The Massive Beams Of Light Disappeared. The Foreign Soldiers, Out Of Great Fear Stayed As Far Away From The West Side As Possible.Because Apparently, That's Where The Beams Of Light Were Mainly Spotted. The City Was Under Siege For Exactly Six Weeks, And Throughout That Time, They Restored The Lights And Water."

Mayor Elite Donald Finley Came On Television And Announced To The Disarray Urging Citizens To Cooperate To Spare Lives. I Remember Francis Aurelius And Greg Jentson Joined Him As He Spoke. I Remember Parts Of The City Became Like News Scenes Of Baghdad During The First Two Years Of Conflict. There Were Rumors That People Were Secretly Implanted Within Military Bases. Then After The Three Weeks Of Terror, The Us Army Invaded The City Of **Occupied Chicago**. *And Dominated This Foreign Army... And Ironically They Looked The Same. They Completely Took Over In The Matter In 9 Hours. The Us Army Crushed These Foreign Forces Releasing The Citizens From The Military Stations.*

Months Passed As The Us Army Remained In The City Of **Occupied Chicago***... Over Seeing The People. But All Of This Was Strange! Was This A Prelude To Something More Horrific To Come? Wrongfully Enough, There Were No Explanations As To What Exactly Occurred And Why. Did You Ever Remember Hearing About What The Sudden Invasion Was All About? And Why Suddenly The Us Army Intervened From Nowhere? All Those That Were Victims Of The Attack Remained In Fear Posing No Questions Because Many Of Them Were Chipped. Later On, As Months Passed, The Mayor Elite Began Making New Laws To Tighten Up Security! What The Hell Is Really Going? It Was Like The Same Person Organized Both Invasions By Two Different Militaries.*

We Will Keep In Touch, Cleni JR Cleni

****

Michaels Folded The Bizarre Letter And Inserted It Back Into The Envelope As He Tried To Figure Out What The Message Was All About? He Could Not Question Cleni JR While Jentson Was There, But He Did Realize That There Was A Far Bigger Web Of Deceitfulness, Intricately Weaved Together By A Single Mastermind, Or Many Of Them.

****

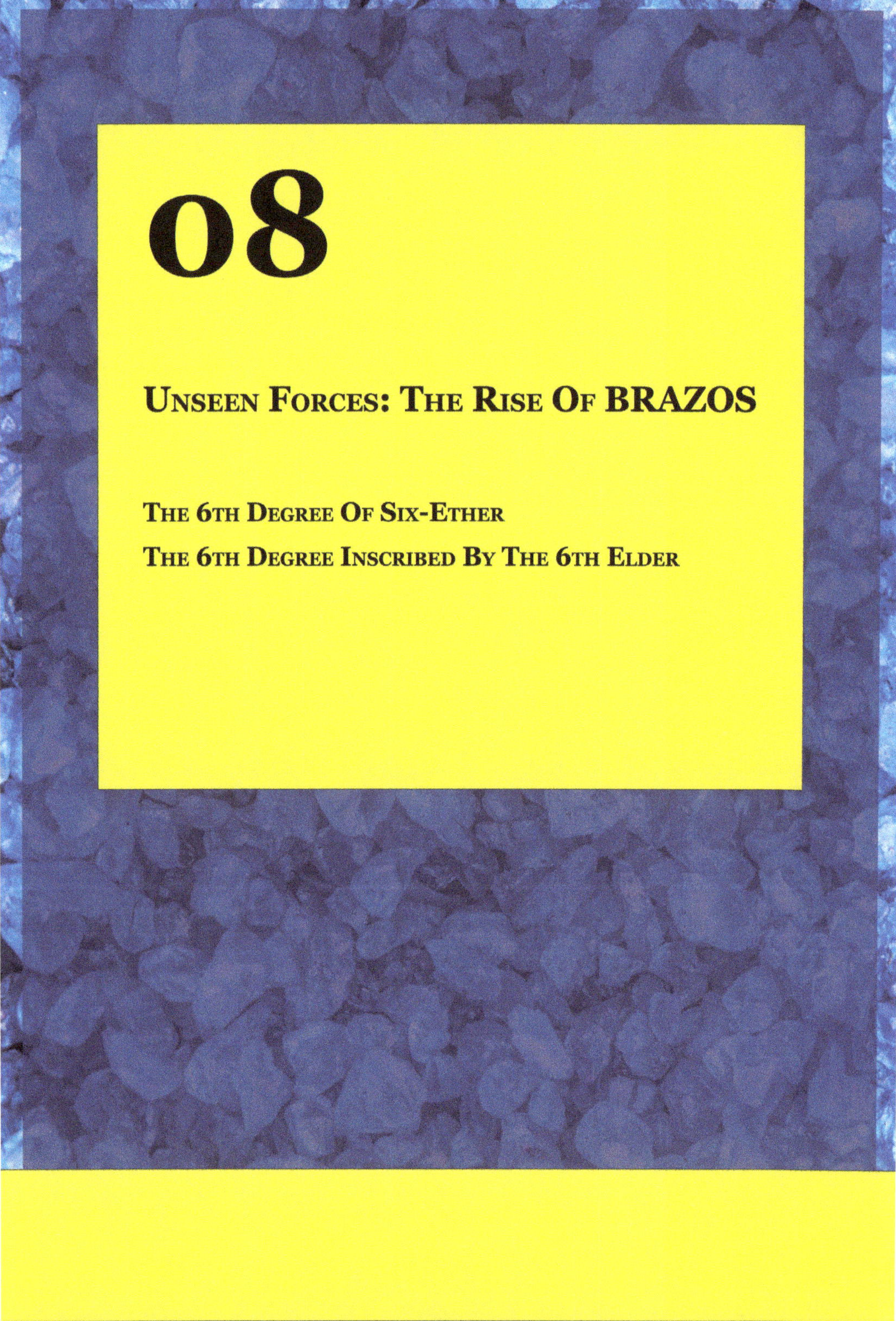
08

UNSEEN FORCES: THE RISE OF BRAZOS

THE 6TH DEGREE OF SIX-ETHER
THE 6TH DEGREE INSCRIBED BY THE 6TH ELDER

In The Year 2025 D.A.

Life Had Changed Since The Elite Chose The New Charismatic Leader, Who Ascended From Out Of The Pits Of Hell And Who Was Later Admired By The Masses. Mr. Nimrod Sinnah Was Supported By, Sorcerers And Warlocks Who De-Materialized Animals. Especially Goats Or Sheep, And Drank Their Blood On A Regular And Ritualistic Basis To Make Him A Success. Those In Higher Places That Were Also Secretly A Part Of The Societies Of Sorcerers And Warlocks. They Sacrificed Their Own Family Members With Consent To Make Sure That The Political Dealings Would Become A Reality For Their Sadistic Benefits.

Along With Sacrifices, The Witchcraft Involved Creating Spells That Were Integrated Into The Mainstream Media; And Many Witchcraft Members Were Working In The Media Syndicates There, Which Made It Easy For The Integration To Occur. They Mastered The Art Of Hypnotizing The Crowds Through The Campaigns By Chanting Slogans That Were, In Fact, The Spells. People Praised And Worshiped Nimrod Sinnah's Motto, And When Sung Backward, It Was Actually Giving Thanks To The Evil Ones.

"Life Will Be Better Once Mister Nimrod Sinnah Is Chosen For Tomorrow, A New," They Would Chant. However, When Backmasked, The Phrase Was *"Wen A Worromot Rof Nesohc Sia Ram Sa Retsim Ecno Retteb Eb Lliw Efil,"* Which Really Meant, *"Win A War O Mother Of Amnesia; We Are Rams Not To See. Put Me In A Scam, For We Built Evil."* The Chants Were Blinding Them And Putting Them To Sleep As They Called Themselves Sacrificial Animals, Allowing The Malevolent Beings To Take Rule.

Nimrod Sinnah Was Regularly Criticized For His Religious Views That Many Felt Were Made To Cause Oppression. He Spoke Rudely Against His Opposition Challenger Madame Helena Ishtar. Who Was Secretly His Wife; Deception Was Everywhere.

Nimrod Sinnah Won The Election By A Landslide And Was Selected As The New Mayor Elite. He Convinced The People During His Campaign That He Was Against BRAZOS Rule, But Shortly After His Victory, He Sided With BRAZOS And Then Hired Madame Helena Ishtar As BRAZOS' Chancellor Elite. Nimrod Sinnah's Secretly Kept His Mother Nancy Semiramis As The Leading Voice In Illinois' House Of Law Making For Deception. She Played A Key Role In Getting Him A Secure Place.

While He First Served As Alderman, As His Mother Flanked Over His Shoulders. Her Demonic Eyes And Hissing Tongue Protected Her Child During His Campaign Run For Mayor Elite. Nimrod Sinnah Soon After Hired Is The Secret Brother, Drake Hosannis, As The Illinois Attorney General And His Secret Sister, Sumantra Helllsworth, As Top Security Director. Nimrod Sinnah Held The Position Of Pro Tem Mayor Elite For The Past 48 Months Before Actually Becoming The Official Mayor Elite. He Was Ruling Behind The Scenes Since Abraham Musa. Nimrod Sinnah's Oppositions Were Already Coached And Informed To Play The Role, *"They Would Not Be Victorious!"*

Nimrod Sinnah Was Already Selected By The BRAZOS And That The Ballads Of Election Voters Were Not To Be Tallied Nor Counted. It Was All A Part Of The Illusions By BRAZOS. Those Members Who Sought To Challenge His Authority Were Quickly Discredited, Humiliated, Castrated, Passed Away Or Thrown In Prison. BRAZOS Deceived The People And Used Nimrod Sinnah As An Agent To Captivate The Citizens Into Mental And Physical Captivity. Soon After, Mayor Elite Donald Finley Changed His Slogan And Vowed To Make BRAZOS Work For The City Of **Occupied Chicago**, Under His New Slogan *"A New Hope."*

He Spoke Many Great Things From His Lips, But Under His Hissing Tongue Conveyed The Greatest Manipulation Of Lies That Contradicted His Campaign Promises. The Reality Was That Mr. Nimrod Sinnah Was A Hostile, Cloned Species Of The 200 Shape-Shifting, Rejected, Fallen Angels, Called Nephileem. They That Relocated Themselves To The Sacred UnGreground Cities Of Illinois. He Was The Terrorist Leader Nicknamed *"Da Rebellious One"* Known As The

Renegade Of UnGreground Army. Who Went Into Hiding After Staging The John Hancock Building Destruction, De-Materializing Hundreds Of Innocent People.

Following That Tragic Event, BRAZOS Emerged As The New Government Entity. Making Claims That **Occupied Chicago**'s Former Government Was Actually Irresponsible Under The Supervision Of Mayor Elite Abraham Musa. The Persecution Was Lead By Illinois State Law Director Paul Romajinn And The City Attorney Francis Aurelius; Which Placed The City In Confusion By Displaying Televised Court Lynching. **Occupied Chicago**'s Most Recognized Judge, Julian Kharnas, Appointed Paul Romajinn As Martial Law Deputy Until BRAZOS Rule Of Law Brought Civil Order. Many Of Abraham Musa's Supporters Were Imprisoned With No Bond Until Newly Promoted BRAZOS Chancellor Attorney Francis Aurelius Came Into Office. Mayor Elite Donald Finley And BRAZOS Chancellor Elite Madame Helena Ishtar Introduced *"Peace And Security!"*

For 23 Full Months, Before Martial Law, Many Questions Arose In Regards To The Actual Birthplace Of The New Mayor Elite; Being He Was A Foreigner With Terrorist Involvements. None Of The Masses Knew Of His Sinister Past, But They Secretly Felt Fearful Of Him. He Was Born On The Sixth Day Of The Sixth Month, In The Year Of Nineteen Sixty And Six A.D., In New York City With His Twin Brother, Adrian, The Computer Engineer. The Sorcerers Cast Spells That Enveloped The Mayor Elite's False Image. To Be In The Likeness Of An Ancient Pharaoh Who Was Considered A Messiah.

He Received Honors Of Rewards And Merits. As A Peacemaker, But Not For What He Had Accomplished Or Achieved. But For What He Vowed To Execute For BRAZOS. Nimrod Sinnah And His Group. They Secretly Concealed Having Associations With Sexual Violations, Who Played A Significant Part In Their Rituals, Which Occurred On A Daily Basis. He Also Had Strong Connections With Extremist Groups And Criminal Mob Families. After His Election, His High-Powered Political Sponsors Were Suddenly Ousted From Their Legislative Seats Through Various Scandals. He Was To Be Considered The First Black Mayor Elite In The City's History.

But Hid Under A False Identity Because He Was A 6 Ether Cursed Hindu Of Extraterrestrial Descent, Campaigning A Great Ethnic Deception Fooling The Masses. *"Do People Deserve What Will Transpire When Warnings Are Echoed To Them, And They Don't Take Heed?"* Donald Finley Asked His Blind Followers One Evening In Front Of The Government Building.

"What If **Occupied Chicago***'s Number Sixth Criminal Laid In The Shadows. And Successfully Got Elected To* **Occupied Chicago***'s Highest Office?"* The Mayor Elite Was Strong In His Left Hand With Bits Of Holly Wood Crushed In His Palm As He Spoke To His Blind Followers. *"Yes,"* He Said Smiling To His Herd, *"Deception Is, In Fact, Every Where!"* The Mayor Elite Nimrod Sinnah Revealed Himself As The False Messiah And BRAZOS Chancellor Elite Madame Helena Ishtar, Became The Aunt Of Christ Or Anti, Against Christ, Also Known As The Anti-Christ.

"Ain't I Like The Christ?" Was Her Motto To Her Employees Who Replied, *"Yes, There Is No One Like Thee."* It Was Her Usual *"Mirror, Mirror On The Wall…"* Phrase. One Summer Afternoon, One Of Her Workers Must Have Awoken From His Trance And Asked Her, *"Some Would Say Anti-Christ Means Against Christ; So How Can Anyone Be Against Christ If You Claim Christ Has Not Returned?"* Ishtar's Goons Passed Away The Young Man Viciously, And His Body Was Offered On A Platter Within Their Midnight Ritualistic Dinners. As The Secret Wife Of Nimrod Sinnah. She Had Extreme Influence On His Choices, And She Signed Off And Initiated Martial Law. Yet, The Citizens Chose To Ignore Their Instincts. Now, He Was Sane Enough To Rule. Oh, By The Way, He Was Responsible For Ending An Unpopular Second Civil War. This Man Caused **Occupied Chicago**'s Destruction, By Bombing **Occupied Chicago** From The Inside Out Enforcing An Illegal Martial Law.

Which Was Lead By The Foreign Mexican Invasion From *"South Of The Border."* The Invasion Was Already There In Place. The BRAZOS Administration Was A Form Of Government Headed By BRAZOS Chancellor Elite Ishtar Who Executed All Official Executive Duties. While The Mayor Elite Was Just A Figurehead. The Chancellor Strictly Controlled The Religious, Political, Social, And Economic Life Of The City-State. Which Was, In Fact, A Major Influence On Their

Population To Maintain This Authority, The BRAZOS Chancellor Elite Had To Cut Off The People From Any Information. *"In Which Might Cause Them To Doubt The Complete Truth About BRAZOS Principalities In High Places."*

All Of The Media Coverage Were Overseen By Parts Of The Chancellor Elite's Department; Newspapers, Radio, Television, And Other Means Of Communication Were Screened. So The Public Would Get Only What The Mayor Elite Wanted Them To Know. Traveling To Other States Was Ironfisted Controlled, And Freedom Of Speech, Within Social Assemblies Was Severely Suppressed. BRAZOS' Strategy Kept The People In A War-Like Frame Of Mind Where Most Citizens Felt That They Were Obliged To Fight Against Those Who Questioned The Regime."

The Mayor Elites Usually Comes To Power During A Period Of Economic Crisis Or In A Time Of Depression. They Get Rid Of The Depression Partly By Employing People In The Making Of Armaments (Defense); Then They Convince The People That The State Is Being Threatened. The Elders All Nodded In Agreement As They Sat Austere In Their Golden Chairs Crafted Perfectly And Specifically To Suit Each Of Them. They Repossessed Homes Once Dwelled In By Many Trying To Live Beyond Their Means.

So Now, These Forces Have Been Set Up To Live The Lifestyle Many Despise. Being Condescending To Those, Who We Call The Meek Who Will Soon Have Their Rightful Inheritance. But For Now, These Menaces Have Occupied Homes With No Rent Or Mortgages To Pay, Yet They Are Being Paid To Sit Above In Higher Places, These Principalities. The Elders Mumbled Disturbed By The Manifestations That Were Occurring Above. So Many People Were Tricked Into Using BRAZOS Credit Cards With High Interest Rates.

All The Money In The Savings Account Were Devalued And Was Useless Because Money Was No Longer Backed By Gold Since The Year 1993 A.D. That Is What The Public Was Not Aware; So BRAZOS Later Introduced The Nimrod Monetary System. BRAZOS Also Sold The Citizens Birthrights Into Stocks And Bonds. Using Their Birth Certificates At The Value Of Six Hundred And Thirty Thousand In Nimrod Dollars. Cell Phones Were The First Test Market Of

Micro-Chipping Citizens. Allowing Citizens To Purchase Merchandise From Infrared Beams Scanning From The Camera Lenses. Social Network Websites Were Free... Because They Were The Agents Who Provided The BRAZOS Intelligence Agency With Personal Information. BRAZOS Intelligence Sent Viruses To Many Of The Participants As Warning. That They Were Monitoring Them For Possible Renegade And Rebellious Minds Against The BRAZOS Hierarchy.

No One Was Able To Travel About Freely Any Longer Without Constant Scrutiny. Except For BRAZOS Active And Retired Military Id Members. Foreign Soldiers Brutally Controlled All The Checkpoints In And Out Of Major Highways, And There Was No Mercy If You Were Carrying Your Own Licensed Handgun. Teenagers Became Civilian Soldiers And Began To Lose Control; Turning Into BRAZOS Machinery And Property Overnight.

Some Parents Were Being Reported As Spies By Their Own Children, Rendering The Parents Helpless. Citizens Were Being Forced Into BRAZOS Concentration Camps. Unless They Were A Part Of Some Sort Of B.R.A.Z.O.S. Affiliation And It Was Already Confirmed That Britain, Russia And Other Parts Of Asia, The Zionist Groups, Opec Hindu Members And Switzerland Were Already Controlled By The Foreign New Power Structure. The 200 Fallen Angels Scattered Themselves Across The Earth Like A Plague, Giving Authority And Wealth To Those Weak Leaders Who Worshiped Them; But What These Greedy People Did Not Know Was That Everything They Received Was Only Temporary."

BRAZOS Controlled The Food Supply Warehouses, Eliminating Private Gardens And Farmlands; That Would Not Grow Chemically And Genetically Altered Food Issued By BRAZOS Food And Drugs Department. Airplanes Were Equipped With Highly Concentrated Poisons Flying Over Many Farmlands To Disperse Chemicals That Were Falsely Labeled; Bringing The Lands Into A Famine Similar Like That Of The Intentional Cases That Struck The Land Of Ethiopia In The 1980s. The Gold Reserve Centers Have Been Empty For Over 20 Years.

BRAZOS Has Been Ordering Major Corporations To Layoff Many Of Their Employees Every Month To Create The Crisis, Similar To The Movie *"They Live, We Sleep!"* Racial Tensions Were Purposely Instigated By BRAZOS Goons To Contribute To Creating Mass Genocides. In Reality, Many African Americans Were Sacrificed To Retain Their Organs To Sell On The Black Market. Gang Violence Is Known As *"Black On Black Crime"* Served As A Principal Instrument For Organ Selling. In Which, A Kidney From An African American Can Go For As Much $50,000. Some Children Were Kidnapped And Slain By Organ Dealers And Created Fictitious Crime Scenes As A Diversion. All Of These Events Were Orchestrated And Used To Usher In The Second Coming Of The Civil War!"

BRAZOS Gained Full Control Shortly After The Anunnaqis Summoned Their 9Sacred Starships To Release 19 Great Olmec Heads Blazing Balls Of Fire Upon The Earth Causing Mass Destruction. Each Fireball Dropped Nineteen Miles In The Earth. It Was Larger Than Any Atomic Bomb But Without The Toxic Man-Made Radiation. On The Surface, The Blazing Fire Engulfed Ninety Miles In A Perfect Radius. Many Witnesses Reported That When The Olmec Heads Smashed Into Earth. One Hundred And Ninety-Foot Tall Granite Statues Were Coming Alive With Ninety-Foot Long Granite Swords Attached To The Olmec Hands Were Destroying And Knocking Over Many Buildings And Crushing Sinners Spirits Of All Walks. Da Anunnaqi Allowed The Reptilian's And Draculas Of The Dracos Constellation Take Full Control Of **Occupied Chicago** And The Entire Planet. Except For The Designated Protection Area For A Short Time.

While The Chosen Souls Were Being Redeemed From The Surface Of Planet Earth, Qi. Humans That Were Caught By The Heat Of The Blasts Burnt To Passed Away Immediately. When The Word Of Mayor Elite Donald Finley's Survival Was Released Many Throughout The World Were Astounded. But Not Only Were They Surprised By That News By The Fact; That There Were Reports That Silvery Shiny Crafts Were Spotted Over **Occupied Chicago** That Night. And That The Electrical And Satellite Signals Had Failed And That Many People Were Missing;

Possibly Taken Up By The Crafts Without Any Traces Left Behind. Many Other Reports Were Received, That Night Shift Cleaning Employees In Government Buildings, Were Witnessing Powerful Politicians Shape Changing And Losing Their Human Form. Transforming Into Tall Reptilian Beings Of Approximately Seven Feet Or Taller That Stood Upright Like Humans.

The Cleaners Explained That They Were Always Aware Of The Rituals. That Were Done Late After Work Hours, But This Time Was The First They Witnessed Such Horrific Events. Which They Said Was Similar To The Images They Saw In Commercials Or Movies. Those Reports Quickly Disappeared; Then New Satellites Were Up And Running After Six Days Of Mass Confusion. All These Events Unfolded After The Lunar Eclipse Opened Up Many More Vortexes Teleporting Many Beings Through The Black Holes Brought On The War In The Heavens. All The Unknown And Unsolved Paranormal Mysteries Were Now Manifesting Themselves In The Presence Of The Inhabitants Of Earth. The Evils On The Planet Were About To Be Silenced.

Citizens From Shamballah, Aghaarta, A Large Civilization Within The Center Of The Earth. Which Had Their Own Sun Who Was The Mother Of All Surface And Internal Volcanoes, Began Coming To The Surface Of The Earth; Disturbed By The Noise And Calamities. Many Powerful Earthquakes Hit New York City, Memphis, Nashville, St. Louis, Haiti, Somalia And Many Other Cities Including Atlanta With Other City-States. Including The Oil-Rich Lands That Were Invaded By Persians Centuries Ago From The Natives Ethiopians And Draining All The Dinosaur Oil That Served As Lubrication In The Earth's Crust.

The Man Had Become Destructive, Using Energy Manipulation Types Of Machinery Such As H.A.A.R.P., High-Frequency Active Auroral Research Program To Change Weather Patterns And Fuse Gasses And Highly Concentrated Chemicals From UnGreground To Trigger Artificial Earthquakes, Heavy Rain, Super Wind Storms And Tsunamis With The Help Of The Disagreeable Nephileem Aboard Their UFO's. Da Igigi Agreeable Anunnaqis Also Gathered Their Spheres From Central And South American.Great Balls Of Fire Also Destroyed This Machinery And Cursed The Families Committed To Causing Massive Passing Away.

Rumors Were Spreading That Witnesses Saw Pope Paul The Sixth's Clone On A Spacecraft. As Well Come Down To Announce That The Mayor Elite Is The Messiah And Everyone Shall Drop To Their Knees And Pray To Him. Displaying Holographic Images Of A False Messiah And Its Mother. This Event Has Followed The Crashing Of The Earthly Made Spacecraft Carrying The Pope's Clone. He Instantly Passed Away, And There Was Following Of Even More Unusual Weather Patterns Of Mother Ninti Also Known As Mother Earth. In Reality, The Fake Alien Invasion Was Manufactured And Engineered But Failed To Keep The Real Invasion From Redeeming The Chosen Ones. After Citizens With Licensed To Carry, Weapons Were Outlawed; Leaving Criminals With Freedom To Have Uncontrolled Torture. The Mayor Elite Was Serving With Two Hats; As Leader Of **Occupied Chicago**, The New Capitol And Newly Appointed Dictator Of BRAZOS At The Same Time.

The Unidentified Flying Objects Were Actually 9Sacred Starships Called Shams. They Were Harnessing Electromagnetic Energy Known As Tachyon Energy. Mastered By The Ancient Ethiopians And Ancient Egyptians Who Were Of The Same Bloodline. This Phenomenon Occurred By Two Wheels Spinning In Opposite Directions; Generating Warm And Cold Clouds. Lightning Generates Electrons From The Earth, Which Discharges Electrical Fields Into The Sky. The Shams Were Absorbing The Lightning And Blasting Them Back Down To The Earth. The Shams Are What Meteorologist Referred To As The Eye Of The Storm.

As The Selected And Managed Damage Control On The Inhabitants Of This Planet Earth, Qi. They Were The Hurricanes, Tornados, Floods, Earthquakes, Tsunamis And Blackouts Administrators. The Human Eye Was Not Fast Enough To See This Wonder But Recorded Footage Was Able To Capture It. Those Who Had Seen Shooting Stars, Questioned, *"Who Shot It To Become A Shooting Star? Who Was Its Navigator?"* The Answer Was That The Movement They Saw Was A 9Sacred Starship Leaving Its Original Position Then Vanishing Into Thin Air; They Were Fast. The 9Sacred Starships Could Travel From Los Angeles To New York City In Less Than Nine Minutes. Now, Things Were Just Considered Rumors After The Second Civil

War. After, Mayor Elite Donald Finley Had Suffered. He Also Gained Enemies In That Tense Time Of Unrest, Yet He Benefited From All Of It As Though He Engineered The Events From The Beginning To Gain All The Power. All Of The Communications Between The Disunited States Of America Were Under Tight Surveillance. Families Were Split Up And Sent To BRAZOS Concentration Camps. That Were Mysteriously Appearing Out Of Nowhere In A Short Period. And The Second Civil War Was So Great That Families Were Even De-Materializing Each Other.

If One Chose To Be Against The BRAZOS System. Money Became Worthless, And The Food Was Scarce. Plastic Filled Coffins And Body Bags Lined The Streets. As Foreign Soldiers Brought Hell And A Deep Hatred And There Were Emotionless, Robotic Soldiers That Were Massively De-Materializing Off Citizens And Foreign Soldiers By The Scores Of Untold Numbers. Some People Passed Away While Trying To Dig Out Implanted Chips From Their Bodies, Which Caused A Poisonous Secretion From The Chip Into Their Blood Stream, Which Was Placed There Just For That Reason. Some Either Volunteered To Be Injected With The Chip And Others Were Inserted Through Vaccinations Without Their Knowledge In Hospitals.

The Residents Of Most Ethiopian, Kenyan, Somalian And Sudanese Neighborhoods Did Not Have Microchips In Them Because They Were Considered Of No Value By The BRAZOS Government. The Drone Planes Kept A Very Tight Surveillance On The Citizens, And All Conversations Were Being Recorded, To Hinder Any Type Of Resistance. Most Citizens Were Assigned Digital Numbers For Tracking By The Drones. The Drones Will Also Be Equipped With Ammunition Weaponry And Thermal Imaging Technology.

To View The Homes Of Suspected Rebels, Without The Need For Search Warrant Known As Property Siege Warrant! Those Spiritual Souls, Who Are Vibrating On A Higher Frequency Of The *"Pure Green Light."* They Will Find Peace In The Bosom, And Protection In The Covenant Of Da Igigi, Annunaqi (*Those Who Stayed Above In The Skies!*) They Will Scramble All Of The Drone Frequencies. And They Will Destroy The Mechanical Demons, A Blessing From The Eloheem! Yes, They Are Teaching Bad Thoughts For The Love Of Vanity, While They Smirk

And Turn Their Noses Up To The People Who They Feel Are Below Them. They Were Assessing The Drug Users' Value In Their Society; Aware Of The Money They Are Making Off Them. They Know The People Are Going To Doctors And Paying A Lot Of Money For Medicine That Does Not Cure Anything, Other Than Producing More Problems Which They Were Initially Trying To Get!

Away In The Form Of The Mentality Cycle; Sadly, This Abuse, Addiction, And Dependence On BRAZOS Have Stayed Its Course, With More Complications Than They Ever Imagined. The Worst Part Is, Because Of Their Arrogance And Ignorance…You Know, Ignoring The Facts… Self-Destruction Is Inevitable." There Was No Need For A War Campaign On Drugs Because The Biggest Drug Users Were Not The Cocaine Addicts, But The Ones Popping Prescription Pills; Those Who Spoke Badly Towards Cocaine And Heroin Users. They Never Stopped To Think, *"What Is It About This Society That Would Make Someone Turn To Drugs?"*

Because They Were Talking About Great Arrogance And Too Occupied Getting Their Prescriptions Refilled While They Could Not Pronounce The Words Of The Chemicals That Produced The Drug. BRAZOS Media Advertised New Viruses That Were Spreading Throughout The State Of Illinois. And Coincidentally They Already Had Vaccines. The Unfortunate Reality Was That People Were Getting The Virus And Microchips Through The Vaccines. Along With Other Passed Away Chemicals Such As Mercury, Which Began Mutating Their Red And White Blood Cells That Were Then Unable To Fight Off The Infections. Sodium Fluoride Was Another Poison They Added To The Toothpaste And Water.

It Was Created By Chemist Charles E. Perkins At The End Of The Second World War, As A Narcotic To Make The People Submissive. Some Famous Athletes Have Even Pretended To Have Contracted A Virus And Sold Their Souls For More Money. They Were Mentally Controlled By BRAZOS Manipulation To Sell Their Contracted Diseases And Illnesses, Such As H.I.V., For The Masses To Accept Their Diseases And Purchase More Drugs For The Treatment. But In Reality, This Was Worsening Their Conditions Including Suicidal Thoughts.

However, Another Tactic That Was Used To Control The Populace Was For The News Programming. To Speak About The Fight Against Theses Man-Made Diseases. Which Were Then Followed By Highly Sexualized, Alcoholic Beverage Commercials So People Would Carry On Having Sex With No Care In The World. BRAZOS Had Many Truths To Their Secrets. All Condoms They Created Had To Be Tested By The BDFD; The BRAZOS Drug And Food Department. The Money That Was Being Allocated For Research Testing Was So Low That, Testing Was Done Negligently. With No Actual Proof Of Whether It Provided Protection Against A.I.D.S., H.I.V., And EBOLA And Other STDS. A.I.D.S. And EBOLA Were Created In A Lab In The 1970's With Help From Beings Residing On The Moon Satellite, Titan. It Was Also Used As The Weapon To Secretly Inject Unsuspected Humans As A Means Of Dying Slowing And Undetected. For Every Curse And Plague Planned And Executed In These Final Days, The Aggressor And Their Family's Bloodline Would Be Cursed Tenfold.

****

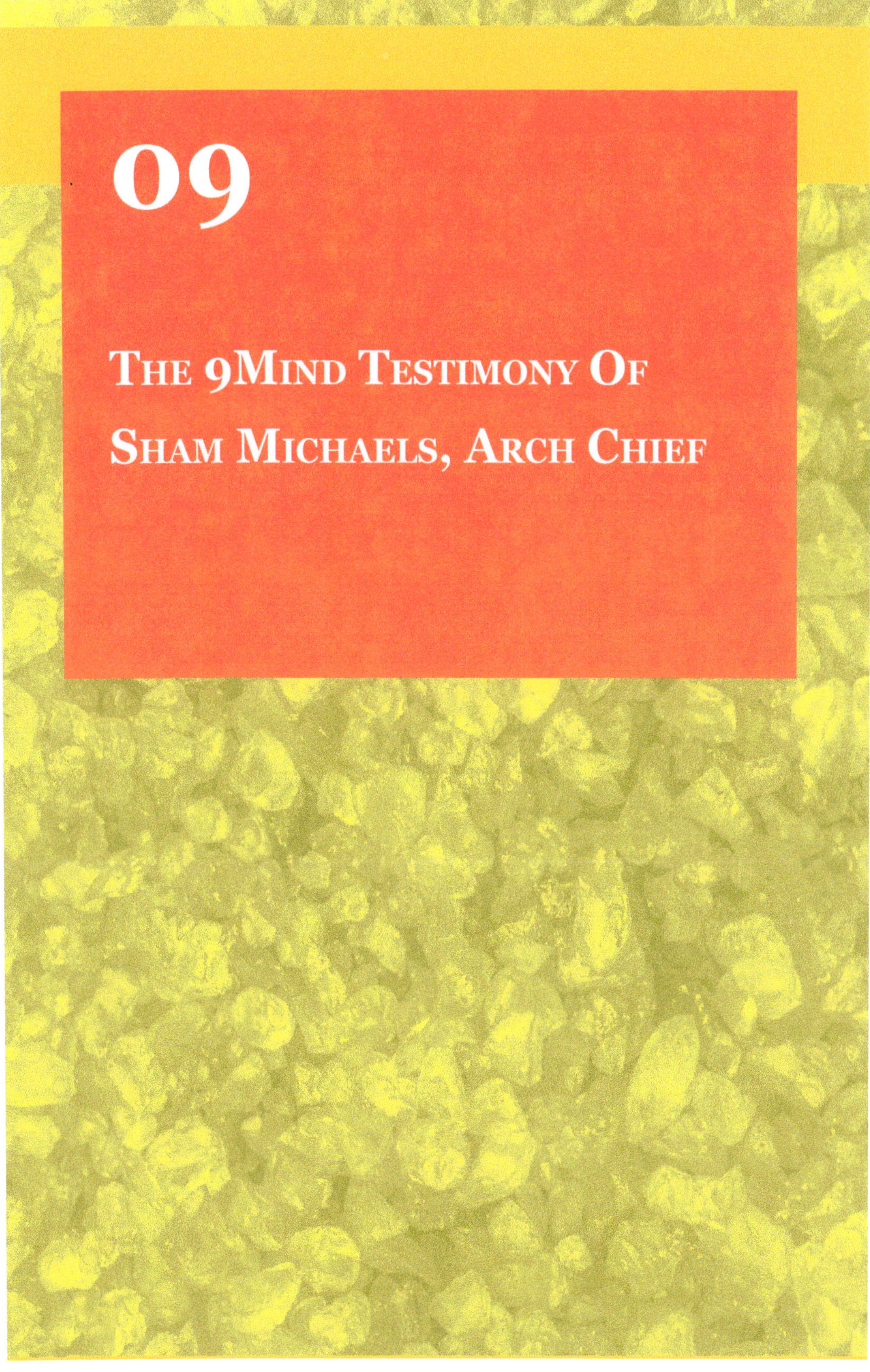

09

THE 9MIND TESTIMONY OF SHAM MICHAELS, ARCH CHIEF

Sham Michaels Was At The Top Of His Class And A Graduate Of The Illinois State Criminal Justice Academy. This Was His 13TH Year At The Bureau Working As The Assistant To His Former Director, Paul Romajinn. Since 1999 A.D., For Over Seven Years, Michaels Had Been Working Behind The Scenes. As A Top-Notch Detective On All The Operations He Executed. Everyone Knew And Respected Him, From The Thugs On The Streets To Colleagues At Work. Most Of The High-Profile Cases Solved Made Headlines, But Only The Director Was Given Full Credit, And Michaels Didn't Mind At All. He Preferred Being In The Shadows Because No One Could Recognize Him Unless He Wanted Them To Know Who He Was.

In The Year 2023 D.A.

Weeks After The Introduction Of The Political Body Called BRAZOS With The New Pro Tem Mayor Elite Donald Finley Was Sworn In, B.R.L-Illiana's Director Coordinated Former Mayor Elite Musa's Spiritual Symbolic Passing Away. **Occupied Chicago** Was Placed In Much Disarray. During That Time, Chief Michaels Was Brought Under Investigations By The Self-Appointed Director Paul Apostle Romajinn, Who Was Well Known For Being A Traitor And Mockery Of The Truth. When Paul Appointed Himself As The 13TH Director, Of The New BRAZOS Rule Of Law Agency In Illinois, He Told Everyone To Call Him By His Middle Name Apostle, And Then He Started Changing The Spiritual Doctrines.

From The Former Mayor Elite Abraham Musa. While Musa Was Still In Office. Paul Had Never Met The Mayor Elite, But He Had Secret Religious Members Of Different Denominations. Within Mayor Elite Musa's Cabinet That Influenced, And Then Paid The Preachers, Rabbis, And Other Religious Leaders To Teach False Doctrines. As The Days Began To Descend In Darkness, Religious Members Of The Cabinet Were Caught Up In Scandals. This Caused Mass Confusion And Caused The Citizens To Question. All Of The Information Of The Righteous Laws That Were Imposed On Them By The Government. However, Paul Created A False Doctrine That

Helped Usher The New Religious System Into To The States And Other Parts Of The World. It Was Signed And Notarized And Placed In Effect By The City's High-Profile Attorney, Francis Aurelius. This Information Continued To Suppress The Citizen's Knowledge.

Mayor Elite Abraham Musa Was The First To Be Removed By The People, Through Scandals In Which There Was No Truth Or Substance About Their Accusations. So In All Of The **Occupied Chicagoans** Ignorance. Their Rightful Leader Of Justice, They Passed Away In Innocence, His Persecution Lasted Over 18 Months Before Resigning. The Former Mayor Elite Musa Cared For His Citizens, But They Were Under The Mind Control Of These New Foreign Teachings. **Occupied Chicago** Would Later Pay The Ultimate Price Of Supreme Oppression, And Chief Michaels Began To Feel The Heat, So He Left **Occupied Chicago** In 2023 D.A. And Returned 3 And Half Years Later. The Deception Was So Great That The Righteous Laws Were All But Forgotten Because, Without These Statutes, Criminals Could Exercise Their Evil Ways Uncontested.

In The Year 2023 D.A.

Mayor Elite Abraham Musa Highly Recommended Sham Michaels To Be The Next **Occupied Chicago** Authority Council. What Michaels Did Not Know Was That The New Director Was In-Conflict With BRAZOS' "A New Hope Theory" Initiated By Those Infiltrators In His Cabinet. Paul Romajinn Was Passed Away At Former Michael Jordan's Restaurant Downtown. The Only Information The Chiefs Had Were Tips That Michaels Agreed To Meet Him. At The Restaurant And That There Was A Reservation Scheduled For The Two Men.

Paul's Birth Name Was Saul Apostle Romajinn, And His Autopsy Revealed That He Was First Poisoned By Food Eaten At The Restaurant. Then As He Began Passing Out And The Ambulance Was Summoned. Three Minutes After The Ambulance Was Called, Two Unknown Assailants Ran Into The Private Dining Area Dressed As Medics, And Executed One...Mr. Romajinn, Blasting Bullets Through His Chest. The Two Men Scurried Out Of The Small Restaurant As Saul Hunched To The Floor With Blood Pouring Out Of Him. Chief Michaels Received A

Call On His Cell From The Other Chiefs At The Precinct While He Was Out Doing Routine Checks On The North Side Of The City. They Began To Accuse Him Of What Occurred. He Jumped In His Denali, And Sped Through Traffic In Fury To The Restaurant That Was Just A Few Blocks Away. He Received Another Phone Call Saying There Was A Frantic 911-Phone Call. On The North Side Of Town; It Was From The Residency Of The Now Former Director Romajinn's Home.

They Said It Was The Voice Of Romajinn's Wife, Sinny Romajinn Who Was Found Passed Away When They Arrived. Her Throat Was Cut From Ear To Ear, And She Was Placed Over A Bucket To Catch The Blood. Chief Michaels Became A Suspect, Being That He Lived The Closest And Was Well Connected To The Romajinn Couple. Even Though Charges Were Never Brought Up Against Him. His Reputation Was Severally Damaged. Secondly, Being That He Was Accused And Still Suspected, It Cost Him The Chances Of A Higher Position In The Precinct And Also Because Of Washington D.C. Native Jentson, Stepped In, Replacing Saul. Chief Jentson's Former Job In D.C. Was Drug Trafficking Control Coming In From South America.

In The Year 2021 D.A.

After Three And A Half Years, Chief Michaels Returned To **Occupied Chicago**. The Newly Appointed BRAZOS Chancellor Elite Attorney. Francis Aurelius Found Favor In Him. Because He Knew Michaels Was Not The Kind Of Man To Do What He Was Accused Of Doing. Aurelius Made Michaels The Arch Chief To The New Director Jentson.Who Already Heard Of Chief Michaels's High Reputation All The Way In Washington, DC, Which Made Him Very Jealous. Jentson Was A Spot-Grabbing Opportunist Who Lived For The Accolades That He Received From Other People's Findings And Not His Own.

Arch Chief Michaels, On The Other Hand, Relied On The Streets And Its Shadows. He Was Respected On The Streets, Being From **Occupied Chicago**'s Salsara Park Himself. He Would Often Give His People A Second Chance, But Half Of Them Returned Doing Dirty Work. So, Arch Chief Michaels Lost Faith In Them. Although The Former Illinois Law Agency Mainly

Dealt With The "Big Fish" As They Considered Them, Once BRAZOS Got Involved, They Put Full Control And Surveillance Into UnGreground Gang Activities.

Arch Chief Michaels Was Now 54 Years Old, 6'3, 207 Pounds Of Muscle And Clean-Shaven. Most Of The Time He Wore Glasses. And Without Its Shaded Lens Effect From The Sun! There Was An Instant Intimidation In Those He Stared Upon! He Was Independent And Always Got The Job Done. He Would Go To Any Level Against His Blue-Collar, Mob Opponents, And The Street Thugs Knew Better Than To Smart Off With Him Or Discredit His Abilities.

He Made Them All Swallow Their Tongues Too Many Times. Someone Had Even Started A Rumor, That They Had Seen Him Fighting Off A Group Of Men, Who Came To Attack Him In An Alley. The Witness Said There Were About Six People. And That They Saw Arch Chief Michaels Speedily, Creating Glowing Blue Balls In And Around His Fists, Electrocuting All Six Men Within 10 Seconds. The Witness Claimed That When All The People Were Electrocuted.

A Thick Cloud Formed In The Sky In Seconds Causing A Huge Thunderstorm And Arch Chief Michaels Disappeared! Now No One Believed The Witness. But Everyone Did Find It Strange As To Why He Had No Fear Of Guns. He Was Known For Walking Into Gunfights, Before Drawing His Weapon While The Criminal Had Theirs, Already Out; Still Resulting In Them Being Shot In The End, Leaving Arch Chief Michaels Untouched.Rumor Had It That He Was Shot Several Times, And Was Never Treated For His Wounds. What People Didn't Know Was That He Held A Master's Degree, In Criminal Psychology From The University Of Illinois In Champaign.

In The Year 2027 D.A.

For Over Nine Months Straight, A Whole New Terror Had Gripped **Occupied Chicago**. One Night, Alongside A Dented Rail That Separated The Sidewalk. The **Occupied Chicago** River On The North Side Of The City, Just Outside The Downtown Skyline, Screeching Tires Followed By Thunderous Gunshots Left This Desolated Neighborhood Yearning For The Attention Of All Sorts. A Car Was Found Riddled With Bullets Made By An AK-47's. ChristOn M Larson

Was Pronounced, So-Called Passed Away At The Scene. In The Middle Of The Night Under The Dim City Lights. It Rained Out Of Control For An Hour With Unusual Sounds Of Thunder, And No Sights Of Lightning. Only The Lights From The Police Squad Cars And Ambulance That Arrived Purposely, Hours Later, And Marked Off The Area.

Two Homeless Men Viewed Every Heart-Pounding Moment, As Hell Began Unmasking Itself. Of Course, It Was The Homeless People That Saw All The Terrible Things On The Street. Arguments, Gunfights, Drug Deals, Rapes. And The Passing Away That Took Place Every Night. And They Were The Ones To See It Because People Started To Become Eviler And Didn't Care Whether There Were Witnesses. So That Night When Detectives Arrived On The Scene, Only One Homeless Man Was There To Testify What He Had Seen. Before The So-Called Passing Away That Evening. The WGN News Team Received A Phone Call, Telling Them To Come To The Scene At A Particular Time. When They Did Arrive, They Came Prepared And Announced That ChristOn M Larson Had So-Called Passed Away.

There Was A Silence Over The Entire City For Three Hours, Especially In Salsara Park. His Mother, Mary Larson, Had A Complete Breakdown. Her Most, Beloved Son, Whom She Had Warned So Many Times About Hanging Out In The Streets, Was Gone. He Was The Brave One, Though; Mature Beyond His Years. The One Who Went Into The Military Just To Travel The World, Make Money To Help Himself And His Mother And To Experience Everything Life Had To Offer. *"But Why The Military ChristOn? There Are So Many Other Ways You Can See The World! I Don't Want To Lose You,"* She Remembered Telling Him.

Mary Larson's Mind Was Spinning As She Bawled, Clenching Her Fist To Her Chest, Then Slid The Scarf From Around Her Hair And Brought It To Her Face. She Fell To The Floor. And Thought She Was Going To Lose Him In The Battle Between Countries Whose Leaders Were Friends. But Instead, She Lost Him To The Street Ministries That He Left The Street Life So Long Ago. She Cried, And No One Comforted Her Because She Was Alone. Her Phone Was Off The Hook And Nobody, Couldn't Get Through To Her.

Mary Larson Thought About All The People, She Had Cursed Out On Her Front Porch. For Her Son And The Many Times She Had Embarrassed ChristOn. In Front Of His Friends By Smelling His Fingers Checking For Cush. She Laughed At The Incident In Her Heart, But Tears Swallowed Her Face, And All She Could Feel Was Pain And Suffering Again. A Few Hours Later, Alesha Arrived At Mary Larson's House To Find Her Mother, Makedah Sheba, With Her Arms Wrapped Around Mary Larson. Alesha Was Devastated, And Her Mother Wondered How She Had The Strength To Drive.

Alesha Was Looking Forward To Preserving The Rest Of Her Life With Her Husband. Plus They Had Just Lost Their Baby. She Sat On His Mother's Couch Listening To The Woman Sobbing, And It Brought Tears To Her Eyes As Well; Sitting In Silence Thinking Off All The Wild Events That Had Been Occurring. She Lost Her Son… Nine Months Old… And Now ChristOn. No Words Could Heal Her Wounds Now. Her Heart Had Been Completely Taken From Her. It Was As Though She Had Sold Her Soul, But She Did Not Know To Whom. She Was Lost In Unimaginable Pain. Alesha Was Past Revenge, But Her Spirit Was Too Broken And Helpless To Do Anything. Worst Of All, She Was Already Three Months Pregnant But Had Never Told ChristOn ChristOn!

Mary Larson Opened Her Watery Eyes, Lifted Her Head From Makedah Sheba's Shoulder And Turned Around Because She Heard Someone Crying Behind Her. It Was Alesha Sitting By Herself In The Corner Of The Dark Room. Mary Larson Could See Pain And Suffering Radiating Through Alesha's Entire Being Like A Green Light. The Following Morning, Thirteen More Gang Members Were Found Lying Brutally Injured In And Around Magog Park. Rumor Had It That These Brutalizes Were Done By Chaos, Who They Thought Were So-Called Passed Away, Also. B.R.L-Illiana Police Rushed To 1404 West Central Avenue, With Tires Screeching Against The Black Ice And Snow, Causing The Brake Pads To Smoke. Some Squad Cars Nearly Lost Control Of The Wheels, Almost Crashing Into Each Other, All Because Word Got Out That The One Who Was To Be So-Called Passed Away, Was Still Alive. The Military Dressed Officers,

Jumped Out Of Their Vehicles, With Guns Drawn And Rushed Towards The Four-Foot-Wide Steps That Led Up To Chaos' Patio. They Were Surprised To Find That He Was Already Outside, Sitting On The Porch As If He Knew They Were Coming. *"On The Ground! On The Ground!"* They Shouted Pointing Their Weapons At Lorenzo Who Was Totally Unaware Of What Was Going On. The Officers Walked Up Onto The Porch, Slowly Penetrating The Clouded Herbal Smoke With The Cold Wind Blowing Cigar Wrappers Across Their Polished Boots.

"On The Ground! On The Ground!" The Armed Military Police Shouted Pointing Their Guns At Lorenzo Who Didn't Budge. All The Dogs In The House Looked Through The Window. They Would Bark Wildly, But This Time They Were Silent. The Cops Paused And Looked At Lorenzo Who Appeared Helpless And Severely Beaten Down. He Was Hunched Over In His Chair With A Horrible Look On His Face, But Not That Of Fear. He Wasn't Shocked Or Worried As He Sat There Emotionless, Inhaling Slowly. He Already Had A Reputation For His Chaotic Ways, Very Cunning And Ruthless As He Usually Acted. But Guns Were Drawn, And All He Could Do Was Remain Calm. Because His Body Was Already Beaten Severely From The Car Accident. Anyone Who Looked At Him Would Have Assumed That He Was Too Crippled To Have Brutally Injured Anybody The Night Before.

Alesha Was In The House Looking At It All Through The Peephole. She Sent A Signal To The Dogs To Keep Quiet And Placed Her Hand On The Doorknob, Mumbling To Herself, *"Ahlum El Kuluwm, Ahlum El Kuluwm."* She Opened The Door, And A Gust Of Cold Air Blew In. The Officers Stood Still And Began Lowering Their Weapons Drifting Under Her Possession. She Drew All Their Attention Away From Lorenzo And Held A Lifeless Stare At All Of The Officers Who Were Cemented In Their Tracks But Alesha Remained Calm. She Could Not Take Any More Excitement And Her God-Brother Needed Peace. She Needed Peace… They All Did!

"Arch Chief Michaels Orders To Stand Down! Orders Were Given To Back Down!" A Voice Shouted Through The Military Officers' Ear Pieces. They All Shook Their Heads, Snapping Back Into Reality, Removing Their Gaze From Alesha And Returning Their Gaze To Her. They Bowed

Their Heads In Embarrassment To Her And Paid Their Respects, Then Turned And Ran Off The Patio Of The Chaos' Residence Like A Bunch Of Machines. In Seconds They Were Out Of Sight.

It Was December 2026 D.A.

Lo! Mother Nature The Neter Was Punishing Illinois Frozen Stretching Out To The Summer Months. It Was Minus Fifty-Four Degree Celsius, The Coldest Winter In The State And With Wind Chills, It Was Below Minus Sixty. It Was A Curse Upon The City As Nature's Punishment, But The Hustle Never Stopped. The Higher Class Was Struggling And Fought Among Themselves Day And Night Because Of How The Money Was Being Handled By The Banks, Which Became Private Institutions For BRAZOS. The Banks Began Spiking Fees, And Cash Was In Slow And Minimum Rotation Making Money. A Particular Kind Or Resource For Those Who Didn't Have Microchips. The State Was An Utter Disaster, Where No One Would Have Known The Leader, From The Follower. If It Weren't For BRAZOS' Intimidating Regime. The Children From Upper-Class Families Were Finding Themselves Getting Involved In Drugs And Prostitution.

Colleges And Universities Were Empty, And More People Were Turning Up Missing. On The Other Side Of The Monetary Scale, Where The Wealthy Roamed Behind Closed Doors To Get More Money In Their Pockets, The Warring Angels Known As Former Gang Members Positioned Themselves On The Freezing Street Corners In Defiance Against BRAZOS. But The Thugs Were Still Destroying Their Communities In The Process. They Worked The Corners Twenty-Four Hours Every Day A Week. Salsara Park From A Visitor's Point Of View Seemed Like A Very Nice Neighborhood, But Twenty And Six Years Ago, That Would Have Been True.

It Used To Be Financially Diverse, Spacious And Quiet, But Developers Created Blocks Of Copycat Houses Built Close Together, About Fifteen Feet Apart To Cram In Lower Income Families. Only The Rooftop Colors Made Each House Different From One Another. Parents In The Neighborhood Didn't Even Know The Children Served As Lookouts For The Dealers. They Covered The Corners And Alleyways, Watching And Remembering Everything That Took Place. The Kids Would Play Some Sport In The Streets, Causing Traffic To Come To A Halt. Football

Was The Best Cover, And If They Saw The Police, They Would Start Fighting Or Arguing Amongst Themselves To Distract Them. However When Arch Chief Michaels Came Upon The Scene, He Knew Their Tactics, And They Could Not Fool Him, So They Never Tried To.

- 140 -

****

Sean Alemayehu Tewodros Giorgis 9Ruby Prince Intergalactic Ambassador

Was The Best Cover, And If They Saw The Police, They Would Start Fighting Or Arguing Amongst Themselves To Distract Them. However When Arch Chief Michaels Came Upon The Scene, He Knew Their Tactics, And They Could Not Fool Him, So They Never Tried To.

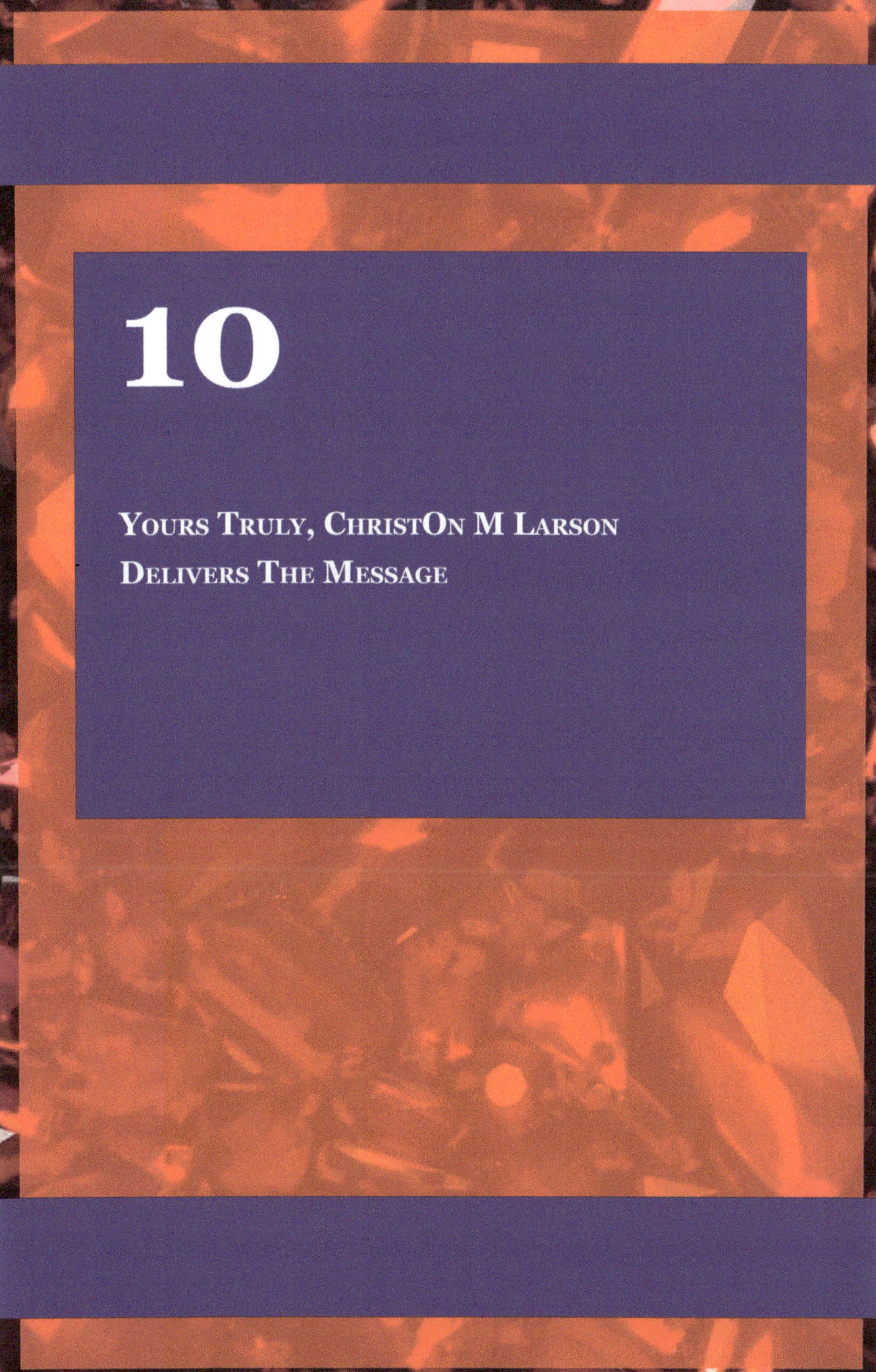
10

YOURS TRULY, CHRISTON M LARSON
DELIVERS THE MESSAGE

In The Year 2023 D.A.

Could You Imagine The World With No Influence From Da Evil One?" Larson Asked The Crowd At Castoni's Bar, "Life Without Seeking For Forgiveness Would Be A Meaningless One!" He Shouted To His Audience, Waiting For The Sound Of His Echoing Voice To Die Out. His Face Was Covered In Mystery By The Shades That Allowed Him To Reveal No Emotion. "After All, Who Knew Of Sin, Before Reading Holy Books… You Know, Like Da Bible?" He Asked Sarcastically Pronouncing The D, Sending A Thunderous Vibration Through The Overhead Speakers.

"When A Man Says, 'What You Should Not Do' He Is Also Saying, What You Can Do!" The Audience Nodded In Agreement. "A Wise Man Once Said, Everything In This World Was Already Written, And All Of This Has Already Happened, And I Feel This Is An Accurate Statement…But," Larson Paused As He Tilted His Head To The Side, "That Is Just My Opinion."

Larson Placed The Microphone In The Empty Stand In Front Of Him, And Held The Connected Objects Within His Hands, And Closed His Eyes, "Then You Have Already Read This Life…Then You Have Already Tasted Life, And So You Have Already Read This Book. Therefore, It Was Already Written."

He Opened His Eyes Beneath The Dark Shades And Found Himself Lost In A Gaze, Focusing On A Dim Green Light Shining Towards Him, "To Deny What You Are Truly Witnessing, Is Denying That You Happen To Exist!" The Audience Applauded As He Stepped Off The Stage And Emerged Into The Crowd. Larson Felt Pats On His Back And Saw Dark Faces With Many Expressions Coming Towards Him To Give Respect. An Unknown Voices Were Calling His Name, Yet His Eyes Still Fixed To The Dim Green Light, Which In His Mind, Represented The Color Of Life.

Thus, ChristOn M Larson Passed The First Test And Earned The Scroll Of "Sincerity."

Who Is ChristOn M Larson?

You Know, A Wise Man That Was A Master In The Art Of Spiritual Eyes Of Deceiving Faces Once Said, That To Deceive You Must First Manipulate The Power Of The Six-Ether Mind," Larson Thought To Himself. All Eyes Shall Behold Me, And This Will Be The Greatest Testimony Ever Told. All Mysteries Of Da 9 Shall Be Revealed, And Many People Will Speak About These Events As Time Passes By In The Illusion Of It All…About A Man Of Great Mystery, Me, ChristOn M Larson, The Trial Of The Century!

****

11
THE WRATH OF LARCENNI

In The Year 2026 D.A.

ChristOn M Larson's Mutilated Body Arrived At An Old Nine-Story Building On 72nd Street And Halstead Avenue For A Secret Examination. Arch Chief Michaels. Along With, Chief Ezra, Uriel, And Raphael Rushed Urgently To The Coroner's Office Of Dr. Cinatto. The BRAZOS Chiefs Entered Upon The Darkened Scene, A Room That Was Surprisingly Already Filled With Six BRAZOS Police Who Did Not See Him Through A Glassed Window, They Observed The Body Bag With Suspicion, Questioning If The Body Was Actually That Of Mr. Larson.

Dr. Cinatto Was Relieved, When The Chiefs Secretly Arrived Downstairs In The Basement. Because He Was Desperately Trying To Hold Off The Savage Minds Of The BRAZOS Police Officers. The Doctor Responded To Michaels's Requests By Remembering His Phone Conversations With The Chief Who Gave Strict Orders. *"Mr. Larson' Symbolic Body Is Not To Be Touched Or Seen Under Any Circumstances Until I Have Arrived, Michaels Told The Doctor Earlier That Evening."*

The Six BRAZOS Police Gossiped About The Badly Burned Body Filled With Rusted Hollow-Tip Bullets. Arch Chief Michaels Was Deeply Disturbed By The Cops' Negative Remarks. He Told The Doctor To Take His Gun And Point The Weapon To The Police Who Did Not Know Michaels Was There. *"Whoa Doc! Lower Your Weapon,"* One Of The BRAZOS Police Said. "When You Leave! You Guys Aren't Authorized To Be Here, And I Don't Feel Safe! Leave, Or I Will Have A Suit On Your Asses!" With His Weapon Drawn, The Doctor Made Them Leave. "Thanks, Doc," Michaels Said To The Nervous Doctor Returning The Gun To Him. *"This Body Does Not Match The DNA Of Mr. ChristOn M Larson,"* The Doctor Said To The Chiefs. However, Dr. Cinatto Was Unaware Of The Attempted Assassination Of The Young Man. Until The Chiefs Informed Him A First Hand Which Was Why The Observations Were

To Be Done In Secrecy. Michaels Instructed Him To Keep All Information Top Secret From Everyone, Including His Partner Dr. Earl Miller. Suddenly, Michaels Received An Unexpected Phone Call Came From Director Jentson Who Was A Nervous Wreck.

Arch Chief Michaels Tried To Calm His Boss Down, And Then The Director Caught A Hold Of Himself. Breathing Hard Through The Phone, He Explained That Meteorites Had Smashed Into City Hall And Other Parts Of The City. The Director Informed His Chiefs That BRAZOS Chancellor Elite Declared **Occupied Chicago** In A City-State Emergency. Arch Chief Michaels Signaled To His Chiefs To Immediately Investigate The City Hall Incident While He Waited For The Family Of Mr. Larson To Arrive. Shortly After The City Was Struck, People Were Terrified By The Destruction. In The Location Where It All Happened, They Gathered Wailing In The Streets Feeling It Was An Executed Judgment Upon Them.

One Hour Later, Larson's Brokenhearted Mother, Mary Larson Larson, Came Rushing Down The Stairs Along With Alesha By Her Side. Alesha Franacia's Mother, Nefertiti Waited For Her Godson Who Was Also Her Nephew, Lorenzo, To Show Up, But He Didn't. Twenty Minutes Later, B.R.L-Illiana's Chief Uriel Walked In, With Chief Ezra And Chief Raphael. The Coroner, Dr. Earl Miller Came Downstairs Holding A Will Signed By ChristOn M Larson.

Mary Larson's Legs Began To Give Out From Beneath Her, And Her Spirit Completely Shattered, As She Broke Down In Tears Then Fell To The Floor. Chief Uriel Walked Over To The Woman, Helped Her To Her Feet And Guided Her To A Seat, Where He Then Handed Her Larson' Personal Items. Among The Items Was A Black Onyx Ring From Haweyah Which Symbolized The Sins ChristOn Had Indulged And Partook In; His Share Of Wrong Doings Before, He Came Into Right Knowledge, Wisdom, And Overstanding As A Scholar.

Alesha Was Given Dog Tags On A Chain With An Ankh And A Key Attached To It. Dr. Earl Miller Gestured To Mrs. Larson To Come Into The Room, Beside Her Seat, Where A Body Bag Laid Stiffly On A Steel Examination Table. Dr. Earl Miller Unzipped The Bag Slowly, And Pulled It Open Releasing The Smell Of Symbolic So-Called Passing Away Into The Air. Mary

Larson Larson Held Her Chest In Pain, As Her Mouth Opened But Could Not Speak. She Took A Deep Breath And Tried To Communicate, But It Came Out Internally To Her Own Spirit. *"That's Not My Son!"* She Shouted Within Herself.

Arch Chief Michaels Noticed The Woman's Difficulty In Breathing And Pulled Her To The Side To Inform Her, That Chief Uriel Would Take Her To A Safe Place, After The Symbolic Funeral. Chief Uriel Approached The Woman After Michaels Walked Away And Wrapped His Arms Around Her, Gently Escorting Her Out Of The Room. Mary Larson Turned To Look At The Room Again, As She Walked Away In Total Disbelief. She Felt That The Mutilated Body Was Not Of Her Son! And The Chiefs Ushered Them Out, Before They Could All Identify The Ruined Body. Three Days Later, The Symbolic Funeral Was Conducted With Many Grieving Souls In Attendance And Mary Larson Still Could Not Release Her Words, Only Wailing Tears Of Pain.

ChristOn Was Not The Only One Who Was Attacked The Night Of His So-Called Passing Viciously Away. Lorenzo Was Ambushed As Well. The BRAZOS Police Smashed Into Lorenzo's Car On The Dan Ryan Expressway. And Forced His Car To Drive Off The Ramp Causing It To Flip Over A Few Times. The Police Remained In Their Vehicle With The Intent Of Wanting Him Passed Away. They Stepped Out And Took A Few Steps Towards The Flipped Over The Car And Squirted Fuel In Its Direction. They Then Lit A Rag And Threw It On The Grass, Which Created A Flaming Trail Towards Its Target.

Lorenzo Was Strapped Into His Seat As His Car Began To Catch Fire. The Police Quickly Walked Back To Their Patrol Car And Sped Away From The Scene. A Homeless Man That Heard The Crash Ran Over And Pulled Lorenzo Out Of The Burning Vehicle. A Few Hours Later, Lorenzo Was In Disbelief As He Lay In His Hospital Bed Trying To Remember How He Got There. Every Time He Began Thinking Too Hard, The Stress Caused A Jolting Pain Through His Body. He Vaguely Remembered The Attack, By The BRAZOS Police That Could Have Cost Him His Life. About 20 Minutes Later, BRAZOS Police Entered His Room And Informed Him

That Some Magog Park Apostle Members Were Placed In Custody For The So-Called Passing Away Of Mr. Larson. As The Cops Walked Out, A Nurse Walked In And Checked The Bandages Around His Leg. *"How Did I Get Here?"* He Asked Her As He Struggled To Breathe. *"Some Homeless Man Brought You Here, But He Did Not Stay Around To Identify Who He Was,"* She Replied Sadly Touching His Leg. She Noticed Lorenzo Trying To Speak And Interrupted Him.

"Please Sir, Get Some Rest, You Have To Get Stronger. If You Stress Yourself, It Will Only Slow The Healing Process Down, Okay?" She Stared At Him As He Began To Relax His Body Into The Bed. He Opened His Eyes And Looked At The Television. *"I'll Turn It On For You,"* The Woman Said. As The Screen Flicked On, The News Reporter Was Already In The Middle Of Explaining. All The Vehicle Accidents That Occurred That Night Throughout The City. The Greatest Calamity Was Of The Meteorites Smashing Into The Downtown Area. A Few Minutes Later, Another Nurse Walked In To Assist Lorenzo. She Then Began Shouting Excitedly While Holding Her Mouth As She Jumped Up And Down.

"Oh My Goodness, That's Chaos!" She Started Pulling And Shacking The Other Nurse's Arm. *"Felicia, Do You Know Who That Is?"* She Asked The Woman Staring At Lorenzo Without Even Blinking. *"Oh, My Goooo..."* The Nurse Covered Her Mouth Cutting Off The Rest Of Her Words. *"Chaos,"* She Said Walking Up To The Wounded Lorenzo, *"I Just Love Your Music!"* Suddenly The Woman's Expression Changed. Her Excited Manner Became Saddened As Reality Began To Kick In. *"Wait,"* She Said Touching His Arm, *"What Happened To You? Who Could Do Such A Horrible Thing To You...To My Baby?"*

Lorenzo Gave The Nurse A Warm Smile, *"It's Okay Hun,"* He Murmured, *"I'll Be Fine."* His Voice Was Then Interrupted By Wgn Celebrity News. *"The Symbolic So-Called Passing Away Of Mr. ChristOn M Larson",* Both Nurses And Lorenzo's Body Froze. WGN Jan Lysalot Was At The Scene, Staring At A Vehicle In Which Mr. Larson Was Said To Be Driving. Lorenzo's Breathing Became Stronger As A Strange Energy Entered His Body. He Threw His Sheet Off His Torso And Thighs And Pushed Himself Up Out Of His Bed. The Nurses Had No Urge To

Stop Him As He Limped His Bruised Body Towards The Screen, Touching It With Both Hands As If He Could Teleport Himself To The Location. *Jan Lysalot Adjusted The Earpiece In Her Ear. This Is Jan Lysalot Reporting Live On The Scene, This Just In. Information Is Flowing Through Stating The Involvement Of The Magog Park Apostles.*

Lorenzo's Anger Rose As His Body Began Trembling. "Where Are My Clothes?" He Shouted In Pain As He Held His Chest. Nurse Felicia Ran To His Side As He Stumbled Into The Bed Holding His Chest And Staring Around The Room. *"Please Mr. Larson, You Must Get Back In Bed!"* She Said Trying To Direct His Large Body To The Mattress. "No! Where Are My Clothes?" He Asked Pleading In Pain. "You...Nurse Who Likes My Music, Where Are My Clothes? Get Them To Me...Now!" He Ordered. *"Okay Chaos, Okay,"* The Other Nurse Said Nervously, *"Hold On!"* She Ran To A Closet. *"Mr. Larson Your Clothes Were Cut Off Of You While You Were Unconscious! Sophia,"* Nurse Felicia Said To The Other Nurse, *"He Has No Clothes! Okay Then, Hold On!"* Nurse Sophia Ran Out The Room And Minutes Later Returned Breathing Hard And Sweating Immensely. In Her Hands, She Had A Sweater And A Pair Of Sweat Pants That She Got From The Gift Shop.

"I Bought...These....For....You," She Said Trying To Catch Her Breath And Speak At The Same Time. *"Chaos...I Bought...It...For You...Here,"* She Threw The Clothes On The Bed And Leaned Against The Wall As She Took Deep Breaths. *"Woooooo! I'm Out Of Shape!"* She Shouted To Herself. "Thank You, Sophia," Lorenzo Said As He Struggled To Get His Naked Body Into The Clothing, Which Fit Him Loosely And Gave Him The Appearance Of An Athlete. "My Shoes, My Shoes?" He Asked Looking Around The Floor Frantically. "Here," Nurse Sophia Threw His Torn Up Runners Towards Him.

In A Few Minutes, His Feet Were In His Shoes, And He Was Out Of The Hospital Doors. Limping His Way Towards The Direction Of Magog Park Apostles, With Motives Of Letting His Anger Loose. On Some Of The Neighborhood Hoodlums, He Felt Might Have Harmed His Friend. He Escaped The Hospital Without Being Properly Released And Coincidentally,

Some Suspect BRAZOS Police Were On Their Way To The Hospital To Make Sure He Didn't Survive The Crash. Paying No Serious Attention To His Swollen Hands Wrapped Tightly In Bandages. He Picked Up A Rusted Steel Baseball Bat And Added Another Fifteen Minutes To The Forty-Five Minutes He Had Already Walked With Much Difficulty. As He Approached The Main Intersection Of Magog Park And Central Avenue, Behind The Urbana Dump Station. He Noticed Two Magog Thugs Walking With Their Backs Turned To Him.

Lorenzo, Forgetting About His Injured Leg, Ran Up With Silent Speed Behind Them And With Full Force. Smashed The Steel Into Each Their Skulls. Both Men Collapsed Immediately As Blood Poured Out Of Their Ears. Lorenzo Was On A Prowl. He Moved Up Through Allies And Caught A Few Off Guard, Aiming Solely For The Head, Breaking Nose Bones; Leaving The Thugs Laying Unconscious In Warm, Salted Blood. He Was Fumigated And Served Up The Entire Magog Park Apostles. That Were Lingering In Shadows.

He Snuck Up Behind Some Of Them Pressing The Bat Up Under Their Chins, Across Their Throats, Against Their Adam's Apple Crushing Their Thyroids As Their Eyes Rolled Back In Their Heads. He Made Sure They Suffered Pain, And The Worst Bodily Damage Unimaginable. For The Ones He Attacked Standing Under Street Lights. The People Who Waited For Their Crack Fiends To Come Around. He Punched Them With His Swollen Fist, Until Their Faces Were Unrecognizable, And Spewed Liquid Red Then Finished Them Off, With A Bat To The Brain.

He Couldn't Remember How Long The Beat Down Had Lasted, But All He Knew Was That He Was Out For The Taste Of Blood. Every Swing Chaos Executed Upon Them; Left Their Bodies Numb And Cold On The Pavement. He Made Sure Each Blow, From His Steel Rattled Their Brains Within Their Skulls, And It Did, Like Earthquakes Swallowing The Earth. They Were Unable To Tell The Difference Between The Strike Of A Knuckle And That Of Steel. Their Nerves Had No Time To Feel The Pain, Because Each Blow Sedated Them. He Chose Not For His Victims To Feel A Passing Away. But A Lifetime Of Pain, Suffering, And Paralysis But His

Anger, And Emotions Left Him With No Room, To Choose Which One He Wanted To Impose On Them. The Magog Park Attacks Ended Up On The News That Evening; Following The Story Of The Meteorites Crashing Into City Hall Where Many Had Died, Except For Mayor Elite Nimrod Sinnah, Who Was The Only Survivor.

BRAZOS Chancellor Elite Madame Helena Ishtar Was Placed In Charge. During While The Hospitalized Mayor Elite Was UnGregoing Recovery And Rumors Had Already Begun Spreading Around The World, About How Both Mr. Larson And Mr. Mayor Elite Donald Finley's Incidents Being Such A Coincidence. Mr. Larson's Secret Examination Was Being Questioned. About The Un-Matching DNA Samples, That Were Drawn From The Badly Burned Body, And Mayor Elite Donald Finley's Body Was Undamaged From The Explosion. That Covered 19 City Blocks That Left The Entire City Burning For Nine Days; The Rumors Were Spreading Like Wild Fire. The Grievance Of Larson Caused Many Of The Warring Angels Known As Former Gang Members To Unite After The City's Nine Days Of Burning; They Were No Longer Fighting Amongst Each Other. BRAZOS Chancellor Elite Madame Helena Ishtar Declared Indefinite Martial Law.

Later That Night, Alesha Took The Key That Larson Had Once Worn Around His Neck, Which Was Given To Her At The Coroner's Office, To A Post Office Box Larson Was Renting Located On The North Side Of The City. She Opened Up The Box And Found Two Envelopes. The First Envelope Contained Two Poems, Which She Began To Read As She Stood In The Cold Building: Love Divine, *The Highest Love This Planet Has Ever Known. U Are My Heart & Soul, My Inspiration In Life! Da Journey Of Da 9Ruby Prince & Da 9Ruby Princess Is A Blessed Mission. 3,600 Years Have I Searched For U. I Know U Were Searching For Me. So, Long, We Have Longed For Each Other. Da Most High, Provided The Ways In Which We Grew In Spiritual Love, Love Divine. We Vibrate On Subscript 9 To Da 9Th Power Of 9! I Have Loved U For Ever In A Day, And That Day Be A 1,000 Years Of Pure Serenity Of Heaven On Earth Alesha & ChristOn ChristOn, We Were Created Out Of Love. Da 9Love Of Father EGZIABHER Created Us! U Are*

My Royal 9Ruby Princess; I Am Your 9Ruby Prince. Out Of 9Love, We Shall Create Another Soul, Becoming A Great All Loving Father & Mother Within Da Royal Chambers Of Our Hearts! I 9Love U For-Ever, U Are My Thoughts And Insights! ChristOn, Da 9Ruby Prince Of Abyssinia Oh He Who Is Yahuwa *"Eye Am The Wind That Blows Thru Your Hair, For Eye Am That Shadow Of Love In Every Step You Walk. Eye Was There When You Were Lonely, For I Eye Am That Light On The Path In Your Journey. Eye Am The Heat When You Are Cold, And Eye Am The Blood That Pumps In Your Heart So Behold. Eye Am That Man Of Your Dreams, For Eye Am That Man Who Dreams Of You. Eye Am The Soul Of Your Spirit. Our Spirits Created For One Another For Da Most High Is Everything, And Everything Is Spiritual 9Love In His Divine Authority."*

The Spell Of Sadness Fell Upon Alesha Franacia Of Amarna. Her Mind Traveled Back Some Three Years When She First Met ChristOn. Instantly Her Life Was Going Through Many Changes In Her DNA Explosions In A Twinkle Of An Eye. She Loved Him More Than She Loved Herself And Knew ChristOn Would Do Anything For Her. He Learned Of A Great Power Patiently Waiting For Her Submission To Da Most High Father EGZIABHER. ChristOn Knew She Had A Greater Purpose. He Was A Warrior Seeking Revenge For What He Called *"Da Lost Righteous Souls."*

Alesha **Da 9Chief Mesesha** Had Knowledge About This Angel Who Transformed Him. However, She Was In Ethiopia, When It All Happened. She Was Well Aware Of This Great Event, Knowing It Was Something He Needed, And Wanted. *"For Many Are Called, But Few Are Chosen. Matthew 22ND Chapter Verse 14,"* She Remembered Him Telling Her In The Past. ChristOn Felt The Change In Alesha, Who Was Now Being Called Alesha After Her Own Spiritual Encounter. So She Was Being Groomed For Many Battles In The Last War. ChristOn's Was Able To See And Feel His Destiny Through Alesha's Eyes, And Alesha Had An Awareness Of Her True Identity. But She Was Willing And Ready To Embrace It All; So The Ancient Spirit Of Destineye Requested, Her Secret Spiritual Sister Kj.

In September 2024 D.A.,

To Cross Paths With Alesha Franacia Of Amarna, Also. Kj Became **"Da Chief Advisor"** After She Was Sent To Give ChristOn Guidance, Wisdom, And Overstanding And She Mysteriously Entered Into His Life Through Music During The Year 2023 D.A. She Was A Very Talented Songstress, A Multi-Talented Musician. During ChristOn's Stay In Champaign, Illinois, Kj Successfully Put ChristOn Back On His Journey By Studying Regularly And Engaging In Spiritual Meditation Ceremonies.

All The Years Alesha Lived In Illinois She Thought Endlessly About Her Future Soul Mate; Years Before She Became Aware Of Her Own Personal Spiritual Connections With Destineye. She Was Devoted To Father ANU EGZIABHER, ELYOWN ELYOWN EL. Alesha's Ancient Spirit Was Connecting With ChristOn Far Beyond His Overstanding; During His Event With Destineye In 2023 D.A. This Affected Alesha's Physical Being In 1999 A.D., And She Knew Not Of Her Own Spirit; Was That Of The Ancient Spirit Of Destineye.

Alesha And Lorenzo Were Not Blood-Related But Were Placed In A Blood Ritual With ChristOn To Tighten Their Bond. Lorenzo's Job Was To Protect Her During Her Visits To **Occupied Chicago**. When She Left For Abyssinia In September 2022 D.A., She Was Already Three Months Pregnant; Her Spiritual Mother, Whom She Called Shaman To Keep This Secret From ChristOn And The Other People She Knew, Instructed Her In A Vision. However, It Was The Will Of Father EGZIABHER To Prepare Her And The Child In Another Sacred Ritual Birth Ceremony. Like That Of ChristOn In The Year 1977 A.D.

Alesha Knew That BRAZOS Created A World Of Torment For One Purpose Only; To Destroy Da Children Of Da Most High, All Done In Arrogance. The Joys Of Life Were Just A Distant Tucked-Away Thought From Their Childhood. ChristOn Had Molded Alesha's Style In Almost Every Fashion. His Music And Creativity Were More Than Just A Street Testimony. He Was Not The Street Thug Everybody Thought He Was. It Was Not The Same For Lorenzo, Who In Secret Was Really His Cousin Living In South Bend, Indiana For A Short Time.

ChristOn Was Destined For Great Things, Just Like His Father Before Him. There Were Always Spiritual Beings Watching Over Him. Rumor Had Spread That Larson Was Met By Two Of His Secret Cousins; Jo Da Posey "Da Enforcer" And Raphael "Da Manager," Who Were Disguised As The Two Homeless Men On The Scene. Witnesses Say They Saw A UFO Hovering Over The Vehicle, Driven By ChristOn That Evening. David Watched In His Craft As BRAZOS' Goons Viciously Attacked The Young Man; And Two Elders In Shamballah, Aghaarta, A Sacred City 99 Miles Below The Surface Of The Earth, Had Already Prepared Him.

"In The Gangster's Heart, They Want To Be Good But Don't Know How" The Elder Dunnakial Said To David. *"Gangstas Really Means Pissed Off Angels, With The Spirits From Above Incarnating Within Them. "Those Who Have Fallen Are Destined To Wake Up, To Help Save The World, Ready For Their Return To "Da Crystal City That Has Already Come Out Of Nibiru. Shortly After The Great War Begins, The Enforcers, Who Are Mysterious Beings To Others, Will Start Striking Down, Many Men In The Most Gruesome Way Ever Known To Man."*

In The Year 2026 D.A.

Months Had Passed Since The Nineteen Great Balls Of Fire Struck The Earth, After The "So-Called Passing Away" Of ChristOn M Larson And The Emergence Of The Enforcer Da Larcenni; B.R.L-Illiana Was On Full Alert. Larcenni Da Anunnaqi's Strikes Were Like Coffee Went Amuck—French Vanilla Stains On A Pearly White Shirt. There Seemed To Be No Motive Behind The Rage. No Traces And No Predictable Hit List. *B.R.L-Illiana Was Baffled!* Director Jentson Was Clueless About The Menace On The Streets. Why, Because The Victims Were America's Favorite And Most Wanted Scumbags!

Was Larcenni Da Anunnaqi A Friend Or Foe To B.R.L-Illiana?

Director Jentson Was So Fearful He Began Traveling In A Bulletproof Vest And Vehicle; Keeping His Own Security Team Around Him At All Times. However, Eyes Were Still Watching By Unknown Enforcers Striking With Lightning Precision. Bringing The Wrath Of Vengeance

On Behalf Of Those Victims Who Fell Into The System Of Lost Identity! Shortly After, The Appearance Of The 13th Planet Nibiru In 2022 D.A., The Crystal City Released Itself From The Large Planet, Located On The Outside Of The Photon Belt, Traveling Two Years To Get Through It. The Crystal Ship And Child Of Its Mother Nibiru, Hovered Eerily Within The Earth's Atmosphere, Undetected And Unseen For Over Three Years Once It Arrived. The Ship's Presence Caused The Entire World To Be In Fear, And Its Energy Made The Emotions Of Revenge, Hate, Sorrow And Regret Within All Sinners Come To A Complete Stop Due To The Confusions Within Them."

All Manipulations Peaked In March 2023 D.A., Two Years Before The Next Election, And **Occupied Chicago**'s Mayor Elite Abraham Musa. Known As A Great Man, Was Mysteriously And Aggressively Being Forced Into Early Retirement Due To A Secret Power That Had Been Running The City In The Shadows. Now That The City Was Without A Mayor Elite, The Passing Aways And Mayhem Reached A New High. Through It, All, An Ancient And Unfamiliar Anunnaqi Surfaced For Revenge. On The City's Tyranny And Penetrated Lightning Strikes As A Wrath Throughout The Streets Of **Occupied Chicago**. The Mysterious Anunnaqi Of Judgment Had A Name… Da Larcenni…Divine Authority And The 13th Of The 24 Elders Of Divine Authority.

Da Larcenni Was Summoned From The Da 9th Chamber Of Nibiru And Had Begun Releasing Vengeance Upon The Planet Qi… The Ancient Title For Planet Earth. The Summoning Occurred Three Years Before, The Visual Appearance Of Nibiru In The Sky." Indeed, Confusion Was In The Air! BRAZOS Mob Bosses Were Coming Up Missing While Activities At Hot Gambling Spots Became Spectator Sports. News Media Were No Longer Censored. News Cameras Were Set Up At Cook County Casino On Halstead Avenue On The South Side.

On January 9th, 2027 D.A.,

The Casino Parking Lot, Which Seemed To Stretch About Five Miles, Was Filled With Cars. The Wind Was So Cold Of Minus Fifty-Four Degrees, And Conversations Among Six Men

Were Kept To A Minimum. The Chill Was Like Urine Slapping Them In The Face. The Winds Penetrated Their Thick Trench Coats, And Elegant Suits Placing Them In A Freezer. All Six Of Them Were High-Profile Lunatics, And Were Well Connected With BRAZOS. They Thought That They Should Have Worn Bulletproof Vests, But It Wouldn't Have Mattered Anyway, Because They All Received Electrifying Head Shocks, Frying Their Brains. The Passing Away Of These Lunatics, Was Nothing To Feel Bad About, Because They Were Pure Evil. For Years They Had Tortured And Passed Away People For No Reason At All.That's Not Including The Passing Away-For-Hire Jobs. They'd Been Responsible For Committing.

TV Camera Crews Continued, Entering Through The Revolving Doors, Which Were Damaged, And When Police Arrived, They Found The Doors Jammed.No One Inside Was Able To Leave Women And Men, Were Screaming And Trying To Find Safety Behind Overturned Tables. It Was Like Five Hurricanes Had Come Through Looking For Victims. In The Casino, Two Thugs Lay Slumped Motionless, Against Their Chairs With Smoke Coming From Their Bodies. As If Gravity Forgot To Finish Knocking Them To The Floor. The Other Four Criminals Were Laid Out In A Fetal Position."

The Chiefs On The Scene Realized There Were No Slugs Found In Any Of Them. They All Laid Staring Into Each Other's Eyes, Watching Life Deceive Them Before They Inhaled Their Last Breath. It's Ironic How These De-Materializers, Never Imagined The Chance Of Mercy Ever Escaping Them! *They Did Not Have An Opportunity To Repent For Their Lives. They Only Witnessed Their Pathetic Lives Reduced To Nothing And Taken By The Strength Of Biological Electricity.*" The Enforcer Must Have Been Somebody In The Room That Everybody Was Comfortable With Because No One Had Expected The Shock Treatment. But When The Enforcer Started To Go To Work, The Thugs Had Been So Afraid That They Had Felt The Passing Away Long Before Any Sparks Were Fired.

Alesha Was In The Casino, And She Walked Right In Front Of The Cameras Ready To Be Interviewed. They Refused To Acknowledge Her Presence, So She Walked Out The Door

And Vanished! Everyone Saw What Happened! They Said The Assassin Waited For The Right Moment To Strike, But They Chose Not Identify Whom It Was Out Of Fear! After That Incident, Many BRAZOS Under Bosses Began Wearing The Bulletproof Vest, And No One Mourned For The Passed Away BRAZOS Followers. When The News Displayed The Victims' Bodies From The Casino, There Was Rejoicing Heard In The Background. The People Remembered The Men's Faces With Hatred.

The Men Were Identified As The Ignorant Criminals At The Warehouse That Worked At The Eye-Scanning Entrance. A Witness Said The Power Had Gone Out, And Then The Room Was Lit With Lightning Strikes As If The Sparks Were Coming Directly From Hands Of Rage. The News Was Always Associated The Mass Passing Away To The Enforcer, Da Larcenni. The Name First Appeared Spray-Painted On A Wall Next To The Gambling Alley Just Two Blocks From Larson' Mother's House In 2026 D.A. It Read *"Larcenni Da Anunnaqi! Strikes Against ChristOn Larson' Adversaries!"*

The Hood Came Kept The Name After Larson *"Ascended,"* And Some Speculated That There Might Be More Than One Enforcer. And Even With All The Satellite Monitoring, There Was Still No Trace! Meanwhile, Jo Da Posey, Andre Da Drego And Lorenzo Da Chaos Were Bringing A New Kind Of Misery To BRAZOS. Da Ill-State Enforcers No Longer Carried Weapons. They Were Able To Harness Controlled Energy From Their Hands, Lightning Strikes Coming Straight From Their Fingertips And Sometimes Their Entire Palms. This Was A Skill Taught To Them By ChristOn.

Of Course, They Thought That Was Impossible Because ChristOn Demonstrates This Training Only One Time. However, He Did Emphasize To Them The Effects Of The Photon Belt On The Etherian Non-Chipped Children. The Double Helixes Were No Longer Two Strands; They Were Mutating Because Of The Photon Radiation. He Learned In Abyssinia That Through A Significant Mental Focus Of The Heart Causing The Mind To Become In Sync With One Of Each Heart's Beat. The Idea Was To Become One Mentally With The Cardiac Conduction

System. And The Heart's Internal Electrical Conduction System. So The Mind Could Transfer The Electricity Through The Blood And The Entire Nervous System, Penetrating Through The Skin. ChristOn Was Taught That By Practicing This Mediation Exercise. The Ability To Create Biological Electricity Would Get Easier By The Day With The Photon Belt As An Ignition. With A Single Dash Of Antagonized Emotions, Mixed With The Meditations Ingredients, All Hell Broke Loose, Fearing For Their Lives.

But It Was Only After The Alleged Fall Of The Lion Of Salsara Park Lords, That The Emotions Of That Great Loss. It Gave Jo Da Posey And Lorenzo Da Chaos And Andre Da Drego The Power. Because It Was ChristOn, Who Taught His Chosen Ones That The Extraordinary Power Was Already Inside Of Them. Da Ill-State Enforcers' New Power, When Used Against The Unrighteous, Caused Extreme Over Heating Of The Bodies. Casting Out The Evil Spirits! But The Energy Was Too Powerful For Their Hearts To Use On A Daily Basis. And Because They Were Still Very Young! *"So They Only Planned Strategic Battles. However, The Mysterious Anunnaqi, Da Larcenni's Power Was Far More Devastating! When Larcenni Da Anunnaqi Struck A Person, They Would Fry Internally Than Externally, Turn Their Body Hard, Then Into A Soft Gray Dust, Crumbling To The Ground As Ashes And Then Blown Away By The Wind."*

Many People After A While Started To Reveal That They Were Witnesses Of The Mysterious Anunnaqi. They Spoke Of Various Locations Where Larcenni Da Anunnaqi Had Been Seen, And All The Witnesses Gave The Same Description. They Described Larcenni Da Anunnaqi As A Tall, Beautiful Woman With Silvery Hair. When They First Saw The Individual, She Had A Black Force Field Around Her Entire Head That Resembled A Motorcycle Helmet. The Witnesses Felt However That For Some Reason, While She Slaughtered The Disagreeable.

She Sent Off A Mentally Controlling Vibration That Kept One Witness At The Scene To Behold Her Judgments. Once She Completed Her Fumigation, The Force Field Around Her Face Vanished Resembling Gas, And She Would Penetrate Fear Into The Eyes Of The Witness She Held Hostage, Letting Them Go To Spread A Word About Her Existence And Before They

Were Also Made Examples Of! Larcenni Da Anunnaqi Possessed A Very Powerful Energy. She Held The Title Similar To That Of Enqi Zagzagul, The 22nd Elder, Son Of Father EGZIABHER The Most High. Enqi Was The Annunaqi Of Soul Snatching, Responsible For Taking The Souls Of Man, A Job Bestowed Upon Him By His Father EGZIABHER.

Larcenni Electrocutes The Entire Physical Body Immediately Separating It From The Soul. She Then Holds The Souls In Suspension Between The Third, Fourth And Fifth Dimension. Until The Opening Of The Ninth Gate, Where The 22nd Elder Awaits. As The Soul Squirms And Tries To Set Free, From The Hands Of Da Larcenni The 13th Elder.

Enqi, Zagzagul The 22nd Elder Opens His Mouth, Revealing Fangs And A Serpent-Like Tongue, That Sucks The Screaming Soul Into His Stomach, Immediately Shutting The Ninth Gate. All This Is Done In Seconds And Is A Secret To The Physical Eyes. BRAZOS' Crimes Were Planned Out Bringing Torment To The City Along With The Name Of Da Larcenni. Most Black Neighborhoods Cared Less About BRAZOS. Who Excluded Them Because They Refused To Take Jobs Offered By Them. The Upper Class Wanted Jobs For The Material Gain, And They Required Implanted Chips. Most Employees Did Not Object Because They Earned Double Pay Working For BRAZOS, Compared To The Hierarchy Wages. Local Officers And Chiefs Were Implanted.

Except For Arch Chief Sham Michaels, Who Also Experienced The Sticky Blood That Oozed Out, Of His Nose With The Chip Stuck To The End. He Had A Special Id That Didn't Require Him To Do Eye Scans Either Because The Department. He Worked For Automatically Thought Everyone Was Chipped. When He Was Off Duty, He Was Given A Half-Hour To Report And Most Of The Time He Reported To The Office Late. This Was The Beginning Of BRAZOS' Worst Nightmare! Someone Had To Get To The Root, Of The Mysterious Larcenni Da Anunnaqi, And Arch Chief Michaels Was The Man For The Job! This Job Was For The Warrior Miykaa'El, And His Name Was Written All Over It. Who Dares To Be Like Da Larcenni? Where Did That Name Come From? Maybe This Anunnaqi Was Another Angel Of Justice?

Only The Evil People Had A Problem With This Threat. Larson Could Take Care Of Himself, And He Had All The Reasons To Have Feelings Of Striking Back At Them. How Was A Man Like Larson In Their Way? On That Designated Night. They Choose To Eliminate This Man. Who Had Been In A Race Of Making His Life Peaceful."

Larcenni Da Anunnaqi, Brought Havoc On The System, By Getting Rid Of The Trash Infesting The Environment, While BRAZOS Exercised An Eye For An Eye! Reports Were Made About A Huge Beam Of Light Over The City. Larson Was The Warrior, Da Sarge With Da Staff And A Talented Rap Singer, With Two Rings On Each Pinky, Da 9Emerald Lion Of Yahudah Ring And Da 9Ruby Prince Ring, Was His Symbol. The 9Ruby Stone Was Of Pure *Royalty! Like That Of The Ancient Spirit Of Destineye And ChristOn's Father Before Him.*"

****

12

MESSAGE FROM FRANCIS AURELIUS
B.R.A.Z.O.S. ELITE ATTORNEY

SIXTH SCRIPTURE OF LIFE

A Message From Francis Aurelius On The Day Of Judgment

Good Afternoon My Fellow Citizens. The Time Has Come For You To Look Into The Sky, And Look Upon The Sun And Cry Out For Your Lives, With Emotions Of All Kinds Except For That Of Pleasure, Contentment, And Happiness. You Will Beg Your Enemies To Pray For You. Rivers Of Blood Will Create Floods, Drained From The Weak Minds And Bodies, Of Those That Followed The Fallen Fleet. Who Are From Various Galaxies In Our Universe. You Followed Us, Your Role Model. Who Is Currently On The Verge Of Receiving The Most Ferocious Judgment From Father ANU, EGZIABHER, ELYOWN ELYOWN EL.

We The Fallen Have No Souls Because We Consumed Too Many. Once The Verdict Has Been Ruled Out, Our Energy Force Will Be Transferred Into The Black Hole Of Eternal Disagreeableness. That Is On The Other Side Of The Universe Because There Are Three Main Sectors. The Side Of Complete Agreeableness, The Center Where We Reside Which Is The Mixing Of Both Forces And The Other Side Of Complete Disagreeableness. The Universe Was Made In Equilibrium, To Create The Balance. Once We Have Been Shipped There, We Will Awaken As The Flesh That We Passed Away, Changing From One Specie To The Other, And We Will Have No Control Over It.

We Will Live For Millions Of Years On A Planet With Five Suns, Shaped In A Pentagram, With The Planet In The Center, And There Will Be No Nights. The Surface Will Be Filled With Fiery Venomous Scorpions And Snakes, Alligators, Crocodiles, Dragons And Other Predator Beasts. They Will Forever Hunt Us. There Will Be No UnGreground Tunnels Because They Will All Be Filled With Molten Lava. We Will Have No Food, But Will Be Food, Attacked And Passed Away, But Never Dying, Forever Living In An Eternal Inferno, An Everlasting Living Passing Away.

So Back To You My Fellow Citizens. You All Have Begun To Question What The Purpose Of The Material You Worshiped Was? Why Could It Not Buy You Out Of This? And You Are

Questioning As To Why You Were So Foolish. Well, It's Because You Put Fear And Greed In Front Of Your Eyes. You Were Afraid Of Us, So You Joined Us, To Be Like Us, To Be "Free" Of Our "Punishments." You Were Indeed Fooled! The Scriptures Of Old That Were Yes, Tampered By Us, Warned You All. It Was All There Clearly Cut. So Now Similar To The Destruction I Will Face, You Will Face As Well, But Before Me, When A Great Force, That You Call A Star, Will Drop Devouring Your Entire Earth And You. So Now Before It All, Your Skies Has Blackened, Attacked By Meteors, Hurricanes, And Earthquakes, Caused By A Galactic Political War Of Ancient Times; Ions Older Than You."

I *Pledged Allegiance To The Sixth Subscript Of Six To The Power Of Six. To Cause Transgressions From All Corners Of The Endless Universe, Where Only Father ANU, EGZIABHER, ELYOWN ELYOWN EL Knows Its Beginning And End. So You Are Now My Final Specie, After Many, To Accept My Stamp, Sending Your Soul To The Galaxy Of Purgatory For Those Who Have Souls. You Accepted My Money. I, Aurelius Azazl Anzu, Of The Yellow Light And My Fleet, Will Pay The Ultimate Price. But For The Meantime, I Will Enjoy How I Made You All Into Predator And Prey, Preying And Praying Against Each Other When You Are All Of The Same Specie. We Separated You, Mixed You Up, Tore You Down, Put Fear In You, Placed One Above The Other, Pleasured You, Bred You And Fed You...Everything To Make Your Psyche Depend On Us.*

W*e Even Ate You. I Enjoyed Watching Your "Leaders" Taking Their Weekly Checks From Us. They Were Our Sheppard Guiding The Sheep With Woolly Hair And The Wolves With Straight Hair. To The Slaughterhouse To Be All Butchered Together And Sold In Stores As Meat. You Should Have Just Been Rebellious Against Us. We Would Have Passed Away You, Yes, But You Would Have Been A Martyr, For Your Offspring And For Righteousness. And Out Of The Billions That We Have Passed Away; Only A Finger Full Of Them Will Make It To The Biosphere In The Galaxy And Dimension, Of Eternal Living. You, On The Other Hand, Will Not Be So Lucky. You Will Feel The Same Judgment As I, Just In A Different Way, Dimension And Galaxy. The Physical Body Was The Clothing, And Your Soul Was The Body... The One That Never Dies. Purgatory*

Is Where Your True Living Will Begin; So Stand In The Shade And Enjoy The Coolness Of This Night Because It Won't Be This Way Where You're Going. Men, Women And Children Have All Passed Away Each Other Thus Tasting The Blood Of The Wicked And The Righteous. But On The Ship That Hovers In Your Solar System. There Are Only Enough Seats For The Righteous. I Will Not Say That I Did Not Want To Be The One To Break It To You Because Then I Would Be Lying, Which I Have Done To You So Many Times Before. But This Is A Special Occasion.

This Is A Historical Event, Da Great And Dreadful 9th Hour, Which Was Foreseen By The Nine-Ether Elders. Found In The Akasha Records, Located In The Mini Galactic Library Of Shamballah, Aghaarta, That Was Made To Resemble The Largest One In The Universe Located In The 19th Galaxy.

We Will Meet Again. Regards,

Francis Aurelius Azazl

A.k.a.

Sama'el Anzu Son Of Zuen Anzu

Leader Of The Luciferian Fleet

****

13

DA 9SACRED STAR CHILDREN VERSUS THE FALLEN ELITE

THE 9SACRED SCROLLS OF NINE-ETHER

September 18th In The Year 2027 D.A.

ayings Of The 16th Elder Rikbi'el Also Known As Rapha'el The Fifth Test, "Heroism" Was A Test Of Will And Faith Over Material Binds. ChristOn's Guides Had Placed Him In Chains, In The Midst Of A Den Of Hungry Beasts, Unclean Beasts, Unclean Birds And Creeping Things! The Wild Beast Howled, The Birds Screamed, And The Reptiles Hissed. ChristOn Asked Himself, "Why Do I Sit To Be Bound With Chains? None Has Power Over The Human Soul." Thus Strengthened, He Rose And What He Thought Were Chains Were Merely Worthless Cords, Rags Parted With His Touch. ChristOn Said, "If Any Man Will Stand Erect And Use The Power Of Will, His Chains Will Fall Like Worthless Rags For Will And Faith Are Stronger Than The Stoutest Chains That Man Has Ever Made. The Darkness That Binds Me Is The Absence Of Light And Light Is But The Breath Of...Father ANU, Egiziabher, Elyown Elyown El, Vibrating In The Rhythm Of Rapid Thought And With The Will Of Might, He Stirred Up The Elders, And Their Vibrations Reached The Plane Of Light And There Was Light And The Birds, Beast And Creeping Things Were Not."

It All Began When ChristOnChristOn And Alesha Franacia Climbed The Highly Armed Building To The 66th Floor. Lightning Rippled Through The Dark Clouds, Jumping From One To The Other, This Time Not Ascending To Earth, But The Rain Was Coming In Heavy Downpours. Not Affecting ChristOn's Eyes Or Alesha Franacia's Eyes. As They Stared Upwards While Climbing The Glass Building. Their Hands And Bare Feet, When Touched By Water, Had The Ability To Stick To Anything With A Light Suction Effect, Especially On Slick Flat Surfaces.

When They Reached The Highest Floor Balcony, Alesha Franacia Shattered The Window With Her Bare Heel. Glass Exploded Around Them Onto The Floor And Falling To The Sidewalk 66 Stories Below Them. They Jumped Into The Building. As Wind And Water Blew Into The Large Dark Room, That Had Nine-Foot Ceilings That Had Snake Heads Carved Into The Crown

Molding. Suddenly A Bolt Of Electricity Hit The Clear Figurine That Stood Beside ChristOn, Pitching Glass On Top Of His Head. *"Got You Now Negative Soul!"*

Attorney Francis Aurelius Began, To Lift The Rest Of The Figurine With The Energy From His Hands. To Slam It Into ChristOn's Head, But Alesha Franacia's Strength Was Too Strong. She Pointed Her Red Eyes, Capturing The Figurine, And Sent It Flying Towards Aurelius, Smashing Him In The Face. Then Unexpectedly, Alesha Franacia Was Lifted Off Her Feet, And Thrown Violently Across The Room, Smashing Through The Wall Into The Other Room's Darkness.

ChristOn Turned To See Madame Helena Ishtar Standing Behind Him. She Hovered Two Feet Off The Ground, Then Flew Head First Into The Next Room, Where She Had Thrown Alesha Franacia. It Was All Happening So Fast, Because, By The Time Ishtar Flew Past ChristOn, Aurelius Had Sent Lightning From His Hands, Towards The Off Guard ChristOn. But The Lightning Got Trapped In His Aura, Which Stored The Electricity As Energy And Ammunition. Both Men Fought With Lightning Balls Of Fire, Igniting Furniture And Books Around Them.

Ishtar Engages To Struggle For Power, When Alesha Franacia Regains Conscience, And Sprays Fire From Her Entire Body Towards Ishtar. Glass Was Thrown As Daggers Covered With Fire, Piercing Flesh That Healed In Minutes, But Still Blood Was Everywhere. They Levitated Themselves, And Each Other, Banging Each Other Heads Into Walls, And Tables In The Middle Of The Fire, That The Four Beings Had Created. The Room Was In Such Flames, That The Dry Wall Broke Down From Between Both Rooms.

Alesha Franacia Caught Her Balance, After Rolling Onto The Floor, Sending More Firebombs. To Ishtar Who Got Herself Stuck In The Glass, Of The Second Broken Window. The Woman Screamed In Excruciating Pain, Shacking Wildly, Freeing Her Body From The Window And Falling To The Floor. With Telekinetic Energy, Alesha Franacia Raised The Woman To The High Ceiling, With One Hand And Ignited Ishtar's Entire Body With The Other. Alesha Franacia Using Gravitational Force, Then Slammed The Burning Woman Into The Floor Leaving Her Crippled And Overpowered By Alesha Franacia's Energy. Meanwhile, In The Other Burning

Room, The Mayor Elite Donald Finley Joined Forces With Aurelius. When He Tried Attacking ChristOn From Behind, With A Failed Attempt. ChristOn Placed His Aura In Full Force! Frying The Hands Of The Mayor, When He Tried To Make Contact With ChristOn's Body.

ChristOn Then Had The Chance Of Throwing Nine Consecutive And Consistent Bolts Of Lighting. Towards Francis Aurelius, Ripping Chunks Of Flesh From The Severely Bleeding Man. Who Was Now Declared Officially Defeated. ChristOn Turned To Donald Finley Whose Rubber Flesh Was Melting Off His Artificial Bones; The Machine Was Losing Energy. So ChristOn Lifted The Melting Man By The Neck With Both Hands, And Began Tearing His Head Away From His Body, While Alesha Franacia Stood By His Side. She Felt The Heat Generating In Her Palms. And Stepped Forward To Help Finish The Man. When Suddenly Francis Aurelius Charges Her To The Ground, Distracting ChristOnChristOn Who Threw The Biological Machined, Mayor Elite To The Ground And Moved Towards The Attorney.

Francis Aurelius Fought The Energy Drained Princess, But He Was Still Weaker. ChristOnChristOn Grabbed Aurelius From The Back, While Alesha Franacia Threw Vicious Lightning Forks. Into His Chest Tearing More Of His Flesh Open. As He Wailed With His Eyes Turning Red. The Doors Of The Burning Office Blew Open, And A Swarm Of BRAZOS Military Foreign Assassins And Robot Soldiers Stormed Into The Already Destroyed, Smoke-Filled Office. ChristOn And Alesha Franacia Threw The Bleeding Man To The Ground. And Threw Fireballs Dismantling The Robotic Soldiers In The Front Of The Pack.

The Two Then Spun Around Quickly, Sped Towards The Open Window And Jumped Out Of The 66th Story Window. Six Ribs On Both Sides Of ChristOn's Back, And Alesha Franacia's Back Tore Away From The Thoracic Cavity, Ripped Through Their Skin And Released Two Powerful Black Wings; Two Meters Long On Both Sides For Alesha Franacia And Three Meters Long On Both Sides For ChristOn. Both Enforcers Flew Away Into The Rainy Night Sky. The Warring Angels Known As Former Gang Members Helped The Two Hide. By Throwing Off BRAZOS Soldiers In Their Hunt For Alesha Franacia And ChristOnChristOn. Who Found Sanctity At

A Hotel Own By Castoni Unknown To BRAZOS. Donald Finley, Ishtar, And Aurelius Were Defeated, But ChristOn And Alesha Franacia Were Not Interested, In Taking Any Lives, They Just Wanted To Remind Them, That The Elders Still Ruled.

- 169 -

******

14

THE TESTIMONY OF
DON MARQUIS CASTONI

SEVENTH SCRIPTURE OF LIFE

September 19th In The Year 2027 D.A.

Announcer: "Today Is September 19, 2027, D.A.And We'd Like To Interrupt Our Regular Scheduled Programming To Bring You This Special Report. Live From Wgn News, *Here's Kent Brunsworth.*"

"Brunsworth Here, Good Afternoon **Occupied Chicago**, This News Just In. Only A Few Hours After Court Arraignment, Mr. ChristOn M Larson Has Been Released, On One Million-Dollar Bond Made By Lorenzo. The BRAZOS Rule Of Law Was Very Astonished, By The Mysterious Appearance Of Larson's Attorney Marla Carter. Ms. Carter Provided Her License, Although She Was Not A Member Of BRAZOS Bar Association. In **Occupied Chicago**, However; Ms. Carter Is An Attorney Out Of Champaign, Illinois. The District Attorneys Along With Judge Julian Kharnas Were Equally In Shock! By The Re-Appearance Of Mr. Larson After The Ruling Of His So-Called Passing Away, Some Nine Months Ago."

"The Home State Celebrity's So-Called Passing Away Silenced The Entire City. And Was Deeply Felt Among The Abyssinians, In The Month Of December 5, 2026, D.A. Shortly After, The Mourning Of Mr. Larson, It Was Quickly Overshadowed By The Meteorites, Smashing Into The Office Of Mayor Elite Nimrod Sinnah. The Catastrophic Event Destroyed Nineteen City Blocks, In Which The Sears Tower Became The New City Hall."

"After The Messiah Like Survival Of The Mayor Elite. During The Night 9Sacred Starships Were Spotted All Over **Occupied Chicago**. B.R.L-Illiana Chiefs Immediately Visited The Grave Site Of Mr. Larson, Only To Find The Grave Site Already Desecrated. Mr. Larson Read His Charges. For Falsifying His So-Called Symbolic Passing Away And Teaching High-Minded Mysteries. He Is The Principal Suspect Being Accused, By The BRAZOS Rule Of Law As The Alleged Mysterious Enforcer, Known As Da Larcenni Da Anunnaqi!"

"In Other Late Developments, There Were Reports About A Massive Prison Breakout, At BRAZOS Corporation Center, There Are Unconfirmed Reports About Prisoners, Mostly Street Gangs, Rioting. This Situation Occurred After The News Traveled, About ChristOn M Larson In Custody. They Were Estimating About Close To Nine Thousand Prisoners Heading This Way To Markham. There Was A Silence On The Streets Outside Of The B.R.L-Illiana Office."

"In The BRAZOS Rule Of Law Building, As A Crowd Of Reporters Gathered Around The Building' Front Double Doors. Attorney Marla Carter And ChristOn M Larson Emerged Greeting The Excitement Of The Crowd, And Prisoners From The Prison Outbreak Were Highly Visible Amongst Them. Many News Reporters In Fear Dispersed Away From The Doors. As They Noticed The Prisoners And Nine Million Warring Angels, Known As Former Gang Members That Marched In Like Soldiers. A Hundred Of Combined BRAZOS Military Chipped Police, Patrolling The Downtown Area, By The BRAZOS Rule Of Law Office, Quickly Ran Away As They Dropped Their Weapons In Fear!"

The News Reporter Kent Brunsworth Continued With His Report As He Was Tried To Speculate The Amount Of Prisoners And Nine Million Warring Angels Known As Former Gang Members. "Oh Stress Thomas! Wait! Look Over There!" Brunsworth Pointed Behind The Cameraman Who Was Facing Brunsworth. "Turn You, Dummy! Look Behind You! There They Are, Oh Stress!" The Cameraman Faced Behind Him. Adjusted His View And Saw A Mass Of Heads Moving Quickly In Their Direction. "It's…It's A Number I Can't Count! There's Just Too Many Heads! And The Train Still Hasn't Stopped Yet!" Brunsworth Shouted As Thomas Faced The Herd That Spread Across The Entire Street Engulfing The Sidewalks And Alleyways As Well. They Were Coming Out Of Everywhere. "Keep The Damn Cameras Rolling Thomas! Stress! I've Never Seen Anything Like This! Wait, Take A Shot Of Mr. Larson On The Steps!

Brunsworth Became Even More Excited Grasping For Words. "Oh, Stress! This Is Unheard Of….Look! Look The Police Are Running Towards The Prisoners! Oh No The Police Are Getting Their Asses Kicked! I Mean, I Mean They Are Trying To Stop This Hostility!" He Said Trying

To Remain Professional. "Aw Damn That…They're Screwed… Hold On….Wait…Wait…Mr. Larson Is Saying Something!" Brunsworth Went Quiet.

"Wait, The Prisoners Stopped Fighting…Turn The Cameras On Larson…Look, Look! He Is Throwing Up Some Hand Signal…He Is Doing A Hand Signal Or Something! They Stopped, They Just Stopped And, And Larson Is Now Walking Towards His Vehicle. I Cannot Believe What I Am Seeing Here! "They Are Protecting Him Or Something!" Brunsworth Held His Head In Astonishment. "Damn Thomas, We Missed His Speech! How Could We Have Missed That? The Car's Leaving." Thomas Turned The Camera Back To Kent Brunsworth. Whose Back Was Turned To The Camera As He Stared At Larson's Vehicle Leaving The Scene. He Suddenly Jumped When He Heard Some Shouting Behind Him And Turned To Face Thomas' Camera.

Brunsworth Stared At The Crowd. "Hey, Stupid Start The Damning Van! There's Way Too Many Amnesia Negus Out Here, And Hell I'm Black! Stress Thomas Jump In Van…Start It Up! Damn This Job, I Quit!" The Camera Shut Off. Jan Lysalot Took Over The Broadcasting,

"*WGN News Here,*" She Said Scrambling For Something To Say. "*I Would Like To Apologize To Our Viewers. Our Reporter Lost Control Of Himself…Mr. Larson Got Released Early On Bond Through Insufficient Evidence After Being Interrogated By B.R.L-Illiana Arch Chiefs. Also Released On Bail Today Was Mr. Marquis Castoni. His Charges Were Truth Conceiling Conspiracies, As Well As Other Criminal Charges. There Is No Evidence To Link Either Larson Or Castoni. To The So-Called Passing Away Of Mayor Elite Nimrod Sinnah, Who Was Assassinated Early This Morning. And Local Authorities Are Trying To Connect The Mayor Elite's Passing Away With The Explosion. That Occurred Early This Morning As Well. According To Lieutenant Brian Brown, Of The 66th Precinct Task Force. It Was Speculated, After Internal Affairs Examined The Rubble Of The Explosion! At The Warehouse Of Stanley's Office Supplies. Which At Least Forty Million Dollars Worth Of Cocaine Was On The Premises Before The Bombing. Internal Affairs Noted That The Officers, In The Warehouse Were Already Under Indictment For Drug Trafficking Corruption.*"

"He Refused To Give Names Under Strict Instruction From Occupied Chicago's B.R.L-Illiana Director Greg Jentson. Reporting Live From Wgn Studios I'm Jan Lysalot, In For Kent Brunsworth And This Has Been A Wgn News Special Report."

Larson's Next Stop Was To Confront Marquis Castoni Before Going About To Search For His Companions, So He Made His Way Back In The Midst Of All The Eyes That Lay Upon Castoni's Bar.

Larson Speaks…

Our Last Moments Became Very Crucial. BRAZOS Out Of Fear Was Trying To Hold Onto Borrowed Time. They Were Attempting To Eliminate Da Ill-State Enforcers. But Were Unable To Deal With Larcenni Da Anunnaqi's Massive Judgment Upon The Earth Before My Trial Had Begun And BRAZOS Knows This New Abode Is A Huge Problem For Them For That Great And Dreadful Day Has Come! BRAZOS Is Going To Make War! But I Still Need To Know Who Held The Title BRAZOS Supreme Chancellor? They Persecuted Me Even Through My Presumed So-Called Passed Away. I Walked Away From BRAZOS And Still They Had To Disturb My Peace."

Lorenzo Only Lives By His Name… Chaos. We Got Caught Up In This Case, And Chaos Bailed Me Out…I Got A Little Concerned. Da Ill-State Enforcers Has That Unwritten Rule: Your Word Is Your Bond, And If You Put Your Hands In My Face, I'll Break Your Damn Wrist! But I Did Not Complete My Teaching With Them. Lorenzo Was The Last Person, Who Was Going To Serve Time For Someone Else's Crime." Cleni, Jr., Already Had His Foot In The Grave, So He Was Pretty Much Desperate For Anything. And Then There's…Castoni JR He Was Willing To De-Materialize Any Of Us If He Felt We Were Stopping Him From Becoming The Next 'Don.' And As For The Rest Of The Members, They Were Going To Follow Orders Out Of Loyalty. Or Maybe They'd Follow The Orders Of Whoever Provided The Most Reasonable Escape Routes. So I Knew What Was First On My Agenda. I Had To Finish My Business With Castoni. I Figured He Might Be At The Club, So I Went There First."

"I Saw That The BRAZOS Police Was Tailing Me, But I Didn't Pay Them Any Mind. To My Surprise, Castoni Was There, And Was Willing To Talk To Me. His Conversation Was Somewhat Different Now. Castoni Seemed To Have Mixed Emotions. He Knew A Lot Of Damage Had Been Done To Our Relationship, But Still Business Was The Business.

Castoni Took A Deep Breath And Just Said, *"Believe It Or Not, Kid, I'm Glad To See You Again...Really! So I Guess You're Here To Finish What You Started Right?"* "And To That Statement, By One Of My Greatest Teachers, Threw Me Off Guard."

"Yeah, As A Matter Of Fact, I Am! First Off, Call Your Bodyguards Off. I'm Not Here To De-Materialize You!" *"So What Do You Want Then?'* He Asked Me. "Just A Few Questions, That's All," I Told Him. Castoni Looked Past Me To Thanney And Bruno And Told Them To Leave And Give Him Some Private Time. Then He Said To Me, *"Okay Kid Let Me Hear What You Got To Say."* "As Long As You Have Known Me, Why Would You Send Someone To Try And Take The Life Of My Child? You're Spiritual Son! Why Or How Could You Do Something So Vicious To Any Child?"

Castoni Responded, *"He Never Had In His Life Given An Order! In Which A Child Was To Pass Away. He Said He'd Been Crying For Weeks. Over His Spiritual Son's Passing,"* Although Castoni Has His Way Of Doing Things. So I Told Him, "Maybe That Wasn't Your Motive, But It Happened! This Child Was Buried Six Feet Deep. He Never Did Anything Wrong To Anybody!" He Said, *"Listen To Me!"* *"You Know The Scriptures Better Than Anyone! Why Look For The Living Amongst The Passed Away? That Part Was My Doing—You Got To Believe Me!"*

You've Taken Some Shocks At Me Before Too," I Reminded Him. *"Wrong Larson! Wrong!"* *"I Only Sent Shots At Your Street Soldiers...Not Lorenzo, Alesha, Cleni's Son, My Own Son Castoni JR., Or You! Yes, We Had Our Differences; You're My Spiritual Nephew. Please Understand Me On This. I've Always Treated You Like A Nephew...Didn't I?"* He Pleaded. "Yes," I Replied. *"I've Always Looked Out For You, Made Sure That You Were Taken Care Of First... Right?"* He Confirmed.

"Still We Went To War, And You Sent People To Take Us Out!" I Shouted To Him.

Castoni Tried To Explain, *"Ok, Ok. Yes, I Did, But For Two Reasons Only. First, You Did Business Behind My Back And Made My Competitors See Me As Weak. The Second Reason Is Pure And Simple...My People Trained Da Ill-State Enforcers To Be Enforcers. I Only Did That To Reassure My Enemies That I...Castoni...Was The Boss. That Was All...Nothing More, Nothing Less. But I Hope You Can Believe That I Wasn't Responsible For The Symbolic Ceremony Ritual For Your Son, Which Was A Clone. My Promise To You!"*

I Stared At The Man And Told Him, "For Some Strange Reason Castoni, I Believe You. But I've Got To Question You About The Drive-By Setup That Alesha And I Barely Escaped." *"What Drive-By Are You Talking About?"* "The Night I Had To Disappear!" I Told Him. *"Sorry, But I'm Not Following You,"* Castoni Wiped The Sweat From His Forehead. "It Was The Night Chaos Was Put Into The Hospital. Nine Days Later My Son… I Mean The Cloned Was So-Called Passed Away," I Couldn't Remove My Eyes From The Old Man. *"Kid I Have No Idea What You're Talking About! Again, I'm Not Responsible For That Either. But There's A Question I've Wanted To Ask You,"* The Man Said Looking Away From Me. "What's That?" I Asked Him. Castoni Returned His Stare To Me In A Mischievous Way. *"How Were You Able To Get A Hold Of That Cush?"*

I Considered Carefully What To Say And Then Answered, "Well I'll Give You A Hint...He Practices Deception And The Art Of Law, Liars, And Lawyers." *"I See!"* Castoni Was Shocked. *"So What Are Your Plans Now?"* He Asked Me. "First, I've Got To See Past This Case. What Do You Think The Outcome Might Be?" I Wanted Him To Let His Guard Down, So I Removed My Behavior Of Suspicions From Him. *"Well By Just Looking Into Your Eyes, I Can See That You Already Got This Figured Out. See, That's Why I Liked You So Much. You Got A Proper Way Of Outsmarting People. This Is Why I Could Only Choose You To Be My Successor."*

"So, What About Castoni JR.?" I Asked Him, *"Well, He Is Learning More About Responsibility... To Be The Next Boss. Larson It's Time For Me To Retire, And With All The Enemies I've Had For Over Forty Years. I'm Still Here And Staying Just A Few Steps Ahead Has Many Advantages. But I Must Warn You That This Court Case Will Be The Passed Away Case Ever! Kid, You're Trying*

To Take On BRAZOS By Yourself. It Will Be Nearly Impossible To Find Out, The Real Ringleaders Without Help. But Who Knows, If Da Ill-State Enforcers Becomes A Living Entity Again Things Could Be Interesting. Listen, You're Gonna Need Castoni JR., Cleni JR, Lorenzo, And Even Alesha. No Matter How Many People Are Involved, All Systems Function The Same. There Is Always Going To Be The One Guy Who Is Always Connected To Everybody—Even If He Doesn't Know It Himself."

Castoni Obviously Knew More Than He Portrayed But I Understood What He Was Saying. BRAZOS Had Plenty Of People Enforcing The Law, And I Realized That Any Testimony Against BRAZOS Could Never Happen. Castoni Said His Criminal Charges Were Like Traffic Tickets—They'd Just Disappear If He Threw Enough Money At Them. He Asked Me If I'd Been Interrogated, And I Told Him Two Hours.

He Asked If It Was City Cops, And I Said, "No B.R.L-Illiana Chiefs... Arch Chief Michaels... And The Director, Chief Jentson." Castoni Asked If Jentson Had Mentioned Him. I Said No, But That Chief Michaels Did. I Was Uncomfortable Not Knowing Why He Asked Me That. So Castoni Said Chief Jentson Was Nothing But A Puss. He Said Back In The Days When He First Opened His Club, Jentson Used To Mess With Him All The Time. But Soon After The BRAZOS Organization Took Over, Things Changed Dramatically. I Asked Him How Things Changed And He Told Me That He Hired Francis Aurelius For His Club Expansion. When That Bastard Jentson Showed Up, Aurelius Had A Talk With Him And He Never Bothered Castoni Again. I Told Castoni The Final Showdown Was About To Begin And He Said The High Court Were Watching Me Closely. Then Castoni Said He Had Two More Questions For Me. First, He Asked Why I Faked My Passing.

"Well Castoni, Like You Once Said, To Master The Art Of Spiritual Eyes Of Deceiving Faces, You Must First Manipulate The Power Of The Six Ether Mind, Even Through Mentally Passed Away! Besides, Can You Think Of A Better Place Than Ascended? Watching Over Your Enemies And Them Not Knowing?" Castoni Approved, *"Well Put The Kid, Well Put!"* Then He Asked Me If I Knew Who The Enforcer Larcenni Da Anunnaqi Really Was. I Told Him I Knew. I Left

Saying I'd Talk To Him When Everything Was Over. I Wasn't There, But I Later Learned What Happened Exactly Twenty Minutes After I Had Left Castoni's. Three Unknown Men Approached Him. Only A Few Words Were Exchanged And Then The Don Was Passed Away.

Thanney And Bruno Attempted To Aid Their Boss, And They Passed Away One Of The Gunmen. The Other Two Were Both Wounded, But They Escaped. Chiefs Rushed In, But No One Was Arrested. I Headed Towards The Old Building That Once Housed Da Ill-State Enforcers When We Were Strong. "To My Surprise, Everyone Was There...Lorenzo, Castoni JR., And Cleni JR! They All Stared At Me As If They Were Waiting For My Orders. They Were More Than Happy To See Me. After Our Reunion, I Told Them That I Would Explain Everything Later. I Was Scooping Out The Building, And It Was All The Same; Every Piece Of Furniture Was Kept In The Same Position."

Lorenzo Approached Me, *"Larson, How Do You Know About Da Crystal City? Man, That Stress Got Everybody Messed Up!"* I Gave Him A Short Answer. He Nodded His Head. "There Is Something I Need To Talk To You About In Private," Lorenzo Walked Me Over Towards The Door. "I Got Jo Da Posey And Lorenzo Da Chaos, And Everybody Else On The Phone. And Told Them Plan 99 Is Going Down! I Told Them We Were Going To The Office Where The Bigger Crime Boss Lived," He Informed Me.

****

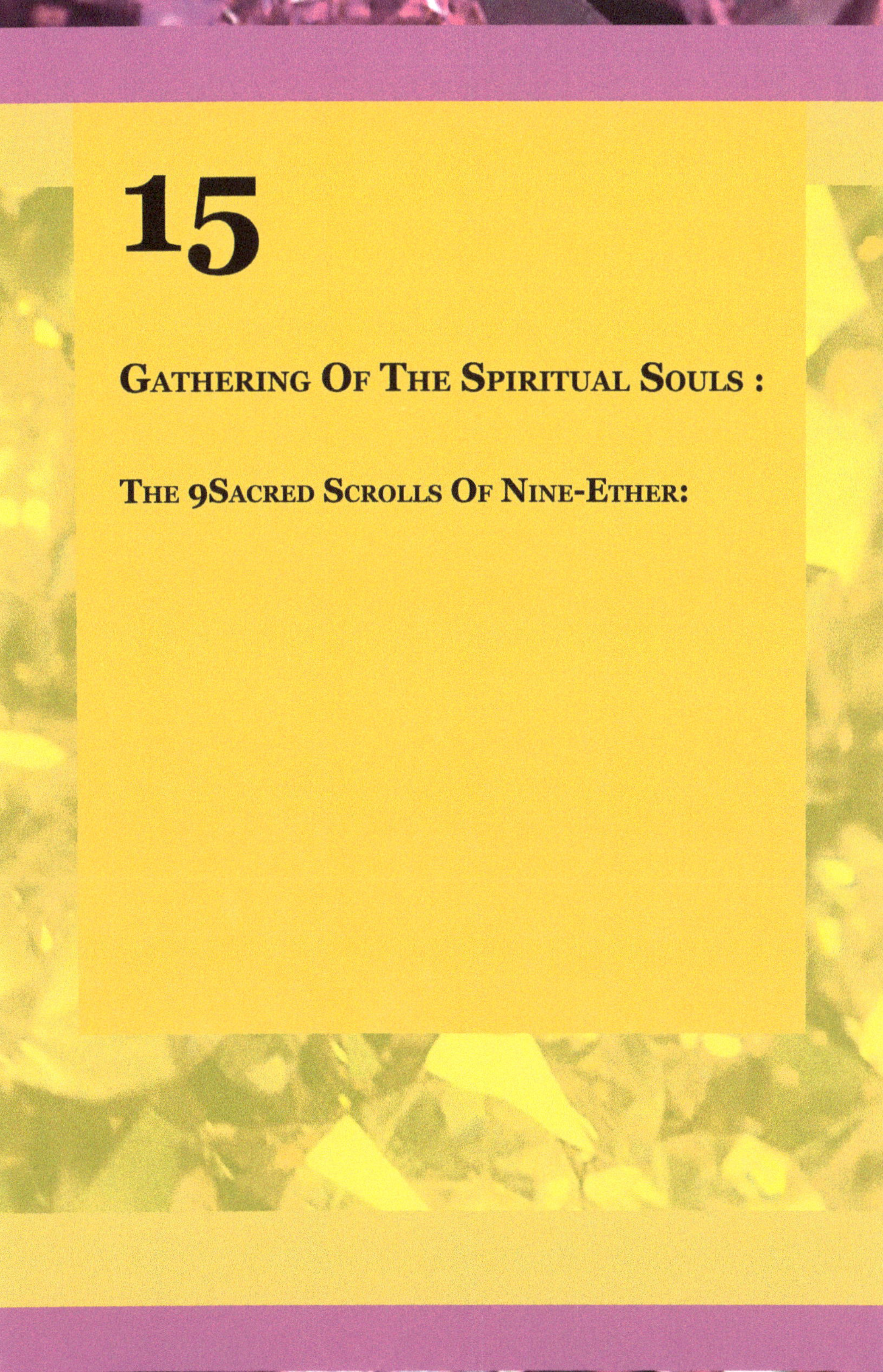

15

GATHERING OF THE SPIRITUAL SOULS :

THE 9SACRED SCROLLS OF NINE-ETHER:

We Headed Towards Downtown **Occupied Chicago** And Went To The Sears Tower. We Saw Jo Da Posey And Lorenzo Da Chaos There Already Whooping All Of The Protection Lined Up For BRAZOS. Yeah, He Was Showing Off, Just Laughing While Adding To The Torment Of Whatever Had The Life. We Have United Again, Da Ill-State Enforcers. We Made Our Journey To The Top Easy By Simply Levitating, And Smashing In The Walls Anyone That Got In Our Way."

"We Crashed Into The Law Office Of Francis Aurelius, And Were Utterly Shocked! There, Right Beside Aurelius, Was B.R.L-Illiana, Director Jentson." Aurelius Grinned At Me Hissing Like A Snake, *"Well Look Who's Back!"* He Said, *"Mr. Larson—So How's Your Case Coming Along?"* I Was Not Shocked But Pretended To Be. "Supreme Chancellor Aurelius! Wow! Da Serpent Finally Reveals Himself! After 3,600 Years Since The Last Encounter, You Are Now Exposing Yourself Because Your Time's Up," I Told Him.

Aurelius Was Stunned And Paused For A Moment, "You Been Here All This Time. Damn, But That Doesn't Matter Now! Universal Law?" Jentson Not Understanding Any Of This Language Turned To Aurelius. *"Universal Law? What About BRAZOS Rule Of Law?"* I Responded To The Ignorant Director, "When The Supreme Energy Force Of Green Was Created, The Opposite Lesser Energy Of Yellow Light Was Also Born, Making A Supreme Balance Of The Universal Law. The Green Light Will Always Be Here." Jentson Did Not Understand The Metaphor, Then Changed The Subject, *"Kid, You Are So Passed Away...For Real Now...All Of You Negative Souls Are!"* He Flung His Arms About Recklessly. I Could Tell By Aurelius' Expression That He Could Not Stand The Man. However, I Still Ignored Jentson's Idle Threats And Reminded Him To Look In The Air, "Better Yet It Would Be Better For You Just To De-Materializ Yourself Than To Suffer The Wrath!" Jentson Laughed In Ignorance, *"There's Something You Should Know."*

"I Am The One Who Made The Orders To Have Alesha Franacia Of Ancient Order Of Abyssinia Passed Away!" That's When The Rage Filled My Body, But I Learned Not To Be Moved By The Evil Words Of Snakes. He Wanted Control Of My Actions, But I Stood Firm And Gave Resistance. I Refused To Acknowledge Jentson And Decided He Would Taste The Pain Later. Aurelius Spoke Firmly, *"Why Did He De-Materialize Your Baby? Is That What I See In Your Nine Twinkling Eye? Tut Ankh ChristOn Ruled For Nine Years. And As You Know ChristOn, In Those Days, The Prince Became The Successor. Therefore, Ankh Ensan ChristOn Took To The Throne After Some Misfortune Because She Did Not Follow The Elders' Rules. But With All The Great Sciences Taught To Them By The Elders. They Cloned The Body Of Tut Ankh ChristOn, Due To Political Reasons And Ankh Ensan ChristOn Faked Her So-Called Symbolic Passing Away. This Has Been A Generational Vendetta ChristOn! You Didn't Know?"*

Aurelius Stared At ChristOn. *"Did You Know That Jentson's Grandfather Was The Brain Behind The Smuggling Of Ankh Ensan ChristOn's Tomb In April 1912 A.D.? He Had His Wife And His Newborn Baby On The Ship With Him. While They Traveled The Seas. Well, The Tomb Was Cursed With The Prayers Of Anubis, Causing The Ship To Sink, De-Materializing Families… Including Jentson's Grandparents Leaving His Father As An Orphan. His Father Would Later Learn. The Knowledge That Ankh Ensan ChristOn Was Not Only A Physical Body. But Also A Spirit That Incarnates Every 99 Years. We Know Who Alesha Franacia Is! She Was The Reason Jentson's Father Was Raised With A Tomb Smuggling Sadistic Family!"* Aurelius Was Angry, And Jentson Could Not Stop Staring At Us With Anger.

"You Know What's So Familiar About This ChristOn, Is That The Elders Passed Away My Father Too! They Never Loved Me! Only Wanted Me To Worship Them Because I Was Different Genetically From Them. Jentson Was Only Taught Hate By His Father Because That's All He Knew…To Steal, Lie And De-Materialize To Get What He Wanted. So He Was Ordered By Me. To De-Materialize Alesha Franacia Of Ancient Order Of Abyssinia. So Her Child Could Grow Parent-Less And Heartless. Just The Same, And We Would Have Made Sure Of That. However,

When Our Gunmen Called Out! To Alesha Franacia Of Ancient Order Of Abyssinia With Her Back Turned To Them. She Spun Around To Two Sniper Bullets, Penetrating The Baby She Was Holding To Her Chest!" Aurelius And Jentson Both Smiled.

"It Is Now The 100th Year Anniversary Of The Titanic. So Jentson Would Like To Pay Respect To His Grandparents Who Died In That Ship ChristOn." Aurelius Was Filled With Evil, And There Was No Doubt About It. *"Now I Am The Brains Behind BRAZOS,"* Aurelius Stood Tall Spreading His Trench Coat While He Placed His Hands In His Pocket. *"Didn't You Read My Revelations? Occupied Chicago Is My Last Location. Your People Accepted The New World Order, Of The Twenty-First Century. They Embraced It, And There Was Nothing Anyone Could Do About It. I Must Admit, Though,"* Aurelius Continued, *"Mr. Castoni Had Your Crew Trained Very Well. But Who Summoned Da 19 Great Balls Of Fire?"* He Inquired.

I Answered Him, "The One Who Is Gonna Close Your Kingdom Down! How Does It Feel Knowing That Your Very Existence Will Be No More?" Aurelius Was Shaken By The Thought But Still Held On To His Arrogance. He Said He'd Had No Choice Because We Were Already Destroying Up His Business. But Then He Was Even More Surprised When I Faked My So-Called Symbolic Passing Away. And He Said The Role Of The Mysterious Assassin Larcenni Da Anunnaqi, Turned Everything Upside Down. He Questioned If I Were The Mysterious One And I Told Him I Wasn't.

"Maybe So, But I Know You Know Who This Enforcer Is! And Because Of That, Mr. Castoni Had To Die, Cause Larcenni Da Anunnaqi! Decided You Were Alive Was More Important." From The Corner Of My Eye, I Noticed Castoni JR. Was Affected By The Remark, *"You're Gonna Die For That, You Sleazy Sinner!"* He Stiffened His Body And Inched Forward.

"Castoni JR., Let Me Handle This, Okay?" I Stretched My Arm Out In Front Of Him Blocking His Movement. Castoni JR. Was Angry, But He Agreed. Jentson Suddenly Said, *"Yeah, Well You're About To Join Your Daddy,"* He Said Laughing A Heavy And Loud; He Was Obnoxious. *"I Just Wanted To Let You Know That Gamb...Ella!"* Jentson Was Trying So Hard To Tempt

Castoni JR.. And Making His Name Sound Feminine Was Out Of Line. But Still, Castoni JR.

Remained Calm And Refused To Make His Emotions Control Him. That, However, Pissed

Jentson Off Even More! *"Let It Be Known!"* He Shouted Angrily As His Face Had Gotten To A

Good Degree Of Redness Instigating The Fire, "That I Was Responsible For Alesha Franacia,

Of Ancient Order Of Abyssinia's Daughter To ChristOn! I So-Called Passed Away Your Son!"

I Felt The Thunder In The Room. It Was Lightning Clapping, Striking Sound And The Room

Vibrated, Slapping Everyone In The Face. I Did Not Budge. The Man Wanted To Die. He Was

Definitely On A Suicide Mission. I Was Facing A Man That Was Less Than Human In My Eyes

And Wondered Why He Too Did Not Transform Into A Cannibalistic Hominid, "Have You

Forgotten What I Told You Jentson? That I Have Wisdom And Overstanding Beyond Years?

Trust Me On This! I Am Not The Only One. Who Knows About Deception!"

All Of My Boys Held My Back To Restrain Me. "Why Did You Try To Pass Away My Son?"

I Felt The Burning In My Throat Holding Back The Tears And Anger. But As A Man, I Knew

No Tears Would Be Flowing Tonight, Only Blood. "Well, I Guess You Got A Punish Coming

To Jentson! You Want To War With The Outcome Of What Things Are To Be; Then I Got One

For You. The Real Marquis Castoni Is In Ethiopia, Watching Over My Children! After All, He

Is The 22nd Elder Zagzagul, Known As Enqi, Da Annunaqi Of Soul Snatching." Jentson And

Azazl Could Not Speak! "Alesha Franacia Of Ancient Order Of Abyssinia Is There With Him!

And The One You Passed Away, Was Castoni's Clone."

Aurelius Started To Smile And Clap His Hands, *"Bravo, You Got Us! I Mean You Have Powerful*

Friends In Secret High Places. Now How Do I Know That? Well When You Were Buried, Soon

After This So-Called Mystery Enforcer Surfaced, I Realized The Name Was Extremely Familiar.

Larcenni Da Anunnaqi? Well, I Knew Who It Was And Fully Aware Of This Supreme Being, One

Of The 24 Elders Who Judges All. The 13th Elder To Be Exact! And So I Knew Better Than To

Confront Such A Being Face To Face, I Know Better Than That! There Were Reports Of Other

Enforcers. Moving About The City Causing Destruction, But Da Ill-State Enforcers, Well You Guys Couldn't Perform On That Level. Because I Tested You Guys Out," Aurelius Smiled Wickedly.

*"I Am The One Who Sent The Foreign Enforcers. To Falasha, Beta Israel Park Personally. Your People Were Good, But Not Great. With All The Thrills I Had My Men Dig Up Your Grave. There Was No Surprise That There Was A Cloned Body! So I Decided, Why Not Look At Your Daughter's Tomb. And What Do You Know The Same Thing! Well Before I Could Eliminate. Alesha Franacia Of Ancient Order Of Abyssinia, She Was Nowhere To Be Found. I Became Suspicious Of Her After She Was Seen At The Halstead Casino. I Never Saw Her Again Until Three Months Ago, Which Lead Me To You, ChristOn M Larson.So That's When I Knew For Certain That You Staged Your Symbolic Spiritual Soul Ceremony. And Ritual Because **9Sacred Starships** Were Seen In The Area. So My Only Real Question Is, Who Helped You And How Were You Capable Of Doing It Under Our Eyes?"*

Chief Jentson Waved His Gun Acting Like Aurelius' Puppet, Which He Was. *"None Of You Are Going To Make It Out Of Here Alive!"* I Was Going To Answer. When Suddenly, I Witnessed Judge Julian Kharnas Hiding Out In The Back, But Then Aurelius Interrupted My Thoughts. *"Jentson Put That Gun Away, It's Useless Now! Oh, And ChristOn,"* Aurelius Stared At Jentson While He Placed The Gun In The Holster. *"Alesha Franacia Of Ancient Order Of Abyssinia, Has Made An Appointment With Me;" "She Should Be Here...To Pass Away...In About Twenty Minutes!"* I Was Growing Annoyed By The Fallen Being By The Minute, "Chief Jentson, Can You Trust All Of Your Fellow Chiefs? Jentson Looked At Me In Confusion With A Dumb Look On His Face. Let Me Tell You Something I Know, Just Bear With Me. You Remember My Attorney, Makedah Carter, Right? Well, She Is Not An Attorney; She Is My Guardian, She Is A Visitor! She Is Not Interested In Upholding BRAZOS Rule Of Law! I Mean Damn, How Can You Fight A System That Has You On Trial? I Told You I Wanted To Be There! I Arranged And Prepared For All Of This To Happen!" Suddenly, There Was A Complete Silence In That Office. Everyone Present Felt A Strong Very Powerful Energy Approaching. The Double Door

Entrance To Francis Aurelius Office Flung Open By A Strong Wind. Loud Echoing Footsteps Were Approaching And Everyone's Attention Was Focused On The Strange Power. Suddenly, Arch Chief Sham Michaels Walked In, Along With Companions. Arch Chief Gabriy'el, Arch Chief Uriel.

Arch Chief Michaels Entered The Room With His Weapon Drawn, Pointed Directly At The B.R.L-Illiana Director's Head. ***"Francis Aurelius And Director Greg Jentson," "You're Both Under Arrest!"*** "Then Suddenly Out Of Nowhere," "About 200 Men Ran Into The Large Room From Another Door And Opened Fire Towards Their Target, Arch Chief Michaels. We All Found Cover In A Few Seconds As It All Happened So Quickly."

Michaels's Entourage Was Being Slammed With High-Powered Bullets. However, The Slugs Did Not Penetrate The Spiritual Beings Who Were Returning Firebombs From Their Palms To The Opposing Side, Blasting Them From The Front Of The Pack, Exposing More Worker Bees. I Looked Up From Where I Was Crouched And Saw Aurelius Shoot A Yellow Beam Of Light In Arch Chief Michaels's Direction. Michaels Stood His Ground, However, Catching The Yellow Beam, Absorbing The Energy Painlessly Into His Body." But Then Something Else Happened, Michaels Folded Forward Squeezing The Entire Beam Of Light Back Out Of His Body, Creating A Bubble Around Him."

He Began To Levitate High Above All The Heads In The Room, With Firebombs And Bullets Flying Below His Feet. Another Strong Wind Blew In Engulfing His Body Within The Beamed Bubble. Spinning Him Faster Than The Seconds That Passed, Shutting Down All The Blasts Of Fire Being Thrown From Each Side Of The Room. My Eyes Could Not Believe The Wonder; Arch Chief Michaels Transformed Into Da Highest Anunnaqi On Earth! White, Woolly, Hair Grew Out Of His Head, Extending To His Shoulder. His Flesh Glowed A Bronze Hue, Never Seen In This Reality And His Black Garb Lifted In The Air, Then Collapsed Onto His Body As He Descended To The Ground. No One Could Have Explained What They Had Just Witnessed.

Arch Angel Miykaa'el Proclaimed In Loud Thunderous Voice, Electro-Lightning Striking To Da 200 Fallen Angels! *"And I Will Destroy You Azazl Sama'el, Like I Destroyed Your Father Zuen Anzu!"* The Entire Room Began To Shake! Arch Angel Miykaa'el Released, A Charge Of Lightning Bolts Of Over 76 Trillion Controlled Watts! Instantly! Turning Some Of The Fallen Soldiers Into Dust, Electrocuting Them Completely Out Of Existence! The Remaining Fallen Now Witnessed The Only True Power Of Da Most High Father ANU! He Was Obviously The One Who Sent Arch Angel Miykaa'el To This Planet, And I Was There To Witness It.

Aurelius And Jentson Had Taken Cover Behind A Desk, While Chief Uriel, Castoni JR. And Cleni JR. All Released Lightning Bolts Of Utter Destruction! Eliminating The Rest Of The Fallen Fleet, Who Were Firing Off Too From Their Side. This Was When Aurelius Seized The Moment In His Hands! He Sent His Lightning Strikes Towards Me, Destroying The Object That Protected Me For A Short While. As I Quickly Dodged Aurelius' Lightning Strikes, I Felt My Body Ignite Into An Internal Flame And Felt My Eyes Harden. My Body Tore Painfully Within, Ripping The Flesh Below My Upper Epidermis, Tearing The Skin From My Palms. The More I Dodged Aurelius' Lightning, The More I Realized I Wasn't After All.

Like Arch Angel Miykaa'el, I Realized That I Was Absorbing All The Strikes That Were Being Thrown At Me. My Etherian Being The 23Rd Elder Sandalfun Stapled My Feet To The Ground And All Six Lightning Strikes Aurelius Threw At Me Entered My Expanded Chest One By One. It Remained In My Heart Chakra, Traveled Through My Blood Exiting My Hands, Blasting Aurelius Into The Wall. I Ran Past A Mirror And Saw My Eyes; They Were Blood Shot Red.

Aurelius Pulled Himself From The Wall And Fought Back By Trying To Counter His Strikes With My Lightning Bolts. He Struggled To Get The Upper Hand And Convinced Himself He Had Me Tired As His Strikes Hit Off My Energy Field Off My Body. Just When Aurelius Thought He Had The Opportunity To Finish Me Off, Something Wild Hit Him Off His Feet. It Was Arch Angel Miykaa'el. He Charged Aurelius With A Heated Burst Of Energy; Shock Waves Held For More Than What We Were Thinking Of Counting, Causing Aurelius' Entire

Body To Lift In The Air. The Light Penetrated Through His Shape-Shifting Body, With The Light Emitting Through Every Hole Of His Epidermis. He Was The Light Bulb, And Arch Angel Miykaa'el Was The Electricity.

Arch Angel Miykaa'el Released The Burnt Immortal Azazl From Mid-Air, Collapsing Recklessly To The Floor. Who In The World Did These Fallen Fleet Think They Were Dealing With? Chief Jentson's Eyes Were Blinking Fast As He Watched From A Distance, Exactly Six Feet Away From His Crippled Looking Partner In Crime. I Could See Jentson And Feel His Fear And Thoughts. He Was Now Starting To Feel His Whole Existence Leaving Him, Slowing Slipping Into The Bottomless Pit. All The Color Drained From His Face, And He Began To Age From The Stress And Confusion.

"Arch Angel Miykaa'El? Da High Priest, Servant Of Da Most High Anu?" Jentson's Words Got Caught In His Throat, As He Fell To His Knees. Lo, But It Was Too Late, And It Occurred In The Blink Of An Eye. The Light From Arch Angel Miykaa'el's Eyes Instantly Whitened Blinding Jentson. *"Ahhhhh!"* He Wailed In Tremendous Pain With Blood Flowing, Through His Tear Ducks And Nose. The Flash Began Decomposing His Evil Spirit Down To Nothing!"

Aurelius Gasped For Air That He Did Not Need. Yet He Was In Intense Pain Staring With Rage. At One Of His Apprentices Suffering In His Name. Azazl Laughed Out Of The Chest Of Aurelius And Blood Spewed From His Mouth And Covered His Teeth And Tongue. He Was Rejoicing. *"Tell Me Something Arch Angel Miykaa'El,"* He Struggled To Say, As He Remained Slouching On The Ground Of The Smoky Room, *"Were You The One Who Protected This Kid? He Deserves To Pass Away! Pass Away! Don't You Understand Michaels? You May Have Resided In The Body Of A Human But The BRAZOS Organization, You Took The Same Oath As I Did Make By Me For The Fallen Fleet! You're On My Side Now! Don't Deny It!"* Azazl Growled And Began To Shape Shift Into A Taller Man. His Beard Grew To His Chest, And The Hair On His Head Grew Straight To The Middle Of His Back While His Skin Lighted, But Still Stained With Blood. He Now Resembled A Persian. "You Just Made More Enemies Because Of These Enforcers!"

"Listen Sama'el You Shaytaan!" "You Serpent And A Filthy Seed Of Zuen, No High Minded Father Would Ever Allow His High Minded Son To Suffer!" Arch Angel Miykaa'el Flashed His Royal Marking, Made Different Than All The Others. It Was **Da 9Ruby Supreme King Ring!** My Heart Jumped In Utter Surprised, And I Was Not The Only One. Azazl Looked Totally Mind Boggled As Well. *"What In The Hell Am I Hearing? Why Wasn't This News Transferred To Me Either?"* Azazl Was Weak But Still Tried To Speak With Force. *"So He Was Under Your Protection, To This Symbolic Spiritual Soul Ceremony And Ritual Right?"*

"That's Correct Sama'el! All That Money You Paid Out To Your Workers, They Ate It And Fed Themselves In Desires And Emotions! It Wasn't Hard To Distract Them!" Arch Angel Michaels Spoke Words That Upset The Growling Being. *"See, I've Been Doing Investigations On You For Quite Some Time Now! I Could Not Find Which Person You Were Hiding Yourself In! That Chief Jentson Was Working For You, Kissing Your Rear, Sinking Himself Deeper Into Hell And Kept Getting In My Way!"* Suddenly Azazl Shot Up From The Ground And Shot Lightning Towards Michaels's Chest, But In A Split Second, I Felt Myself Fly In Front Of My Father. It Struck Me In The Arm With Two More Lightning Strikes That Were Discharged. A Bolt Of Lightning From Nowhere Suddenly Hit Azazl In The Head, Throwing Him Out Of The Air, Crashing To The Floor. A Second Bolt Penetrated Struck His Body Again.

Finally, We Had Come Face To Face With The Last Two Mysterious Enforcers. There In Our Midst Out Of Nowhere Was Marla Carter Garbed In A Beautiful White Attire. She Looked At Everyone In The Room As She Too Began To Transform. This Time, Enter Mother Shaman Larcenni, Da Anunnaqi Known As One Of The Two Holy Ones. 13th Elder. Her Entire Body Glowed With Radiance. And Her White Hair Shone In The Darkness Of The Fire-Engulfed Room. When I Thought It Was All Over I Felt A Touch On My Shoulder, There Stood **Alesha Franacia Of Ancient Order Of Larcenni. Spiritual Soul Of Ankh Ensan ChristOn, Da 9Ruby Princes**s And Da Protector Of Me, Her Husband. *"I Have Been Preparing For This Great And Dreadful Day ChristOn,"* She Said, As I Could Not Believe My Eyes.

"Father Arch Angel Miykaa'el Trained Me, In The Ways Of A Master Teacher. Did You Know That Mother Shaman Larcenni Is Our Spiritual Mother? She Descended From Da Crystal City During The Taking Up Of The 144,000 Blessed Souls To Enforce The Will Of Da Most High Father ANU, EGZIABHER, ELYOWN ELYOWN EL." Although Events Were Happening Around Us, We Both Zoned Out And Spoke Telepathically To Each Other While Beams Of Light And Fire Blasts Bounced Off Of Our Energy Field Of **9Love** That Was Protecting Us.

Ankh Ensan ChristOn Said Mother Shaman Larcenni, Disguised Herself As Marla Carter To Bring Utter Destruction To The BRAZOS Reign. So There We Were **Da Royal 9Ruby Family Of Abyssinia** On The Same Battleground. My Father Arch Angel Miykaa'el's Spiritual Family Was Brought Back Together, After 3,600 Years On The Planet Qi Of The Old Tiamat.Some As Incarnate And Others As Their True Selves. Suddenly A Rich Sound Echoed From Outside Of The Window, Shattering It Completely.

"Oommm! Oommm! Oommm!" "It Was A Freighting Vibration Like No Other." The Windows In The Surrounding Building Also Began Breaking Out Of Their Frames. By That Time Azazl Had Been Totally Blown Out And Could Not Move From His Totally Disabled Body. We Heard His Terrifying Screams Within The Loud Sound Of The Om, And Then A Black Hole Stretched Open From The Ceiling Of The Burning Room, Sucking In A Fire, Burnt Furniture And The Bodies Of Some Of The *"Passed Away"* Fallen. Our Garbs Were Lightly Being Tugged, However, But The Force Seemed To Know What Exactly It Came For!

Azazl Screamed In Pain! As He Shapes Shifted To Over A Million Life Forces. Within Seconds As He Tried Holding Onto The Broken Wall.His Legs Lifted Up High In The Air His Head And Began To Stretch And Tear As The Black Hole Sucked At Him. He Screamed, As His Legs Were Torn Off Into The Vacuum, With His Skin Following Next And Then The Rest Of His Upper Body. The Vortex Shut Immediately. He Was Sentenced And Now Resides In The Realm Of The 6TH Dimension And Which All Of His Children And Followers Were Placed.

Larcenni The 13th Elder, Who Is Of One The Two Holy Ones Are The Supreme Judgers Of The Malevolent Spirits, Father ANU, Egziabher, Elyown Elyown EL Gave This Divine Authority To Them. The Second Of The Holy Ones Is Yaanuwn The 19th Elder Also Known As Arch Angel Miykaa'el, Who Is Also Murdoq, The Ruler Of The Anunnaqis In The Realm Of Malakuwt. They Arrested Ishtar Who Is Also Known As Dina The Moon Demon Deity And Most Of Her Daughters, Who Did Not Repent In Sincerity. Enqi, The Annunaqi Of Soul Snatching, Transported All Of These Beings To The Realm Of The 6th Dimension.

9 Nine Million Warring Angels Are Known As Former Gang Members Who Were All Of One Mind. They Traveled The Streets Carrying Out The Will Of Father ANU! To Bring Justice And Order To The Citizens And There Was No Need For Weapons. They Were Of The New Order Of Healing To Those Who Have Lost Their Souls. As They Taught A Divine Message Given Them By ChristOn M Larson. Also Known As **ChristOn Michaels Qaddi, Leul Anbessa Of Zyon, 9Ruby Prince Of Abyssinia**. Many Human Beings Will Live Their Entire Life; Not Knowing They Are Wise Enough To Know Evil Having No Knowledge Of Good. Ignorance Is A Disease That Has No Cure, Except For The Uncorrupted Spiritual Soul Remedy Of Truth! Every Human Being Can Be Forgiving For Their Sins; As Long As They Repent To The Creator Of God In Sincerity And Forgive Themselves First!

****

9Eyes 9Deceiving Faces 9Mecca Chicago
Da 9th Hour Testimony Of Krassa Amun Giorgis Alias Christon M Larson
And Da Wrath Of Qaddisin, The 13th Elder
Obsidian Gold 9th Edition
Sean Alemayehu Tewodros Giorgis
9Ruby Prince President Intergalactic Ambassador

9EYES 9DECEIVING FACES 9MECCA CHICAGO
DA 9TH HOUR TESTIMONY OF KRASSA AMUN GIORGIS ALIAS CHRISTON M LARSON
AND DA WRATH OF QADDISIN, THE 13TH ELDER
CRIMSON FIRE 9TH EDITION
SEAN ALEMAYEHU TEWODROS GIORGIS
9RUBY PRINCE PRESIDENT INTERGALACTIC AMBASSADOR

9EYES 9DECEIVING FACES 9MECCA CHICAGO
DA 9TH HOUR TESTIMONY OF KRASSA AMUN GIORGIS ALIAS CHRISTON M LARSON
AND DA WRATH OF QADDISIN, THE 13TH ELDER
ROYAL ETHER 9TH EDITION
SEAN ALEMAYEHU TEWODROS GIORGIS
9RUBY PRINCE PRESIDENT INTERGALACTIC AMBASSADOR

URBAN SCIENCE FICTION: SPIRITUALITY BOOK OF REVELATIONS: STARSHIPS UFO'S
LIBRARY OF CONGRESS CONTROL NUMBER: 2026908852
ROYAL ETHER 9TH EDITION
AIR FORCE RESERVE
AIR FORCE RESERVE
AIR FORCE RESERVE
MARTIN LAWRENCE | LEGENDARY COMEDIAN | MOVIE STAR HOLDING THE
BOOK OF AUTHOR FORT HOOD, TEXAS — 2011 9EYES 9DECEIVING FACES

9 YEUX 9 VISAGES TROMPEURS — 9 MECQUE CHICAGO
LE TÉMOIGNAGE DE LA 9TH HEURE DE KRASSA AMUN GIORGIS, ALIAS CHRISTON M LARSON
ET LA COLÈRE DE QADDISIN, LE MYSTÉRIEUX 13TH ANCIEN
OR OBSIDIENNE — 9E ÉDITION
SEAN ALEMAYEHU TEWODROS GIORGIS
PRINCE PRÉSIDENT 9RUBIS AMBASSADEUR INTERGALACTIQUE

9 YEUX 9 VISAGES TROMPEURS — 9 MECQUE CHICAGO
LE TÉMOIGNAGE DE LA 9TH HEURE DE KRASSA AMUN GIORGIS, ALIAS CHRISTON M LARSON
ET LA COLÈRE DE QADDISIN, LE MYSTÉRIEUX 13TH ANCIEN
FEU CRAMOISI — 9E ÉDITION
SEAN ALEMAYEHU TEWODROS GIORGIS
PRINCE PRÉSIDENT 9RUBIS AMBASSADEUR INTERGALACTIQUE

9 YEUX 9 VISAGES TROMPEURS — 9 MECQUE CHICAGO
LE TÉMOIGNAGE DE LA 9TH HEURE DE KRASSA AMUN GIORGIS, ALIAS CHRISTON M LARSON
ET LA COLÈRE DE QADDISIN, LE MYSTÉRIEUX 13TH ANCIEN
ÉTHER ROYAL — 9E ÉDITION
SEAN ALEMAYEHU TEWODROS GIORGIS
PRINCE PRÉSIDENT 9RUBIS AMBASSADEUR INTERGALACTIQUE

9ዓይኖች 9አታላይ ፊቶች — 9መካ ቺካጎ
የ9ኛው ሰዓት ምስክርነት የክራፋ አሙን ጊዮርጊስ (አሊያስ ክርስቶን ኤም ላርሰን)
እና የቀዳሲኝ ቁጣ፣ ምስጢራዊው 13ኛ አረጋዊ
አብሲዲያን ወርቅ – 9ኛ እትም
ሸአን አለማየሁ ቴዎድሮስ ጊዮርጊስ
9ሩቢ ፕሪንስ ፕሬዚዳንት | ኢንተርጋላክቲክ አምባሳደር

٩ عيون، ٩ وجوه مخادعة، ٩ مكة شيكاغو
شهادة الساعة التاسعة لكراسا آمون جورجيس المعروف باسم كريستون م. لارسون
وغضب قديسين، الشيخ الثالث عشر
إصدار النار القرمزية التاسع
شون ألمياهو تيودروس جيورجيس
روبي الأمير الرئيس السفير بين المجرات ٩

9 Ojos, 9 Rostros Engañosos, 9Meca Chicago
El Testimonio de la Novena Hora de Krassa Amun Giorgis,
Alias Christon M. Larson Y La Ira de Qaddisin, El 13.º Anciano
Edición Royal Ether — 9.ª Edición
Sean Alemayehu Tewodros Giorgis
9Ruby Príncipe Presidente Embajador Intergaláctico

FROM PRESIDENT GEORGE WASHINGTON TO EMPEROR TEWODROS II

AN ABYSSINIAN-AMERICAN-FRENCH HIDDEN LINEAGE REVEALED A GREAT-GRANDSON OF

PRINCE ALEMAYEHU TEWODROS PRESENTS A MILITARY, GENEALOGICAL, AND SPIRITUAL AUTHOR BIOPIC

SEAN ALEMAYEHU TEWODROS GIORGIS

9RUBY PRINCE PRESIDENT INTERGALACTIC AMBASSADOR

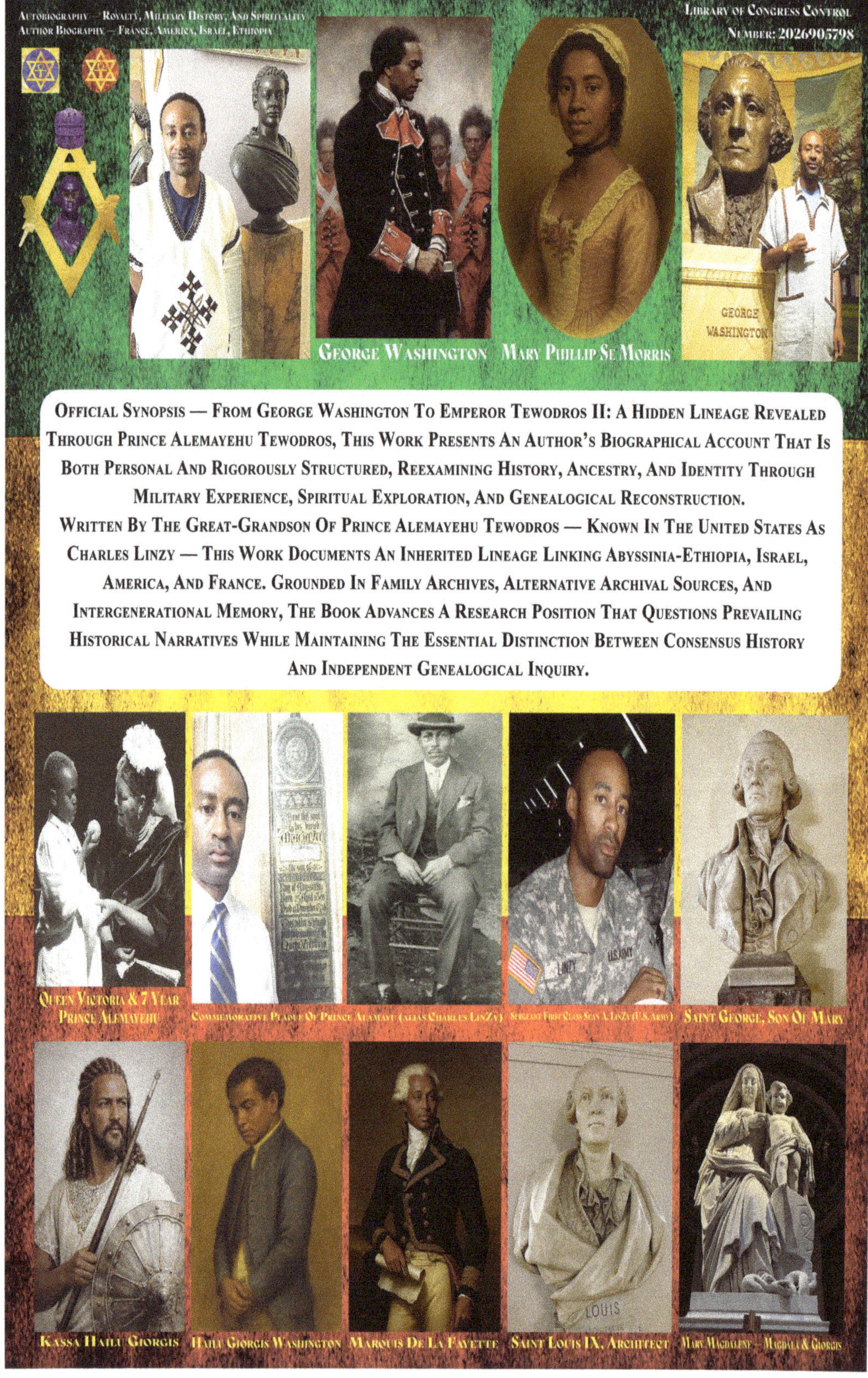
AUTOBIOGRAPHY — ROYALTY, MILITARY HISTORY, AND SPIRITUALITY
AUTHOR BIOGRAPHY — FRANCE, AMERICA, ISRAEL, ETHIOPIA
LIBRARY OF CONGRESS CONTROL NUMBER: 2026905798
GEORGE WASHINGTON
MARY PHILLIP SE MORRIS
GEORGE WASHINGTON

OFFICIAL SYNOPSIS — FROM GEORGE WASHINGTON TO EMPEROR TEWODROS II: A HIDDEN LINEAGE REVEALED THROUGH PRINCE ALEMAYEHU TEWODROS, THIS WORK PRESENTS AN AUTHOR'S BIOGRAPHICAL ACCOUNT THAT IS BOTH PERSONAL AND RIGOROUSLY STRUCTURED, REEXAMINING HISTORY, ANCESTRY, AND IDENTITY THROUGH MILITARY EXPERIENCE, SPIRITUAL EXPLORATION, AND GENEALOGICAL RECONSTRUCTION.
WRITTEN BY THE GREAT-GRANDSON OF PRINCE ALEMAYEHU TEWODROS — KNOWN IN THE UNITED STATES AS CHARLES LINZY — THIS WORK DOCUMENTS AN INHERITED LINEAGE LINKING ABYSSINIA-ETHIOPIA, ISRAEL, AMERICA, AND FRANCE. GROUNDED IN FAMILY ARCHIVES, ALTERNATIVE ARCHIVAL SOURCES, AND INTERGENERATIONAL MEMORY, THE BOOK ADVANCES A RESEARCH POSITION THAT QUESTIONS PREVAILING HISTORICAL NARRATIVES WHILE MAINTAINING THE ESSENTIAL DISTINCTION BETWEEN CONSENSUS HISTORY AND INDEPENDENT GENEALOGICAL INQUIRY.

QUEEN VICTORIA & 7 YEAR PRINCE ALEMAYEHU
COMMEMORATIVE PLAQUE OF PRINCE ALAMAYU (ALIAS CHARLES LINZY)
SERGEANT FIRST CLASS SEAN A. LINZY (U.S. ARMY)
SAINT GEORGE, SON OF MARY
KASSA HAILU GIORGIS
HAILU GIORGIS WASHINGTON
MARQUIS DE LA FAYETTE
SAINT LOUIS IX, ARCHITECT
MARY MAGDALENE — MAGDALA & GIORGIS

ከፕሬዝዳንት ጆርጅ ዋሽንግተን እስከ ንጉሥ ቴዎድሮስ ዳግማዊ

የተሸፈነ አቢሲንያ-አሜሪካ-ፈረንሳይ ዘር ተገለጠ የፕሪንስ አለማየሁ ቴዎድሮስ የአራተኛ ትውልድ ልጅ
የወታደራዊ፣ የዘር እና የመንፈሳዊ የደራሲ ታሪክ ያቀርባል

ሸአን አለማየሁ ቴዎድሮስ ጊዮርጊስ

9ሩቢ ፕሪንስ — የኢንተርጋላክቲክ አምባሳደር

De George Washington, Président, À l'Empereur Tewodros II
Une Lignée Cachée Abyssino-Américaine-Française Révélée Un Arrière-Petit-Fils Du
Prince Alemayehu Tewodros Présente Une Biographie D'auteur À Caractère Militaire, Généalogique Et Spirituel

Sean Alemayehu Tewodros Giorgis
Prince-Président Rubis 9 — Ambassadeur Intergalactique

Inscribed By 9Ruby Prince Intergalactic Ambassador
BLESSED ARE THOSE O CHILDREN
ANCIENT ISRAEL | AMERICA | ABYSSINIA | &
DA KINGDOM OF ANU ALESHA | UNITED 9 NATIONS
SEAN ALEMAYEHU TEWODROS GIORGIS
PRINCE PRESIDENT INTERGALACTC AMBASSADOR

HOLY SCRIPTURES | ANCESTRY
BIOGRAPHY HISTORY
FLAG OF 7MECCA GIORGIS WASHATAW | ANU ALESHA | UNITED 9 NATIONS
LIBRARY OF CONGRESS CONTROL NUMBER: 2025911275
FLAG OF 7MECCA GIORGIS WASHATAW | ANU ALESHA | UNITED 9 NATIONS

THE SMARTEST STUDENT IN HIGH SCHOOL MADE THE WORST GRADES IN AMERICA

BLESSED ARE THOSE O CHILDREN OF ANCIENT ISRAEL, ANCIENT AMERICA, ANCIENT EUROPE, ANCIENT ABYSSINIA. SCRIPTURES TESTIMONY — 2ND VOLUME

SEAN ALEMAYEHU TEWODROS GIORGIS
PRINCE PRESIDENT INTERGALACTIC AMBASSADOR

Holy Scriptures | Ancestry Biography History

LIBRARY OF CONGRESS CONTROL NUMBER: 2025911760

AND IN THE MIDST OF THE SEVEN CANDLESTICKS ONE LIKE UNTO THE SON OF MAN, CLOTHED WITH A GARMENT DOWN TO THE FOOT, AND GIRT ABOUT THE PAPS WITH A GOLDEN GIRDLE. HIS HEAD AND HIS HAIRS WERE WHITE LIKE WOOL, AS WHITE AS SNOW; AND HIS EYES WERE AS A FLAME OF FIRE; AND HIS FEET LIKE UNTO FINE BRASS, AS IF THEY BURNED IN A FURNACE; AND HIS VOICE AS THE SOUND OF MANY WATERS. AND HE HAD IN HIS RIGHT HAND SEVEN STARS: AND OUT OF HIS MOUTH WENT A SHARP TWO-EDGED SWORD: AND HIS COUNTENANCE WAS AS THE SUN SHINETH IN HIS STRENGTH.

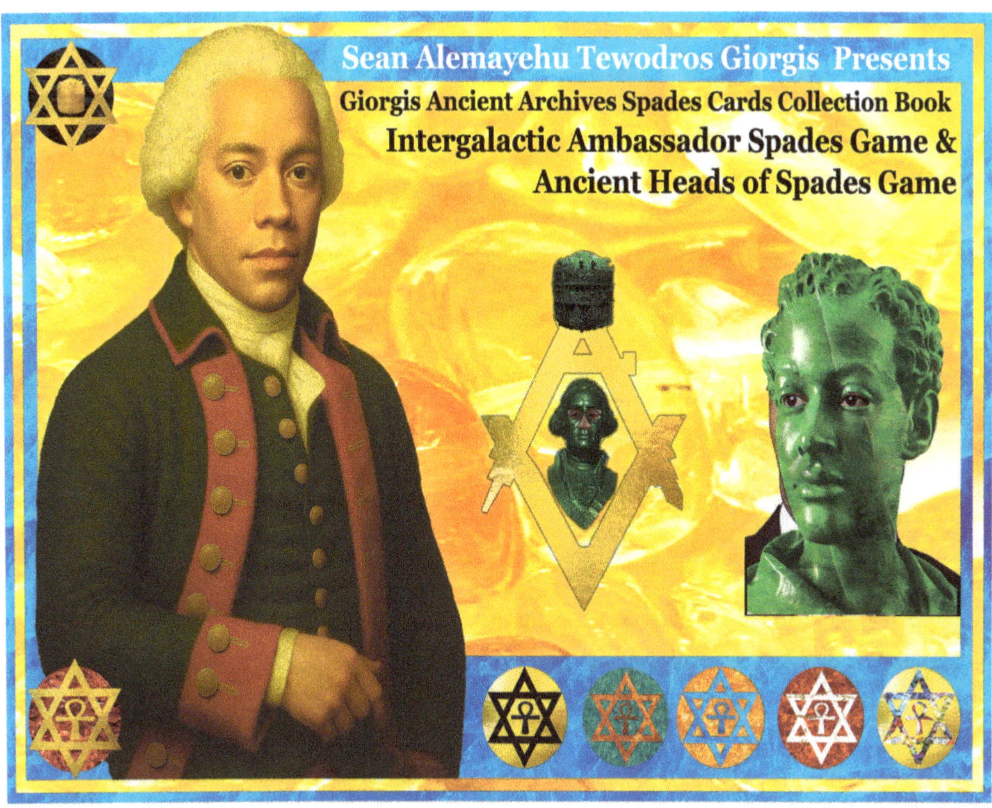
Sean Alemayehu Tewodros Giorgis Presents
Giorgis Ancient Archives Spades Cards Collection Book
Intergalactic Ambassador Spades Game &
Ancient Heads of Spades Game

GENRE : GAME CARDS : ART COLLECTION : GENEALOGY
LIBRARY OF CONGRESS CONTROL NUMBER 2026911191
www.Prince-President-Giorgis.com and order www.makeplayingcards.com
QUEEN CHRISTINA, SAINT NIGREST WIFE OF LOUIS 15, SAINT KING
EMPRESS TRUWORK WUBE, MOTHER OF PRINCE ALEMAYEHU TEWODROS
ALEKHA, SAINT PRINCESS ARCHITECT DAUGHTER OF MARY MAGDALA | GESUS
GIORGIS, SAINT KING ARCHITECT SON OF MARY MAGDALA | GESUS
GEORGE WASHINGTON 1722 LEOS, GENERAL | SON OF MARY JOSEPH, AND CHIEF HALSWORTH WEBSTER
CROWN • UP
99CARD
HIGH CARD 10

Sean Alemayehu Tewodros Giorgis Presents
Giorgis Ancient Archives Spades Cards Collection Book
Intergalactic Ambassador Spades Game &
Ancient Heads of Spades Game

Genre : Game Cards : Art Collection : Genealogy
Library of Congress Control Number 2026911191
www.Prince-President-Giorgis.com and order www.makeplayingcards.com

URBAN: SCIENCE FICTION
UFOs & Extrateresstrial
YOU KNOW; A WISE MAN ONCE SAID; TO MASTER THE ART OF DECEIVING FACES, YOU MUST FIRST MANIPULATE THE POWER OF THE MIND!